BOUND BY A DRAGON

Bound by a Dragon

Book I of The Dragon Archives

Linda K. Hopkins

PROLOGUE

Keira watched as the great beast circled slowly through the sky, blocking the sunlight for a few seconds on each turn. Fire spewed from its mouth and dissipated in the cool air before the flames reached the ground. All around her people shouted as they grabbed their children and ran for their homes. Doors slammed shut, and locks slid into place as buildings were barred from within. Keira shook her head in amusement – a mere door wouldn't stop a dragon!

"Come," Anna yelled, tugging on Keira's arm, but Keira shrugged her off and stared at the monstrous beast flying above the village.

The dragon had taken up residence in the mountains some six weeks back, but it had yet to kidnap and devour a single innocent maiden. But people had long memories, and the stories about the last dragon that had lived in the area were not easily forgotten. For many years it had peacefully inhabited its mountain lair, until one day it had suddenly turned on the village. Half the homes had been destroyed by flame before the creature was killed by some brave soul. The only questionable thing this dragon had done, however, was to take a few head of cattle and a couple of sheep. And since the dragon always left some form of payment for the animal taken – a small bag of gold or a few precious stones – the villagers didn't complain too loudly, despite their fears of a grisly death. After all, the payments always exceeded the worth of the animal. But the villagers remained convinced that it was just a matter of time before the dragon set the village alight and snatched the village girls.

"Come on, Keira." Anna's words broke through Keira's thoughts, reminding her that her parents shared the same fears as the other villagers. "Mother'll be furious if we don't return to the house now."

"Stop pulling me. I'm coming!" said Keira. She glanced at the sky once more, admiring the way the scales of the dragon caught the late afternoon light and threw a thousand rainbows against the sky. The creature was heading away from the village, but before Keira turned away, it twisted its long neck and looked at her. Keira pulled her arm out of Anna's as she met the dragon's golden gaze, then watched as it turned its enormous body in a slow, fluid motion and lazily flew towards the mountains.

CHAPTER ONE

The day was sweltering as Keira sat on her low stool, watching the crowds milling between the narrow lanes. The awning over her table provided little relief from the sun's burning rays, and she pulled the damp fabric of her bodice from her skin in an effort to find some relief. It was market day in the village, an event that occurred every Wednesday and Saturday, come rain or shine, and Keira was minding the table that held her father's carved wooden tableware. It was a task she shared with her mother, but as her mother had gone home to have her morning meal, Keira was at the table alone. She glanced around the marketplace and wondered, not for the first time, what her younger sister was up to. She saw no sign of her, but that was hardly surprising. Just that morning she'd suggested that Anna should help out more at the stall, but their mother was adamant in her refusal.

"Anna is too young to mind the table," Mother had replied. She hadn't noticed Anna standing in the corner where she made a face at her sister.

"Too young? She's sixteen, Mother. Old enough to be married. I started working at the stall when I was twelve."

"Now Keira!" her mother responded sharply. "Don't be

impertinent. I've said that Anna is too young, and that is the end of the discussion."

Keira sighed. Anna did not have a grain of responsibility, so it was probably better if she didn't mind the market stall. But Keira could not quash the rebellious thought that if Anna was not so spoilt, she would probably be more responsible.

Keira rose from her seat, and surreptitiously lifted her skirts in an effort to cool her ankles as she walked to the front of the table that displayed her father's carved wooden tableware. He was a Master Craftsman, and the pieces reflected both his skill and the pride that he took in his work. Each one had been sanded to a surface so smooth, it felt almost soft to the touch, inviting customers to run their fingers over the different items. His wares were sought out by the wealthier families in the surrounding towns and villages, and they even graced the altar of the closest cathedral. The items had been displayed to show off the quality workmanship, and Keira rearranged some of the plates to exhibit the natural beauty of the wood. She glanced around the marketplace as she worked – it was a riotous assault on the senses, where colors, smells and sounds competed for notice. Sellers shouted their wares, adding to the cacophony made by animals penned at the back of the square, while customers raised their voices above the din as they strove to negotiate the best prices. Merchants displayed their goods in every available corner of the square, leaving shoppers only a few feet to negotiate between the stalls as they pushed and shoved past each other. Keira always felt a moment of relief when the market closed for the day and she could escape to the solitude of the forest.

As Keira returned to her stool, she noticed that something had caught the attention of the other merchants, and she turned to see a stranger making his way between the stalls. That in itself was not a cause for comment, as the village was on a busy road that brought pilgrims, traveling bands of mummers and other wayfarers, but this stranger was not like those who usually passed through. He was tall, well built and clean – unlike the others, who were often scraggly and unkempt – and he was well dressed. Very well dressed, actually. He wore a blue velvet doublet over a shirt of silk, with finely woven woolen hose that disappeared into heeled boots that reached to his knees. His hat, perched neatly over one ear, was also made of velvet, with a feather that curled over his other ear; and a sword hung at his side, the sheath studded with jewels. The man was clean shaven and his tanned skin washed – clearly a man of noble breeding. He continued to browse the stalls as he made his way slowly along the narrow path, pausing to examine the different wares on display. Occasionally he would pull out a small leather purse, and Keira could see how the contents weighed down the soft skin. Some of the merchants called out to him, willing him to spread his coin at their stalls, and he stopped to banter with them as they pointed out their wares.

As he made his way closer, Keira guessed that he was about thirty years of age. At twenty-two, Keira was already considered an old maid, but that didn't mean she couldn't appreciate his fine figure and powerful stride which exuded confidence and strength. She wasn't the only maiden with her eyes glued to his handsome form, she realized with a self-conscious smile.

He continued to weave his way between the stalls, and Keira was amused to see that his audience was growing. He was clearly out of place in the nondescript little village that Keira called home, and the shoppers nudged each other as he walked by. She laughed to herself as they openly speculated about the weight of his purse, but he paid no attention to the stir he was causing. Instead, he continued to browse the stalls – buying little trinkets at some; replacing the items with a smile and friendly word at others. He was almost at Keira's table when he looked up and caught her startled glance. She looked away hurriedly, embarrassed to be caught openly watching him, but not before she saw the smile that curved his lips. She could feel his eyes on her, and she nervously smoothed down her simple, homespun kirtle, wishing she had dressed in something a little less plain. In two quick strides the man was at her table, where he looked down to examine the wares on offer. He picked up a bowl and ran his finger over the smooth surface, then lifted his gaze to meet Keira's.

"This is just what I'm looking for," he said.

Keira cast him a speculative look. "You're shopping for plates and bowls?" she said. "Why?"

"To eat from, of course," he responded with an innocent smile.

"But surely you have many plates?" she said. In fact, she wouldn't be surprised to learn that he had plates made from pewter, imported ceramic or even silver. She had never seen such luxuries, of course, but she'd heard about them. And it was well known that Reeve Hobbes was in possession of a large pewter serving platter.

"You're right," he replied, "I do, but I've recently moved into the area, and not all my possessions have arrived yet, so I need some tableware to tide me over."

"Wooden plates and bowls?" she asked again, her suspicions not yet allayed. Her father's craftsmanship was fine, but she knew that it wasn't wood that usually graced the tables of the wealthy.

"Yes."

"Don't you have servants to take care of such trivialities?"

"I do," he said. "My steward is quite capable of handling such matters, but since I'm here, there's no reason for me to not tend to it myself."

A moment's silence filled the air as Keira considered his response. "And where have you taken up residence?" she finally asked. "I wasn't aware of anyone moving into the village."

"Do you always interrogate your customers like this?" he asked with an amused smile. "One would be inclined to think you don't want anyone to buy your wares."

Keira raised her eyebrows, but when she didn't respond, he continued.

"I haven't moved into the village, as you're clearly aware, but rather into Storbrook Castle, a few miles hither. Do you know it?"

Storbrook Castle! The name sent a shudder down Keira's spine. The castle was hidden deep in the mountains, a good thirty miles away; and although few in the village had ever seen the mountain fortress, there wasn't a child who hadn't shivered in fear and delight at its purported horrors. It was rumored that the castle had once been the lair of a maiden-devouring dragon that had roamed through the mountains in days gone by. Children and adults alike whispered about the dark corridors where abducted maidens, held against their will, were forced to do unspeakable things at the dragon's bidding, and where other heinous dealings occurred, too dreadful to be repeated.

"Storbrook Castle," Keira repeated, her voice dropping. "They say the dragon lives in the caves below the castle."

The stranger laughed lightly. "I hate to disappoint you, but I haven't seen any half-gnawed bones around Storbrook. I have heard about this dragon, though." The man glanced around before leaning towards Keira, his hands on the table as he lowered his voice. "How many beautiful damsels have been snatched up by this dreadful monster?"

The man's warm breath washed over Keira's cheek, and she shivered slightly. "None," she said, her voice matching his. "No damsels, beautiful or otherwise, have disappeared from our village or any of the other villages in the area." She paused. "Perhaps our dragon isn't quite so dreadful after all."

"You don't fear the beast?" he asked in surprise, straightening to his full height.

"No, why should I?" she said with a smile. "It hasn't done anything fearful."

"But you must have heard about the monstrous creature

that lived here before?"

"I have," Keira replied. "People say that it lived peacefully in the mountains for many years before attacking the village. But it seems rather strange, don't you agree? Surely something must have provoked it to make it attack so suddenly." She glanced towards the mountains. "As for this dragon, I rather like it!"

The man stared at her in stunned silence for a moment, then swept his hat off with a smile and delivered a courtly bow.

"Please allow me to introduce myself. Aaron Drake at your service." The sun glanced off his light brown hair, highlighting streaks of gold that shot through the brown. It was held in place by a red ribbon, tied at the nape of his neck. His eyes were a light tawny brown flecked with gold, unusual in their lightness. Even his skin seemed to take on a light golden sparkle in the sun. Keira recognized the name Drake – Storbrook Castle had been owned by Drakes for generations, but it had stood empty for years. "And you are …?" he prompted, when she didn't respond.

"Keira Carver … milord," she said. She glanced over her shoulder when she heard footsteps, to see her mother returning from her morning repast.

"Keira," she said, "I'll help this gentleman while you go home and have your meal."

"Yes, Mother," Keira said. She turned away as Mother began to point out the subtle colors of the wood grain and the fine design of the various pieces, but before she left, she glanced over her shoulder at the stranger. While her mother's attention was directed at the items on the table, Aaron looked up and caught Keira's eye, holding her in his gaze for a moment. The look he gave her promised future encounters, and she felt her heart speed up as she quickly looked away, a smile lighting her face.

CHAPTER TWO

Keira lived with her parents in a small house at the end of the village, where they owned a few acres of land. As a landowner, Master Carver was considered wealthy by village standards, and he had ensured that his daughters received a basic education from a traveling tutor. He'd spent a year in their home, sleeping in the tiny attic at the top of the house. In exchange for food, shelter and a few pennies a week, he taught Keira and Anna their letters and numbers. It was this knowledge that enabled Keira to take her place at the stall, where she meticulously wrote down each piece that was sold, keeping a running tally of the numbers.

The only other landowner in the village was the village reeve, Matthew Hobbes, who served the manorial lord by upholding his interests within the village and maintaining law and order in the surrounding area. It was the lord who appointed the reeve, which was a pity, Keira thought. If the villagers were allowed a say in the matter, Matthew Hobbes would certainly not be the man they had chosen. He was mean and vindictive, and used his position to serve his own ends.

As Keira headed home, she pushed her way through the

crowded market and past the village church that overlooked the square. Beside the church was a small, shadowed churchyard, and behind that was a large field with a well-worn path that led into the forest at the foot of the mountains. Keira knew the path well – it also led to a small lake that was a favorite swimming hole for the villagers. Arriving at the house, Keira skirted around the building and entered through the kitchen where Mary was stirring a large pot over the fire. Keira greeted Mary with a smile as the housekeeper bobbed her head.

"Morning, Mistress. 'Ere for your dinner? It's fish pie."

"Wonderful, thank you Mary."

For as long as Keira could remember, Mary had been mistress of the Carvers' kitchen. She lived at the other end of the village, in a small, dingy cottage that was shared between three families. Each morning, she arrived just after sunup to take command of the household, and did not leave until after dark, when the pots in the kitchen shone like new. She delivered her directives to Bess, the young housemaid, in an imperious voice that had the girl running from room to room in fright, but Keira knew that Mary had a soft, motherly heart. When Anna and Keira were younger, she'd scolded them many times when they returned with muddied gowns or torn aprons, but she always slipped a treat into their pockets before sending them on their way once more.

Sometimes, if Keira awoke before Mary arrived for the day, she'd invite the woman's censure by creeping into the kitchen and lighting the fire so that the heat could begin to warm the bedroom above. She'd endured many a scolding about doing work beneath her station, but she knew Mary was secretly pleased at her display of independence.

She slid into the bench at the large kitchen table and waited as Mary placed a bowl before her. A wonderful aroma of fish, herbs and spices, cooked within a crispy pastry, assailed her nose, and her mouth watered as she slid her spoon into the lightly browned shell.

Half an hour had passed when Keira left the house and headed back to the market. In the distance loomed the mountains, stretching as far as the eye could see in either direction. Keira had never been beyond the mountains, and she often wondered what marvels could be seen there. Her tutor had told her once about a large city where hundreds of people lived, and where anything could be bought for a price. Keira's mind wandered back to the stranger at the market. Perhaps he'd lived in the big city. How strange to leave that behind for a remote and mysterious castle in the middle of the mountains! Especially if the dragon really did live in caves nearby. There were few who were not terrified of the creature, and fewer still, Keira guessed, who'd want to live so close to such a dangerous beast. Keira thought of the first time the dragon had flown over the village, some three months earlier. The villagers had fled to their homes in terror, but necessity had forced them from their hiding spots a few days later. It had taken a few more weeks before people began to resume some semblance of their normal lives, but even then, they'd scurried for shelter every time the dragon had flown overhead.

Keira supposed that the reaction of the villagers shouldn't be too surprising. Eighty years may have passed since a dragon had last inhabited the Northern Mountains, but when it died, it had left behind a village frightened and scarred. It had lived in its mountain lair, so the story went, for many years without bothering a single soul. In fact, some even argued that the villagers were quite happy to have a dragon living close by. If ever the village were attacked, they thought, perhaps the dragon would assist them in their defense. But that had all changed when the dragon tried to abduct a maiden from the village. The story was a little murky on the details, but all agreed that the dragon would certainly have killed her if it hadn't been for the young man who'd bravely – and single-handedly – attacked the dragon so he could rescue the maid, then raised the hue and cry that brought others to his side. The dragon had burnt down half the village and killed some of the villagers before finally breathing its last. The woman's fate was unknown, not that it really mattered, the storytellers agreed. The important thing was that dragons were dangerous, and should never be trusted. As though drawn by her thoughts, the dragon glided over the village as Keira reached the market, making the villagers clutch their children closer as it climbed into the mountains.

Keira often saw the dragon soaring through the sky in the days that followed. When it first came to the mountains, the sightings were few and far between, but now it regularly flew over the village, soaring low as if to see what the villagers were doing. Sometimes it flew so close, Keira could hear the massive wings as they cut through the air, and feel the heat that emanated from the beast. She always stopped to watch as it soared past, admiring the way its huge golden wings cut through the blue sky, holding its huge frame as though it weighed no more than a feather. Its golden gaze would catch hers, and she'd hold her breath as she stared back, marveling at the dragon's beauty. It was, she decided, more splendid than anything she had ever seen.

A week passed before Keira saw Aaron again. She was at the market, negotiating the sale of a dozen cups when she looked up to see him standing a few feet away, his light eyes watching her as she worked. He caught her gaze and nodded, but stayed away until she had completed the sale.

"Good morning, Mistress," he said with a smile as he stepped towards the table. "I've come to make another purchase."

"Milord," Keira said with a nod. "I understand you've already purchased enough plates and bowls to feed a large household."

"My cook tells me we need a new platter."

"Your cook? She discusses such matters with you?"

Aaron smiled. "She told my steward, and since I was

coming into the village, I offered to make the necessary purchase."

Keira nodded. What the man did was his own concern. She picked up a platter and handed it to him. "Is this the size you're looking for?"

Aaron frowned. "I'm not sure. I didn't think to ask her the size." He looked up at her. "I'll take it, and if it's too small, I'll come back for something larger."

"Or send your steward."

"Oh, I'm not sure about that! I rather enjoy making my own purchases. I meet such interesting folk! People in the city are so dull and conventional, always doing and saying what polite society demands." His tone was amused, but Keira didn't miss the teasing barb hidden within his comment.

"I've never been to the city," she said, "so I don't know how people act there. I prefer to be myself and speak my mind."

Aaron laughed. "Yes, I already know that much. I didn't intend an insult – you're like a refreshing breath of air."

Keira pointed at the platter. "Are you purchasing this or not?"

Aaron smiled and pulled out his purse. He handed her a few coins, waving away her protest that it was too much.

"Consider it a down-payment on my next purchase," he said, and walked away.

"Who's that?"

Keira turned to see the son of the reeve walking towards her. Edmund Hobbes was a year younger than her, and Keira had known him all her life; in fact, they had practically been raised together. Their mothers had been great friends, until Mary Hobbes had died a few years before.

"Master Drake. He's moved into Storbrook Castle."

Edmund whistled. "Indeed! Why would anyone want to move into that place, I wonder?"

Keira remained silent, wondering the same thing.

Edmund watched the retreating figure for a moment, then turned back to Keira, his blue eyes capturing hers. He was a good-looking man, Keira acknowledged, with high cheek bones and a strong jaw. His lips were full, giving him a slightly sensual look. He leaned closer, his eyes narrowed and his mouth grim. "You aren't becoming too friendly, I hope. He looks like a dangerous man." Before Keira had a chance to respond, he pulled away again and looked over her shoulder. "Madam Carver," he said as Keira's mother drew near, "Shouldn't you be inside on such a hot day? I'm sure Keira would be happy to mind the table alone, although, of course, I'd be glad to offer whatever assistance she requires." Keira groaned quietly to herself. The last thing she wanted was Edmund's company.

"Oh, Edmund, you're so kind," Mother replied, her hand fluttering lightly at her chest. "You're right, of course, it is a frightfully hot day, but I couldn't possibly leave Keira to manage all on her own. Mistakes can so easily be made!" Keira took a deep breath and turned away.

"In that case," Edmund said, "I'll leave you to your work." He gave her a charming smile. "Good day."

Keira watched as Edmund walked away. He stopped to exchange a few words with Sarah Draper, then waved at Gwyneth Jones across the way. They laughed and giggled, pleased at the attention.

"Edmund is such a lovely young man," Mother said. "Always so considerate."

"Where's Anna, Mother?" Keira said.

"Anna? I saw her earlier. I think she was with Jane. Why?"

"Well, perhaps Edmund is right – you should be inside. Anna could help me here, and maybe learn a little more about the business."

Mother waved her hand. "Anna's young. Let her have her fun. I'm happy to stay here and make sure everything runs smoothly." Keira smiled tightly and reached beneath the table to place Aaron's coins in the strongbox.

CHAPTER THREE

Keira pulled away from the huge cauldron over the fire and wiped the back of her hand over a sweaty forehead. She was helping Mary pickle the first cucumbers of the season, and it was hot, tedious work. Delaying it would mean that the fruit was ruined, however, so Keira had resigned herself to the unpleasant task, glad, at least, she had Mary to share it with. Bess was outside, washing the dirty laundry, and as for Anna – well, she'd poked her head in once and reluctantly helped to turn the massive ladle, but when she'd been sent to draw fresh water, she had disappeared, leaving the empty bucket beside the well.

"Ah, that child," Mary had said, shaking her head in dismay when the bucket was discovered.

"She should be dragged back here and tied to the table," Keira said angrily.

"P'rhaps. She's a young'un."

"She's not a child anymore," Keira said. "People shouldn't indulge her."

"Well, you can't blame 'er for taking advantage when no one says no, can 'ee?" Mary said. "And we both of us know it's not you who must say no."

15

Keira sighed. "I know." She fanned away the scalding steam as Mary added more water to the pot. It had been incredibly hot for days now – a heat wave, Aaron had called it. He came to the market regularly, always stopping at the wood carver's store for some item or other. Keira had stopped asking him about his steward – for whatever reason, he preferred to make the purchases himself. Keira hadn't missed the fact that he usually came by when she was alone, and she smiled to herself. Clearly, he was a creature of habit, who did the same things at the same time each day. There were times, of course, when Mother returned before he left. At first, she'd been delighted to have a new customer – especially one who spent so lavishly – but lately she'd begun frowning when she saw him talking to her daughter, and her manner had become abrupt and terse. As if noticing her discomfort, Aaron did not linger over his shopping, but left as soon as the transaction was completed, with a smile in Keira's direction.

Keira let go of the ladle and rested her hands on her hips for a moment. Knots were forming in her back, and she twisted around, trying to loosen them. It would take all day to finish the preserving, and she was already starting to ache. She glanced at the door, wishing she could leave her responsibilities behind as Anna so carelessly did, before taking the ladle once more and stirring the bubbling contents.

The hot weather had still not broken when, a week later, Keira headed out of the house with a basket over her arm, heavy with jars of preserves. They were a gift for Dame Lamb, an elderly, but sprightly widow who lived at the other end of the village. Keira couldn't remember her husband, he'd died so long ago, but she had many fond memories of the old lady. As a child, Keira had sat at her feet as she pedaled the spindle, listening in delight as she told her tales of days gone by, when fairies and brownies still showed themselves to the humans of the world. Keira had listened in

16

fascination, eager to know more about the magical little creatures. If only she had wings like a fairy, she could explore the whole world! When she'd told Dame Lamb, she'd shaken her head.

"There are other things out there, my dear," she said. "Other creatures that aren't so friendly and kind. Monsters that are cruel and vicious. Best to stay close to home." Keira disagreed. One day, she told herself, she'd see what lay beyond the mountains.

"Mistress Keira!"

Keira looked around in surprise, jolted from her musings. She smiled when she saw Aaron Drake. "Milord."

"Milord is very formal," he said. "I think we're well enough acquainted for you to call me Aaron. Where are you headed?"

"I'm taking these to Dame Lamb," she said, lifting the cover off the basket to show him the contents. "She lives at the other end of the village."

"Really! What a coincidence. I happen to be headed that direction too," Aaron said. "Perhaps we can walk together."

Keira lifted her eyebrows but remained silent, accepting his company as she walked.

"Have you seen your dragon lately?" he asked.

She laughed. "He's my dragon now, is he?"

"I've noticed how you watch it whenever it passes over the village," he said. "I think you're quite taken with the creature."

"He is rather handsome."

"Handsome? A dragon! Are you sure you aren't befuddled?" Keira laughed as he continued. "Although, if this dragon has a penchant for beautiful damsels, I'm sure you're at the top of his list."

Keira blushed. "Milord!" she said. "You are being very …"

"Forward?" he finished with a grin.

"Absolutely," she said.

Aaron watched her for a few moments. "You haven't answered my question," he said.

"What question?"

"Have you seen the dragon much?"

"Actually, I saw him this morning. It used to be that we never saw it, but lately ..." Her voice tailed off. "Some villagers are waiting for young maidens to start disappearing." Keira looked at the sky as she spoke, her eyes scanning the horizon as they walked through the village. There was no sign of the dragon, however, and she turned her gaze back to Aaron, startled to see him watching her with an unfathomable expression. The expression quickly smoothed away, and he gave a light laugh.

"I think there is only one beautiful maiden the dragon may be tempted to abduct and hide in its lair," he said. "I think you should take great care in future to hide away whenever that foul monster comes near, otherwise you could well be his first victim."

The color rose in Keira's cheeks, and she glanced away to hide her blush.

"What do you think its lair looks like?" Aaron continued in a low voice. "Is it dark and malodorous? Perhaps there are bones from its victims lying everywhere. And surely it is smoky, too – the walls are probably black from the hellish fire that emanates from the beast with every breath. And gold, we mustn't forget the gold! I imagine that there are treasures piled everywhere, because everyone knows that dragons hoard wealth."

Keira laughed. "Aren't the dragon's caves below Storbrook Castle? Surely you must have explored them by now?"

Aaron shuddered. "Sweet Keira, do you honestly think I should risk my life hunting for a dragon and its lair? You might think the dragon is harmless, but I'd prefer not to become the fiend's next meal. Of course, if the creature abducts you, I'll feel honor-bound to try and rescue you, despite having warned you of the dangers of the monster." Aaron looked at her with eyebrows raised quizzically, a grin tugging at his mouth. "I hope you will feel some small remorse at my early demise?"

"Why, milord," she said. "Do you mean to tell me that the simple villager who killed the last dragon would best you in courage if it comes to a battle against this one?"

Something flashed in Aaron's eyes, but it was gone in a moment.

"Alas, I fear the answer is yes."

"Well," she said, "I don't believe you have any reason to fear. As I've said before, this dragon does not seem interested in harming anyone, so perhaps he will spare your life when you stumble across his lair one day."

"I'm very relieved to hear it," he said, the twinkle in his eye belying his grave expression.

Keira smiled in amusement. "Doesn't Drake mean dragon, milord?" she asked.

"Yes, I'm afraid it does," he said. "One of my ancestors had the temerity to possess a nature as fierce and mean as a dragon. His friends called him Drake and the name stuck. I would have much preferred it if he could have been known as Drake-Slayer. It has a far better ring, do you not agree?"

Keira shook her head. "Don't fancy yourself as Drake-Slayer anytime soon. I rather like our dragon. In fact, I think I feel a bit sorry for him."

"You do? How can such a dreadful beast evoke the pity of such a lovely young maid?"

"Well, he must be rather lonely," she said. "Imagine living all by yourself in the mountains with no-one to keep you company. And every time you come near a village in an effort to make friends, everyone runs away, screaming in fright!"

"What makes you think the creature is coming in search of friends?" asked Aaron in amusement.

"Since he hasn't taken anyone from the village," she said, "I think we can rule out hunger as his reason for frequenting the area. So that must mean he's looking for companionship," she concluded with a satisfied air of certainty; but when Aaron laughed, she flushed in embarrassment. "You're laughing at me," she said sheepishly.

Aaron hastened to reassure her. "No, no," he said. "I'm not laughing at you. You've such a kind heart and a wonderful imagination. I was just wondering how a dragon would try to make friends with a screaming maiden."

Keira grinned in response. "With a bouquet of burning branches, of course," she said. She glanced around to see that they had reached the other end of the village.

"This is the home of Dame Lamb," she said, stopping in front of a small, wood-framed cottage, its bright whitewashed walls contrasting with weather-darkened timber beams. Bright blooms, wilting in the sun, clung to the wall, and the front stair was swept clean. "Thank you for your company, and good day."

"Good day, Keira," Aaron said, extending his leg neatly as he swept off his hat and delivered a courtly bow. Keira dropped a shallow curtsey in response, but before she turned away, Aaron caught her hand in his and lifted it to his lips. His lips brushed against her knuckles, and a tingle ran down the length of her spine. "I look forward to our next encounter, beautiful damsel." He dropped her fingers and turned away, leaving Keira staring after him in bemusement.

CHAPTER FOUR

The front door to the little house was open, and Keira called out a greeting.

"Come in, come in." Dame Lamb hobbled to the door, smiling when she saw Keira standing at the threshold. "How lovely of you to come and visit."

For as long as Keira could remember, Dame Lamb had been old. Her white hair was neatly tucked away at the nape of her neck and hidden beneath a lacy cap, while long, bony fingers clasped the shiny knob of a walking stick which wobbled slightly as she shuffled towards the door.

She nodded at the basket in Keira's hand. "What's that you have, dear? Have you brought me some of those wonderful preserves Mary is so renowned for?"

Keira nodded. "I have." She pulled the cloth off the basket, revealing the contents.

"Wonderful!" The old lady tapped her stick on the ground. "Well, don't just stand there, girl. Come inside and sit down."

Keira followed her obediently, taking a seat on a stool which rocked precariously. Beneath her feet the floor rushes rustled while fleabane and lavender, strewn over the rushes, released their sweet fragrances. She glanced around the room, taking note of the bed that had been placed near the large, open fire.

"Your father moved my bed downstairs for me," Dame Lamb said. "I couldn't manage the stairs any longer."

"I'm sorry," Keira said.

"Tsk, don't be! We all have to get old sometime, child. I've outlasted my husband by twenty years. It's about time I moved on."

"Don't say that," Keira said. "Who would tell us about the faeries if you weren't here?"

Dame Lamb's eyes sparkled merrily. "You, of course, my dear. Why do you think I told you all the old tales?"

Keira laughed. "I thought you were just diverting my attention so I wouldn't interrupt your spinning."

"Well, that too! Now pour us some wine, child. You know where to find the cups."

Keira nodded and headed over to the heavy wooden cabinet in the corner. The shelves were sparse, with just a few cracked wooden bowls and plates, and two clay cups. She took them down and filled them with watered-down wine from a pitcher on the table.

"Not too much, child," said Dame Lamb. "Wine is dear these days." Keira returned some of the wine before handing the old lady a cup. She took a sip, and puckered her mouth. "Dreadful stuff, this," she said. She placed her cup on the table and turned to look at Keira. "Now, my dear, when are you getting married?"

Keira spluttered out a mouthful of wine. "Married, Dame Lamb? I have no plans to get married."

"Well, why not? I was married at fifteen, you know, and like me, you're also getting on in years." She grinned, revealing a gap between her teeth. "It's about time you got married and relieved your father of the burden of providing for you. What about young Edmund? I seem to recall your mother saying once that you were intended for each other."

"Dame Lamb," Keira protested. The old lady held up a hand.

"I know you don't want to discuss this, child, but someone needs to talk some sense into you. What is your objection to Edmund?"

Keira sighed. Dame Lamb was not the only one concerned about her future. It was a constant irritant in her relationship with her parents, especially her mother. She thought back to the last conversation they'd had on this subject, only a few days prior.

"What are you waiting for?" her mother had railed in frustration. "Reeve Hobbes has spoken to your father about finalizing a marriage contract between you and Edmund."

"I don't want to marry Edmund, Mother," Keira had said.

"If not Edmund, then who? Widower Brown? He's expressed a desire to take you to wife many times over the last five years. He doesn't have Reeve Hobbes' fortune, but he does have some money."

Keira had shuddered at the thought. Widower Brown was at least thirty years her senior and suffered from gout. His breath was always foul, and it was well known that he was frequently deep in his cups. She doubted he'd bathed once in the last five years, and she dreaded to think what creatures might reside in his long, bushy beard.

Mother nodded, noting Keira's shudder with satisfaction. "Edmund will make a fine husband, Keira. He's charming and thoughtful, and will give you a comfortable life. One day he'll replace his father as reeve, and you'll have the chance to expand your social circle beyond our little village. You know it was the dearest wish of his mother and I that you two would form an alliance."

Keira sighed. It was true that Edmund was charming and thoughtful – when he chose to be. But he had a mean streak that Keira could not ignore. She thought of young Jamie, a boy from the village. He was sweet and kind, but a little slow in the head, and walked with a gait. She had come across

Edmund and his friend Alan teasing Jamie once, poking him with a stick to get him to move faster. She'd quickly intervened, stepping between Jamie and Edmund. Edmund had laughed, but he'd narrowed his eyes in a way that sent a sliver of fear through Keira. A few days later, someone had thrown Jamie down the well. He was rescued a few hours later, sobbing and incoherent, but when he'd finally calmed down, he refused to name his tormentor. Keira had no doubt, however, that Edmund had been responsible.

That wasn't her only complaint about Edmund. At the annual harvest festival the previous year, he'd grabbed her by the wrist and pulled her into the shadows of the churchyard. He'd stroked her face, then grabbed her chin when she tried to pull away. He'd kissed her then, forcing her lips apart with his tongue, and when she resisted, he slapped her across the face. "You'll be more obedient when you're my wife," he'd snarled, before turning and stalking away.

As she'd stood before Mother afterward, Keira rubbed her hand over her mouth, trying to erase the memory of the kiss.

"Edmund's not the person you think he is," she said.

"Nonsense," Mother had said briskly. "All boys have their youthful foolishness. But he'll make a fine husband."

Keira was brought back to the present when Dame Lamb patted her hand. "There are worse things than being married to that boy, my dear," she said. "Starving at the side of the road would be far less tolerable. If not Edmund, settle on another man and secure your future."

Keira smiled absently. The truth was, she could not imagine spending the rest of her life with anyone from the village. She wasn't fanciful enough to expect a love match, but she did want to like the person she would be sharing a home and raising children with. The image of Aaron rose in her mind, but she pushed it away forcefully. He'd be gone in a matter of weeks, back to the city. She was fortunate that her parents had not yet forced her into marriage, but it was just a matter of time before they took matters into their own hands. Lately the possibility of taking holy orders had become more appealing. As a bride of Christ, she would not be a burden to her parents, and her life would have some purpose and direction. She'd never felt the calling, but perhaps, she reflected, she had not been listening? And a life of prayer and contemplation was infinitely more attractive than the idea of marrying Edmund.

She took her leave of Dame Lamb a few minutes later. She'd only gone a few steps when she heard someone call her name, and she turned in dismay to see Edmund walking towards her.

"Keira. Where are you going?"

"Good day, Edmund," she said.

"I saw you walking with that stranger earlier on. What did he want with you?" A slight emphasis on the last word turned the question into an insult, which Keira chose to ignore.

"We were headed in the same direction, so he offered to walk with me."

"Don't forget you're intended for me, Keira," he said. "I'll not have you make a fool of me."

"Until we're betrothed, you have no say in the matter, Edmund," Keira said, turning away from him. He caught her by the arm and spun her back to face him.

"You think you have a choice, Keira, but you don't. That man would never be interested in the likes of you. We both know you'd never be more than a diversion to him."

"There are others who want to marry me, Edmund."

Edmund laughed. "You mean Widower Brown? You're welcome to marry him if you want, Keira, but somehow I don't think you will. I'm biding my time now because it suits me to do so, but one of these days, you will be my wife."

Keira pulled her arm free from Edmund's grasp and tossed her head. "Perhaps you're right Edmund, but know this. I will make your life so miserable, you'll regret the day your mother and mine ever laid eyes on each other. Hell will be preferable to a life with me."

Edmund smiled. "Ah, Keira, you really think I'll give you the freedom to do what you want? I'll bind you to the bed, and after I've had my fill of you, I'll leave you to sleep on the floor. You'll be no more trouble than a snappy mutt that can be flung outside when he grows too tiresome." He leaned closer, his nose only inches from hers. "So I suggest you take the time before we're wed to learn some respect and obedience." He turned and strode away as Keira watched with a sinking heart. The call of the church was suddenly thundering in her ears, pounding with each beat of her heart. She turned towards home. The sun was already dipping low in the sky, and there were chores to be completed before this day ended.

CHAPTER FIVE

Market Day dawned bright and fair, and Keira watched her father load up the cart with his handiwork. He had crafted some new pieces, beautifully carved with intricate designs of birds and flowers, and these were carefully placed next to the plainer, more utilitarian pieces already in the cart. Keira smiled to herself when she saw them. Father hoped that Aaron Drake would be enticed to part with further coin to purchase these superior pieces. When the cart was loaded Father walked Nelly down the road, steering the aging horse towards the marketplace where he would unload the merchandise before returning home. Keira followed a few paces behind, exchanging greetings with her neighbors as she walked by. Despite the early hour, the villagers were already up and about, used as they were to hard work and long days. A few children ran out to greet her, and she stopped to hear their tales and sympathize over a scratch or scrape.

It was busy at the marketplace when Keira arrived with Father. Other merchants milled around, unpacking their carts as they set up their displays. Keira greeted them with a smile and a wave as she started arranging the table, carefully finding a spot of prominence to display the new pieces. By the time she was satisfied with the display, customers were already starting to file past the market stalls, and Keira sat down on her stool. Her mother would not be coming for another few hours, and Keira enjoyed the small freedom this gave her. At this time of morning, most customers coming to market were there to buy their fresh fruit and vegetables, or to order their meat, so she was not surprised when her display received no more than a few cursory glances. Instead of watching for customers, she leaned back against the table and allowed the sun's rays to warm her face.

Her mind drifted to the conversation she'd had with Edmund the previous day. It had shaken her more than she cared to admit, and she'd barely slept the night before, as the shadows beneath her eyes attested. Sometime during the night, she'd resolved to speak to Father James about taking holy orders. It would mean leaving her home and family and moving to a convent many miles away, but she didn't mind leaving the village behind. She did, however, worry about Anna. As spoiled as she was, her journey into adulthood would not be easy. There were few, if any, who would indulge her as Mother had, and the lessons would be difficult. Perhaps, Keira thought, she would wait awhile before speaking to Father James. Edmund was in no rush to get married, and Father was not pushing her to make a decision. Maybe she could teach Anna some responsibility in the meantime. She could not delay for too long, but she'd do all she could for Anna before she left.

The sound of a cat yowling in pain broke through her thoughts and brought her to her feet. The sound came from the alley behind the market, and she ran towards it, determined to discover the cause of the cat's distress. As she rounded the corner, the sight of three boys tormenting the animal drew an angry shout.

"What are you doing?" She pushed the boys aside and pulled the terrified creature into her arms. "That's Dame Lamb's cat!"

It clawed at her arm, hissing in anger, but she continued to hold it close, stroking its fur and murmuring under her breath as the cat slowly calmed down. Its fur was matted with blood, and as she looked more closely she was horrified to see a piece of string tied tightly around its tail, ripping through the tender flesh. Clumps of fur lay on the ground, and Keira could smell smoke – she shuddered to think what the poor creature had endured. With the cat still in her arms, she rounded on the boys as they stood glowering in defiance against the alley wall. She was not surprised to see Matthew, Edmund's youngest brother, among the boys.

"How dare you treat an animal like this?" she hissed at them, her voice low with anger.

"It's just a cat," Matthew muttered, staring at the ground as he stirred the dust with a grubby toe.

Keira shifted the cat to one arm and yanked his ear. "This is one of God's creatures," she said. "How would you like to be treated like this? And you," she said, releasing Matthew's ear and pointing at his two friends, "you are all horrid little boys to treat a helpless animal like this." She was about to say more, when a voice cut in from behind.

"Don't speak to my brother like that," Edmund snarled. Keira spun around to see him motion Matthew over with a jerk of his head. Matthew moved over to his brother, relief evident on his face, and his friends quickly followed him.

"He was torturing a cat, Edmund," she snapped through clenched teeth. "He deserves to be whipped."

"Don't be ridiculous," Edmund said. "You're the one who should be whipped for interfering where you had no business. They were just having a bit of fun." He advanced towards her, his expression threatening, and Keira took a step back, stopping when she felt her back against the wall. The cat wriggled free of her arms and darted away, disappearing around the corner. The menace in Edmund's expression was evident, and Keira glanced around in search of a means of escape. Seeing none, she pushed herself upright and stared at Edmund.

"Your brother is a bully, picking on a helpless creature, and so are you, Edmund Hobbes."

"How dare you," he snarled. He lifted his hand and drew it back.

"Go ahead," she said. "It will just increase the contempt I have for you!"

She saw his hand flying through the air, and closed her eyes in anticipation of the blow, but it never came. Instead, the sound of a savage growl reached her ears, followed by a dull thud. Her eyes flew open in time to see Edmund hitting the wall and crumpling to the ground in a heap. Beside him stood Aaron, his eyes blazing.

"Get up, you coward," he ordered. "Keira is right, you're nothing but a bully. And only a coward would ever strike a woman. If you come near her again, I'll make sure it is the last thing you ever do."

"Keira is mine," Edmund snarled as he pushed himself up from the ground. Aaron stared at him for a moment, astonishment etching his features, then threw his head back and let out a loud laugh.

"Not only are you a coward and a bully, but I believe you're also deluded," he said. "I seriously doubt that Keira will ever shackle herself to a man such as you, but perhaps we should ask the lady herself." He turned to Keira, his face suddenly serious. "Mistress Keira, what do you have to say to this?"

Keira looked at Aaron for a moment before slowly turning to face Edmund.

"I will never be yours," she ground out with contempt. "Now go. Get out of my sight!"

"You heard her," Aaron said when Edmund didn't move. "Go!"

With an ugly expression of abhorrence, Edmund stared at Keira before he turned and stalked out of the alley. As he disappeared around the corner, Keira slumped back against the wall, her legs trembling.

"I fear I've made an enemy for life," she whispered, struggling to hold back tears.

"Don't be afraid," said Aaron, moving to her. "Edmund knows that going after you will incur my wrath, and he is too much the coward to take that risk." He reached for her hands and Keira allowed herself to be pulled gently into his arms. She leaned her head against his chest. His hand was soothing on her back as he rubbed small circles between her shoulder blades. She lay in his embrace for a few more moments, before she reluctantly pulled away.

"How did you come to be here?" she asked.

"I heard you yelling at the boys," he said, "so I came to lend you my support. I almost lost all control when I saw Edmund about to hit you. If he'd managed to land that blow, he would not have walked out of this alley alive," he added darkly, turning his face away. His jaw was clenched in anger, and Keira felt her heart racing as she realized that his threat was completely serious, and just what a formidable adversary he could be.

"Why do you care?" she asked in a whisper.

Aaron turned to look down at her, his expression softening as his gaze held hers.

"Sweet Keira," he started in a soft voice, but whatever else he was about to say was lost when the sound of footsteps alerted them to someone's approach. "It's your mother," he said with a grimace, "and she's incensed." He stepped back to put some distance between them.

"How …" started Keira, but he held up a hand to silence her.

"Sshh!"

Keira's mother rounded the corner a moment later. She glanced suspiciously between Aaron and Keira, but Aaron just smiled as he swept his hat off with a bow.

"Madam Carver," he said.

Mother responded to his greeting with a curt nod before

turning to her daughter.

"You weren't at the stall, Keira," she said. "Edmund told me I might find you here, along with this man. What do you have to say for yourself?" She folded her arms across her chest, and tapped her foot as she waited for her daughter's response.

"Some boys were torturing Dame Lamb's cat, Mother," Keira explained, "including Matthew Hobbes. I had to stop them. Milord Drake heard the commotion and came to investigate."

"Edmund said that you and he had argued, but seeing you here, alone, in an alley with this man," Mother said, nodding in Aaron's direction, "gives me more reason for concern than the fate of a cat."

"If he hadn't arrived when he did," Keira shot back, her voice rising in anger, "then perhaps Edmund hitting me would have been a reason for concern, Mother."

"Why in the world would Edmund hit you?" asked Mother.

"Because he's a bully," was Keira's instant reply.

"Come now, Keira, I'm sure Edmund wouldn't have hit you. You must have misread his intention." Mother's voice was placating now, and Keira felt her annoyance mounting. A heated response quickly rose to her lips, but Aaron's cold voice stopped her.

"Edmund was fully intending to injure your daughter, Madam Carver," he said, his eyebrows pulled together in a frown of disapproval, "and would have done so if I had not intervened."

Mother turned to Aaron, her expression clearly communicating her disapproval of his interference, but he met her stare unflinchingly, his hard eyes boring into her own. She stared at him for a few moments before dropping her gaze and glancing back at her daughter.

"Come, Keira," she said over her shoulder as she headed out of the alley.

As Keira turned to go, Aaron brushed his fingers against hers. She smiled at him, then hurried after the retreating figure of her mother.

CHAPTER SIX

Keira was working in the kitchen a few mornings later, stringing bunches of herbs from the rafters to dry. It was tiring work, and she swiped the back of her hand over her forehead to wipe away the sheen of sweat that had gathered there. She paused when she heard sounds, then groaned when Edmund's voice reached her. She was about to sneak out the back door when Mary came into the kitchen. "Your mother sent me to call you," she said. "Master Hobbes is in the parlor."

Keira nodded in resignation, and wiped her palms against her working kirtle as she headed to the parlor.

"Father and I snared some pheasants this morning, Madam Carver," Edmund was saying. "I brought you a brace for your kitchen."

"Thank you, Edmund," Mother said with a smile. "You're always so thoughtful."

"You've been like a mother to me, ever since my own passed away," Edmund said. "It is the least I can do for someone I already consider to be family."

Keira resisted the urge to roll her eyes as she entered the room. Mother turned at her approach. "Edmund has come to call, Keira."

Keira lifted her eyebrows. "So I see, Mother."

Edmund passed his eyes over her form, taking in her homely appearance and rosy cheeks. "Keira," he said, "you look as charming as always."

Keira smoothed the colorless, homespun kirtle with her hands. "Thank you, Edmund. I'll remember your appreciation of this gown, and be sure to wear it for you more often."

"Keira!" Mother exclaimed.

"I take no offense, Madam Carver," Edmund said. "I've known Keira for so long that I recognize her attempt at wit. She'll learn what pleases me when she becomes my wife." He turned to Keira. "I'm glad you're home, Keira, as I especially wanted to speak with you. I'm afraid you misunderstood me the other day."

Keira raised her eyebrows. "Did I misunderstand your raised hand?"

"I'd never hit you, Keira. Surely you know that!"

"You also said I should be whipped."

"I was just funning."

"Keira knows that, Edmund," Mother said. She looked at her daughter. "I think you owe Edmund an apology, Keira."

Keira's gaze swung to her mother. "I owe Edmund an apology? I think not!"

Edmund laughed. "It's all right, Keira. I'm quite prepared to forgive you for misconstruing my actions and allowing a stranger to step into our affairs. Although I do think you should know me better by now."

"On the contrary, I believe we understand each other very well." Keira stared at Edmund, and he turned away.

"I rue the day that man came to our village," said Mother. "He's nothing but trouble, mark my words."

Edmund nodded. "Unfortunately, I must agree with you, Madam," he said. "Keira's lack of caution has already allowed her to be taken in by his lies and deceit."

"Indeed," said Mother. "He's wasted no time in trying to drive a wedge between you two."

"Edmund's character is already well-known to me," Keira said. "I need no-one else to influence my judgement."

"I'm glad to hear it," said Mother severely. "Then I trust you understand the great consideration Edmund shows you in desiring you for a wife."

Keira turned to look at Edmund, meeting his upraised gaze. "Yes, Mother," she said, "I understand Edmund's consideration very well. Now if you'll please excuse me, I must go finish hanging the herbs before they begin to wilt." She nodded at Edmund, and escaped with a sigh of relief. He left soon after, and Mother came to find Keira in the kitchen.

"What is wrong with you?" she demanded. "Edmund's patience will run out one of these days."

"Then I long for that day, Mother."

"You're being a fool, Keira. Edmund can provide you a safe and secure future."

Keira smiled wanly. "Then I think I prefer an insecure future to a secure one."

"You're just being stubborn. One of these days you'll come to your senses, and you'll be grateful for Edmund's provision."

Keira sighed. She knew from experience that argument was futile. "Yes, Mother," she said.

Keira finished hanging the herbs an hour later. She washed her face and changed her gown, eager to get away from the house for a while. It was a beautiful, sunny day, but clouds were starting to gather on the horizon, promising a wet evening. Taking her basket, she headed out into the lane and towards the village. Within a short while she was walking along the cobbled street that ran between the stores of the high street. Turning into a covered entranceway, she pushed open the door to the haberdasher's shop, causing the small bell above the door to tinkle. She smiled and nodded at the proprietor in response to his greeting, and headed over to the counter of colorful ribbons and laces.

An hour had sped past by the time Keira emerged from the small shop into the sunlight with bright hanks of ribbons spilling color from her basket. She walked more slowly than before, reluctant to head home now that her afternoon errand was complete. The clouds on the horizon were looming closer, tall stacks of fluffiness, like puffs of seeds on a tall reed. The sun still shone brightly, as though determined to keep the upper hand against the impending rain, but Keira knew it was fighting a losing battle. Soon the clouds would block the warmth and light, replacing them with gloom and damp. Lost in her thoughts, Keira didn't hear the approaching footsteps that fell in with hers until a soft voice spoke in her ear.

"You look like you're a thousand miles away, my sweet. What lands are you busy traversing?" At the sound of his voice, Keira jumped, before looking up at Aaron sheepishly.

"I didn't even see you."

"You should be more vigilant," he warned. "The dragon will drop from the clouds and have you in its grasp before you even know it's there, if you continue to walk so heedless of potential danger."

"I'm not worried about the dragon, but my head was in the clouds," Keira said with a laugh.

"It was?" He looked up at the sky dubiously, before turning his gaze back to Keira. "How could your head be in the clouds, when you are clearly here on this narrow street?"

"You know perfectly well what I mean by that, Aaron Drake," she responded pertly.

Aaron laughed and moved a little closer, allowing his arm to brush against hers. Keira shivered at the touch, all thoughts suddenly chased from her mind as his gaze caught hers. He crooked his elbow, inviting her to rest her hand on his arm, then placed his hand over hers when she did so. He leaned a little closer, his warm breath brushing her ear.

"Tell me what you were daydreaming." His face was so close to hers, Keira was sure that their lips would meet if she just turned a little more towards him. Instead, she looked away, drawing in a deep breath as she marshaled her thoughts. It took a moment, but when she replied, her voice was steady.

"I was imagining what it would be like to ride atop one of those clouds," she said. "The entire world lying below you as you slowly drifted through the sky. I wonder what the world looks like from up there." Keira glanced at Aaron, wondering if he was laughing at her, but his face wore a curious smile. As she spoke, the light of the sun was suddenly cloaked for a brief moment before displaying its full glory once more. Keira turned her face up to the sky again as Aaron watched. "Look how fast the clouds are moving," she said. "In just a single day they travel over villages and fields, across the mountains and past the city on the other side. Wouldn't it be incredible to travel with them?" She turned back to Aaron, her face aglow with delight. "Maybe there are faeries in the clouds that are watching us right now."

"Faeries?" Aaron said in surprise.

"Yes, faeries," she repeated. "Master Rutlidge, our tutor, always scoffed at the idea of faeries. He used to say that educated people don't believe in faeries anymore. Is that what you think?"

"Well," Aaron replied, picking his words carefully. "I've never seen a faerie before."

"Just because you haven't seen one doesn't mean they don't exist," she retorted. "Dragons exist, so why not faeries?"

"Well, you know dragons exist because you've seen them," Aaron pointed out.

"Yes, that's true," she responded thoughtfully. "But until one moved into the mountains I'd never seen a dragon, and I still believed dragons existed."

"That's because others could attest to the existence of

dragons," he said. "After all, everyone in the village knows the stories of the dragon who was here before."

Keira looked at Aaron with a grin as she delivered her coup de grace. "And Dame Lamb can attest to the existence of faeries. She has spoken with them, you know." She smiled shamelessly as Aaron rolled his eyes in defeat.

The pair walked along in silence for a few minutes as the clouds continued to gather, their fluffy white puffs turning more grey and ominous. Aaron pulled Keira's hand further over his arm, closing the small distance between them. Keira turned to him with a smile, then frowned when she saw his solemn, intense gaze.

"What is it, Aaron? You look so serious."

"Keira, there's something I need to tell you." No sooner had the words left his mouth than a large drop of rain fell to the ground, quickly followed by a second and a third. Keira put her head down as the skies opened, releasing a gushing waterfall onto the land below. Pulling her arm from Aaron's, she quickly turned to him with a rueful expression.

"Goodbye, Aaron," she said, and before he had a chance to respond, she dashed away through the torrent in the direction of home, clutching her basket to her chest in an attempt to keep the contents dry. If she had turned around, she would have seen Aaron watching her, oblivious to the rain soaking through his clothes, before he turned around and headed in the opposite direction.

CHAPTER SEVEN

The dragon swooped down low, circling the village. As usual, the villagers were scrambling to get away from the threat, but Keira stood and watched the mighty beast as it glided and swirled through the air, admiring its grace and elegance. The sun glanced off the golden armor of the creature, making it shine lustrously. The unhurried movement of the dragon through the air reminded Keira of the dance troupes that toured the countryside, ready to exhibit their talents for a crowd willing to part with a few pennies. Keira was the only one watching the dragon's performance, but when the creature circled around again it looked directly at her, giving her the impression that the show was exclusively for her benefit. The dragon circled above the village one more time before turning towards the mountains, gliding on a swirling eddy of wind.

Keira was about to turn away when she saw that the dragon was losing height, descending near an open area in the distance. She watched for a moment, then spurred herself to a run as she realized that the dragon was headed in the direction of the lake. It dropped behind the trees as she ran, and a moment later, Keira saw a sudden burst of light brightening the sky, competing with the sunlight before slowly fading away. She pushed herself to run faster, twisting between the trees, hoping that the dragon would still be there when she arrived.

Ten minutes later, panting and sweaty, Keira approached the lake. She slowed down as she drew close, not wanting to disturb the creature, if indeed he was still there. She just wanted to catch a glimpse of him as he rested. Even though she was sure the dragon wouldn't harm her, she knew it would be foolish to act on this belief. Dragons were powerful creatures, known to kill and eat humans; just one swipe of a claw, or breath from his mouth, would see her in the grave. She sidled quietly around the trees and stopped at the edge of the clearing that led to the lake. Peeking between the branches, Keira searched the clearing for the large form of a beast. But instead of a dragon, the sight that met her eyes made her draw in her breath in a gasp.

Standing at the edge of the lake stood Aaron. His back was to her, and he was pulling on a pair of hose over his bare legs. Although a good distance away, he lifted his head at the sound of her gentle gasp and quickly spun around, his glance taking in her form in an instant. Keira stared at him for one horrified moment, then turned and ran back through the trees.

"Keira, wait," he called, but she shook her head in mortification and continued to run. She could hear his footsteps already directly behind her, and she urged herself forward, but to no avail. Before she could go another step, he grabbed her arm, spinning her around on her heel and catching her when she fell off balance. She gasped as her hands fell against his bare chest, then jerked them away as the color rose in her cheeks at the intimate touch.

"Please, let me go," she cried. He released her arm, but kept a hand near her elbow in case she tried to flee again.

"Keira," he said, "it's all right. There's no need to run." Keira looked away, mortified. "What are you doing here?" he asked.

"I ... I thought I saw the dragon landing here," she said. "I sometimes come here to swim," she added when he didn't immediately respond.

"And instead of a dragon, you found me."

"Yes," she whispered, turning to look at him.

He stared down at her, then slowly cupped her cheeks with his hands. They slid down her face, then slipped behind her neck as he pushed his fingers through her long, thick hair. He pulled her a little closer, and the searing warmth of his skin burned through Keira's kirtle. His eyes glowed like burnished gold as he gazed at her, making her breath catch. He lowered his head and gently brushed his lips over hers. Her eyes fluttered closed and she leaned towards him, then pulled away, shocked at her response.

"Please don't," she whispered.

"Why not?" he demanded softly. His gaze wandered back to her mouth, but she shook her head.

"Please," she whispered again. He drew back, his eyebrows raised in question.

"I must go," she said, slipping herself from his hold.

"Keira," he said, grasping her by the arm once again, "please don't run away."

"Aaron." She turned back to him, meeting his golden gaze. "I don't want to be some passing fancy that you quickly forget. Soon you'll be gone again, off to some new place with new hearts to conquer, but I'll still be here, and I don't want to be left a miserable, pining spinster. My heart is the only thing that is truly mine to give – even my maidenhead can be taken against my will, or given away by my parents. And I would give my heart to someone who'd value it, without the risk of it being broken."

"Loving someone is always a risk, Keira," Aaron said, "but if you're prepared to take the risk, then the rewards are beyond telling." He paused, gazing deeply into her eyes, and her pulse began to race. He wrapped his arms around her waist and leaned closer to whisper in her ear. "Sweet Keira, take a risk on me, because I'm in love with you."

Keira pulled back and stared at him in shock, her mind reeling. He returned her gaze steadily as his eyes began to glow.

"Oh, Aaron," she said. "How many other women have you said that to?"

"You're the only one, my sweet," he whispered. He leaned closer, his face mere inches from hers. His warm breath brushed her skin as he spoke.

"I've lived a long time," he said, "far longer than you may suppose, and I won't deny that there have been other women, when the loneliness became too much to bear. But apart from my mother, you're the only woman I have ever loved, and the only one I have ever said those words to."

He stared at her, then lowered his mouth to hers once more. This time she didn't pull away, but instead brought her hands to his bare skin. It was warm and smooth, and she wanted to feel him closer. He lifted his head and stared down at her, then suddenly stiffened when the sound of someone crashing through the trees reached them. His gaze rose swiftly and his expression grew hard.

"Your sister's coming," he growled into her ear before he stepped away, his hands slipping from her waist. Keira looked at him in surprise as Anna broke through the undergrowth a few feet from where they stood.

"Keira," she started, but at the sight of Aaron her eyes widened. She looked back at her sister in disbelief as a sly grin crossed her face. "Mother sent me to find you. I wonder what she'll say when she hears that I found you with a half-naked man hidden in the woods." Anna sniggered, then turned around and raced away.

"Anna," Keira shouted. She gave Aaron a despairing look. "I must go – she'll tell Mother if I don't stop her." Before Aaron had a chance to respond she took off after her sister.

Keira finally caught up with Anna as they approached the village. "Anna, stop! You can't tell Mother," she said, grabbing Anna by the arm.

Anna raised an eyebrow. "Why not?"

"You know she'll forbid me to see Aaron again. And I can't marry Edmund!"

Anna nodded. "Very well, I won't tell her. But you have to make it worth my while to keep silent," she added with a smirk.

Keira hesitated for a moment, then groaned. "Very well! I'll feed the chickens for the next week."

Anna grinned. "Thank you, Keira. You're the best sister there is."

It was afternoon before Keira could escape the house once more, and her footsteps meandered aimlessly towards the woods. She lifted her fingers to her mouth as she walked, and ran them tentatively over her lips. Aaron had kissed her so gently, and the memory of it sent a shiver down her spine. He'd told her he loved her – could it be true? Was it even possible for a man like Aaron to love such a simple country girl? Could she risk her heart with him? It was a silly question, since love, like a thief, had already come creeping in and stolen her heart.

CHAPTER EIGHT

The mist was thick on the ground when Keira crept out of the house at dawn one week later. She glanced back to ensure that Anna wasn't following her, then took off down the path in the direction of the woods. She had fulfilled her agreement with Anna regarding her chores, but wouldn't put it past her sister to sneak after her and check out what she was doing – especially if she could use it against her.

Keira told herself that she was just going for a quick swim, but if she was honest, she was really hoping against all hope that Aaron would be there again. Keira shuddered at her newfound wantonness, dreading to think how her mother would react if she learned that Keira had seen – and kissed – Aaron when he was wearing nothing but his hose. There had been a few meetings at the market since then, but no opportunity for more than a few words of greeting. Still, his smile and the look in his eye made tingles run down her spine.

Keira glanced at the sky as she walked. The early morning sun was burning off the lingering mist, promising another hot, sunny day. She searched the horizon for the dragon, but saw no sign of the huge creature. Lately, it flew over the village on an almost daily basis, and still, no maidens had been reported missing! Keira always stopped to watch it as it circled around in the sky, and sometimes she knew the dragon was watching her, too.

She was so lost in her thoughts that she didn't hear the sound of voices ahead until she was nearly in the clearing. She stopped, tensing when she heard Edmund's voice. He was not alone, and a moment later Keira recognized the voice of Edmund's friend Alan. Keira's heart hammered in her chest, and she took in a deep, slow breath, holding it a moment before gradually exhaling through her lips in an effort to still the pounding. When it was clear that they hadn't heard her, Keira cautiously backed up, holding her breath as she did so, and tentatively placed one foot behind the other. She had only gone a few paces when a twig snapped beneath her foot. The sound echoed through the air, and she froze in fright. She held her breath as the conversation in the clearing stopped midsentence.

"Hey, who's there?" rang Alan's voice through the trees.

"Go check it out, Alan," Edmund said.

At the sound of Edmund's words, Keira spun around and started to run, paying no heed to the noise she was making. She could hear Alan giving chase, and she pushed herself to run faster, but to no avail. In a few moments he caught up with her and grabbed her arm painfully, causing her to trip and fall onto the forest floor.

"Well, look who we have here," Alan said. "I'm sure Edmund will want to know why his future wife is sneaking through the woods."

"Let me go!" Keira tugged at her arm, trying to pull it out of his grasp, but Alan was broad and beefy, and his grip on her was unyielding. He hauled Keira to her feet, and maintaining his grip on her arm, dragged her back towards the lake. Alan threw Keira into the clearing and she landed in a sprawl near Edmund's feet. His eyes widened momentarily before a grin slowly spread across his face.

"Well, well!" he said. "I'm flattered that you went to so much effort to see me. And Keira, since we're all alone, we can have a little fun together!"

Keira pushed herself up to her knees as a cold sprawl of dread mushroomed in the pit of her stomach. She quickly glanced around, trying to discover a means of escape, but Alan anticipated her attempt and placed his foot on her back, forcing her back onto the ground. She spat out a mouthful of dirt and dried leaves as Edmund laughed. He reached down and grabbed a fistful of her hair, painfully pulling her face up to meet his.

"You need a few lessons about pleasing the man who'll soon be your master. And there's no time like the present to start."

Keira looked at him in horror as she pushed herself onto her knees. She knew exactly what Edmund planned to do, and her ire bubbled to the surface. "Never! You'll never be my master, Edmund. Now let me go!"

Edmund's eyes narrowed as he looked at her. Grabbing her arm, he pushed her over in the dirt and turned her onto her back. Before she had a chance to scramble away, he was straddling her.

He wore only a long thin shirt over his damp chest, with nothing beneath it. He grabbed Keira's wrists with one hand and pulled them above her head, pinning them to the ground while he pulled up her skirts with the other.

"No, please Edmund, don't do this," Keira begged, struggling against him.

He yanked her skirts to her waist, then pinched the soft skin of her thigh, twisting his fingers as his nails dug painfully into the tender flesh. She tried to jerk away, but his legs around her waist held her secure. He was hard against her as he started to move, rubbing himself against her pelvis. The feel of his tongue suddenly being forced into her mouth made her wrench her head to the side, and she heard Edmund growl before he landed a sharp slap against her cheek, his nails tearing her skin.

She cried out in pain, but the sound was swallowed by a load roar that rolled through the air like a crash of thunder. Fire sparked around them as embers fell to the ground, and with a rush of wind, Edmund was suddenly off her as huge talons, sharp as razors, encircled his chest and waist. His arms and legs flailed uselessly as he struggled against the dragon's iron grip, while his shirt was ripped to shreds by the claws that dug into his flesh. The relief Keira felt at being released from her tormenter turned to terror as she watched the enormous creature above her. Sparks shot from its mouth, while its huge wings churned dust into the air and made the trees overhead creak and groan against the sudden onslaught of wind and flame.

The dragon made a sharp turn in the air and released Edmund from its grasp. He dropped to the ground below, and his yell of surprise turned to a cry of pain as his body struck the hard surface, knocking over Alan who had been making a valiant effort to flee. Swooping down low, the dragon grasped Keira in its claws, and she shrieked in fright. She lashed out with her arms, trying to free herself from its grasp, but to no avail. Instead, the dragon clasped its claws more firmly around her, ignoring her cries. The creature turned and swooped low over Edmund and Alan, breathing a long stream of fire as it flew past, and they scrambled back in panic as the flames shot to the ground around them. Sparks flew into their hair and onto their clothes, and as a final gesture, the dragon smacked them with its tail as it sailed past them, sending them soaring through the air.

With Keira clasped in its claws, the dragon rose into the morning sky. Unlike the merciless grip with which the dragon had imprisoned Edmund, the talons curled around Keira were gentle even as they held her in an unrelenting grasp. She struggled in vain to free herself from the restraints, twisting and turning in the hope of slipping from the dragon's hold, but a chance glance down at the ground, now rushing far below them, put an effective stop to her struggles. She grabbed the thick leg of her captor, and wrapped her arms around it, suddenly afraid of falling. Although its scales did not extend down its leg, the dragon's skin was rough and incredibly hard, and Keira could feel her hands and arms being scraped raw as she clung to the powerful limb.

The creature pushed itself higher as it soared towards the mountains, leaving the clearing and village far behind. Although the beast cradled her gently in its claws, waves of anger pulsed through the air, and flames spewed from the creature's mouth, warming the air around her.

Dread gripped Keira's heart as she wondered where the beast was taking her, and what it planned to do with her once it got there. The fear grew as she remembered the stories she'd heard as a child. The dragon sniffed the air, then let out a deep sigh before looking down at her, its golden eyes blazing.

"Don't be afraid, Keira," it said. "Unlike those craven curs, I'm not going to harm you, or eat you for breakfast. I would have liked to make a meal of those boys, though," it added darkly, its jaw clenching with fury as it said the words.

Keira gasped. "You speak!" she gasped. "But, you're a dragon! A beast!" The dragon was silent. "Where are you taking me?" she whispered. "Please, just let me go." The dragon's words did nothing to relieve her fear, and her voice trembled. The dragon might have saved her from Edmund, but it could have an even worse fate in store for her. Suddenly, something else penetrated her mind.

"How do you know my name?" she demanded.

The dragon gave a hard laugh. A few moments passed before it responded.

"There's much we need to discuss, Keira," it finally said. "But this is not quite how I envisaged having this conversation. Let me find a good place to land, and then we can talk."

Keira wondered what the dragon considered a good place

to land. Some smelly cave, maybe? The idea wasn't very reassuring, but it did make her think of Aaron – hadn't he said that he would rescue her if she was captured by the dragon? Storbrook Castle was built atop a tall mountain, so perhaps he would see her in the dragon's grasp and set out to rescue her from the creature's lair. The thought make Keira smile, despite her dire circumstance. Her mind turned back to her captor's words: something about the dragon's voice tugged at Keira's memory, but it scattered in her mind before she was able to grab hold of it. Despite her fear, she could not help but marvel at the splendid creature that was carrying her through the air. From her vantage point she could see the body of the dragon, massive above her. Its huge wings spread out above its body, both graceful and powerful, while the strong tail streamed out behind. Flames continued to rush from its mouth, the heat curling around Keira before dissipating in the cool morning air.

The land below them changed from fields to mountains. The dragon began to descend as a large alpine meadow spread out below them. It released Keira a few feet above the ground, and she watched as the mighty creature came to a graceful stop a few feet away. It folded its wings onto its back, and curled its tail as it lay down on the ground facing her. Keira trembled slightly as she gazed at the enormous creature. Even lying down, its head towered above her, power rippling through its massive form. Golden horns stretched backwards from the top of its skull and blended with the sharp spikes that ran down the length of its long neck. The thick tail was as long as the dragon's body and was fiercely armed with more spikes. Even at its tip, Keira would not have been able to wrap her hands around it. The upper part of its body was covered in golden scales, as hard and strong as iron, while the skin beneath looked tough and leathery. Two pairs of legs, thick as small tree trunks, stretched from its underbody; they ended in sharp claws that could rip out the heart of any enemy with ease. It was an awesome and terrifying creature, and Keira's heart drummed out a fearful tattoo as she gazed at the mighty beast, who stared back at her with golden eyes that blazed with flame.

The dragon stared at Keira in silence for a few moments, then bent its neck into a graceful arch and brought its face close to hers. Keira quelled the desire to step back, instead keeping her feet firmly planted as she continued to gaze at the dragon.

"Why did you take me?" she finally asked, shuddering at the thought of what might have been. She lifted her hand to her face, feeling the sting of scratches scored down her cheek. A flash of sharp teeth made her draw in her breath as the dragon replied with a growl.

"I'm sorry Keira," it said. "I should have been there sooner. When I think of what that boy was about to do ..." The dragon stopped and pulled in a breath. "I shouldn't have left him alive."

Keira trembled at the thought. "But why?" she said. "What does it matter to you?"

The dragon stared at her for a long moment, until finally it breathed out a sigh, sending sparks flaring from its nostrils. "Come closer, Keira," it said.

Keira hesitated, wondering what the dragon intended to do with her.

"I won't hurt you," it said.

Keira looked at the mighty beast before her and suppressed a shudder. Its claws rested on the ground, razor-sharp and menacing. She could see its pointed teeth and knew that it could rip her to shreds in an instant, or burn her to a crisp with one hot breath. One swipe of its massive tail could send her flying through the air, or leave her broken on the ground. Keira knew that the dragon could wield mighty power with barely any effort, striking fear into the hearts of many brave men. But as she looked at the dragon, gazing into eyes that blazed like the fire it breathed, she knew she was in no danger.

"I know," she replied softly. ""I believe you, even though you terrify me."

"Why?" asked the dragon in surprise. "You know that I could kill you as easily as you would swat at a mosquito. Maybe I only saved you so that I could have you for breakfast! Maidens taste especially sweet first thing in the morning."

Keira grimaced before slowly replying. "You said you wouldn't hurt me, and I trust you. I've heard plenty of stories about dragons, but you make me feel ..." She searched for the right word. "Safe."

The bony ridge above the dragon's eyes lifted in astonishment. "Come," it said. Keira hesitated another moment before slowly walking towards the beast.

"Touch me," the dragon said softly. "Feel my scales and know that my strength protects you." Keira stretched out a trembling hand and gently placed it against the dragon's neck, her hand small against the giant. The dragon watched her with its golden eyes as she gently ran her fingers over its might armor. The scales were smooth, like plates of gold melded together. Moving slowly, she walked along the dragon's length and down to its tail. The dragon lifted it slightly in response to her touch, then smacked it back on the ground.

"You're beautiful," whispered Keira. "A beautiful drake." The dragon pulled back slightly, its bony eyebrows raised. "Show me your wings," Keira said softly. The dragon unfurled them, dropping the tips until they rested on the ground. Keira's eyes widened at the size of them, stretching out twelve feet on either side of its body. She reached up to touch the massive appendages, slowly running her hands against the smooth surface. She expected them to feel hard and leathery, but they were soft, as though woven from many strands of silk. The dragon shuddered slightly at her gentle touch before bending its head closer, golden eyes gleaming.

"Sweet Keira," it said softly, "you asked me why I saved

you. And how I know your name." The dragon paused, watching her carefully. "You already know the answers, my sweet, because you already know me, as I know you. There is no reason for you to fear me, because I would never hurt you. You see me now as I truly am – a dragon capable of terrifying acts. But Keira, you also know me as something else. As someone else."

Keira stared at the dragon, her mind struggling to accept his words.

"You already know who I am, Keira." He leaned closer, his voice a murmur. "Say my name." She stared at him in silence. "Say it," he said. "Your heart already knows the answer."

"Aaron," she said softly. "Your name is Aaron Drake." The dragon gazed at her for a long moment, his eyes burning into hers as she stared back.

"Ah, Keira," he murmured. "Do I scare you?"

"No," she whispered. Tentatively, the dragon lifted a claw and gently brushed the back of it down her cheek. His warm breath washed over her, smelling of fire and musk. Reaching up her hand, Keira placed it between his eyes, running it down the bony length of his snout. Sparks flew from his nostrils as he stared at her.

"Stand back, Keira," he said, "and look away."

Keira took a few steps back, her heart racing as she continued to gaze at the dragon.

"Further back, over by that rock," he said. "And turn your face away – your human eyes cannot tolerate the light of my change."

Keira walked backwards to the rock he had pointed out, then stared at him for a long moment before turning around. A bright flash of light lit up the area around her before slowly fading away.

"Keep looking away," she heard Aaron call. "I need to clothe myself." She waited a moment, her face turned away, until she heard his footsteps approaching. She turned back to him slowly, shy and uncertain, but when he pulled her into his arms and softly kissed her, she felt her trepidation melting away. He wore a pair of loose workman's trousers, but his chest was bare, his skin golden, and she could feel the heat of him through the thin fabric of her kirtle as he held her close. Her eyes widened in surprise when she saw the tips of wings behind his shoulders, tightly folded against his back. He pulled away slightly to look down at her.

"Are you all right, my sweet?" he asked. She gazed up into his eyes, shining gold, and nodded slowly. Aaron ran his thumb against her lower lip before cupping her cheek. Her mouth opened slightly in response to his touch, and in a moment his lips were on hers again. She gasped at the unfamiliar touch of his tongue against her lips before opening her mouth further in response. The air from his mouth was hot, spilling over her like a flame. Her hands rose to his neck as she wrapped her fingers into his hair and pulled him closer. She heard a faint rustling sound, and saw that he had unfurled his wings, wrapping them around them both like a cocoon, protecting them from the world. She slid her hands to his back and gently stroked the joint of his wings, and he moaned and pulled her tighter, deepening the kiss.

CHAPTER NINE

The sun was high as they lay in the grass of the alpine meadow, Aaron's arms wrapped around Keira as she lay against his chest. His wings were gone, and except for slight ridges along the length of his spine, there was nothing to show that he ever had wings sprouting from his back.

"When you're like this, in human form, can you do the things you can do as a dragon?" Keira asked. Aaron looked at her for a moment before slowly replying.

"You see me as a human," he said, "but I am a dragon – in whatever form I take. The qualities you see as being those of a dragon are always a part of me. I'm not human, Keira, even when I look and act human. Can you understand that?"

"So even like this, you're still … a dragon?" She sat up, pulling her knees to her chest as she gazed at the ground, trying to grasp what he was saying.

"Yes." Aaron watched her for a moment, before shifting himself to face her. He placed a finger under her chin, forcing her to look into his eyes. "Can you accept that, Keira? Can you accept me for what I am?"

Keira gazed at him, her eyes wide, as a slew of emotions assaulted her. All her life, she had been taught to fear dragons. Stories of their ferociousness and cruelty had been a part of her childhood, and although she trusted this dragon, she didn't doubt that the stories were true.

"Do you eat people?"

"Yes, amongst other things. And never the innocent," he replied, his gaze unwavering.

Keira gulped, closing her eyes. "How old are you?" she asked.

"A hundred and five," he replied.

She lifted a hand to cover her eyes, but a moment later felt his warm fingers as he gently pulled it away.

"Open your eyes, Keira, and look at me," he whispered.

She opened her eyes slowly. His face was only inches away and she caught her breath as she stared into eyes that burned fiercely, like flames contained behind a sheet of glass, the color shifting and moving as he gazed at her. They were completely inhuman, but as she looked at him, she forgot her fears. It didn't matter that he was a dragon, that he wasn't human. What mattered was that he loved her. She lifted her hand to his cheek. "I love you, Aaron Drake," she said, "no matter what you are."

Keira hadn't thought it was possible for his eyes to burn any more brightly, but in the moment before his lips touched hers, they blazed as brilliantly as the sun. His warmth radiated through her as his arm slipped around her waist, pulling her closer.

"As I love you, Keira Carver," he murmured. "I loved you from the first moment I saw you, my sweet, and it wasn't in the marketplace." He laughed softly.

"It wasn't?" She pulled back in surprise before realization sunk in. "Of course, it was when you flew over the village."

"That's right," he said. "You showed no fear at all. Just curiosity, and … something else I couldn't quite place."

"It was awe," she whispered, "you looked so beautiful."

"Ah, Keira," he said. He brushed his lips against hers.

"So can you breathe flame when you look like this?" she

asked a moment later.

"I can – look." He lifted his hand and held it a few inches from his mouth, then blew out a stream of flame. It curled around his hand and dissipated.

"Doesn't it burn you?" she asked in surprise.

"Dragons are made from fire," Aaron explained. "The flames cannot hurt me."

"What else is different?"

"My senses are far more acute than yours. My eyesight rivals that of a hawk – I need to be able to see fair maidens from quite a distance, you know."

Keira glared at him, and he grinned. "But I limit myself to the beautiful ones," he murmured into her ear. Keira blushed and pushed him away.

"Can you fly when you're like this?" she asked.

"I can. Should I show you?" He pulled her to her feet and wrapped his arms around her, one hand around her waist while the other supported her weight. She gasped as her feet left the ground, and wrapped her arms tightly around his neck. She closed her eyes for a moment as she regained her sense of equilibrium.

"I won't let you fall," Aaron whispered in her ear.

"I know," she said. With a deep breath, she opened her eyes. His wings were stretched out behind his back, huge and beautiful, and she watched in amazement as they moved through the air, lifting them higher. She felt his gaze on her, gauging her reaction, and she turned to look at him. His eyes caught hers, and her mouth fell open to draw in a breath. It was stolen away a moment later as he kissed her. It wasn't just his eyes that burned with flame – his hands on her back seared her skin, and his lips scorched hers as they demanded a bold response. Keira's hold around Aaron's neck loosened from a death grip as she wound her fingers into his hair and pulled him closer, her need matching his.

The air warmed and the sun sped across the sky as they floated in the silence, across mountain peaks and alpine streams. It was so peaceful, a world away from Edmund. It was Aaron who finally brought them back to reality.

"I should probably get you home before your neighbors start sending out hunting parties to rescue you from the dragon," he said, his tone reluctant.

"You're right!" she said, suddenly alarmed. "I couldn't bear it if people tried to hurt you."

"I'm not worried about me," he replied with a snort. "It would take more than a few humans with pitchforks to hurt me. But people will think that you're in danger, and I don't want that." They were descending as he spoke, and a moment later were back on the ground.

"People cannot know what I am," he said. "I must change back to my natural form."

She nodded. "Of course."

He stared at her for a moment, then grabbing her arms, gave her a hard kiss before pushing her away. "I've never had an incentive to remain human before," he said, "but you make it hard for me to change." He turned around. "I need to unclothe myself," he said over his shoulder.

Keira turned away and waited until a bright light filled the air. She turned back and stared at the enormous dragon standing before her. He cocked his head, and she swallowed hard.

"How do you do that?" she said.

He smiled. "Mind over matter," he said. "Now climb on my back." She eyed him suspiciously, and he laughed. "Stand at my side," he said. She walked over to him, then gasped in shock when he wrapped his tail around her waist and lifted her onto his back.

"Lie down and hold my neck," he said.

"Have you done this before?" Keira asked. "Carry a human on your back?"

Aaron laughed. "No."

"I'm not going to fall, am I?"

"Not if you hold on tightly." He turned his head and

smirked. "There's nothing wrong with my flying, so the fault won't lie there."

She groaned, and wrapped her arms around his neck as tightly as she could.

"Ready?" he asked. He didn't wait for her reply, but unfurled his wings and lifted himself into the air. Keira relaxed her grip slightly as the wind rushed past her face. As long as she remained steady, she could tell it would be difficult to tumble from Aaron's broad back.

"You asked if I've flown with other humans," he said, "but apart from my mother, you're the only human who knows my true form."

"Your mother is human?" she said, shocked.

"Was," he said. "Yes, she was human."

"Oh! I'm sorry. About losing her, I mean." She paused for a moment, considering his words. "So the other women …"

"Never truly knew me, Keira. Only you."

Keira smiled as she wrapped her hands tighter around him. All too soon the village came into view, and Aaron dropped towards a clearing on the outskirts. He landed gracefully, and Keira slipped off his back, sliding over his smooth scales. She walked around to face him and stared into eyes that gleamed gold. She stretched up her hand and laid it against the hard, leathery skin on his face. He returned the gaze, then leaned forward and placed his cheek against hers. His breath was hot against her neck, lifting the hair around her face.

"Keira," he said, pausing for a moment, "you do understand that no-one can know who I truly am? People cannot know that the dragon is more than a mere beast."

"I understand," she said. "I won't tell anyone. But I will tell them that you're good. And that you saved me from Edmund."

He snorted softly. "You'll have a hard time convincing them of that. People can be quite obdurate when it comes to changing their beliefs."

"Well, I can certainly try."

"I'll see you soon, my sweet," he said softly, then pulled back and lifted himself into the air. She watched as he circled above her for a few moments before turning in the direction of the mountains.

As soon as she walked into the village, Keira saw her mother running towards her.

"Keira!" she screamed. "Keira! Thank God – you're alive! We thought that dreadful monster had eaten you." She grabbed Keira's hand, pulling her off balance. "How did you escape? You must hide!"

"Mother, there's no need to hide," Keira said. "The dragon brought me back. And he's not a dreadful monster – he saved me from Edmund."

"Saved you?" Mother gasped. "How can you say that? Dragons are dangerous predators that love to eat girls like you. What has that creature done to twist your mind like this? Edmund told us how he almost lost his life fighting the dragon as he tried to save you. Why are you making up these lies?"

At these words Keira came to a stop, yanking her arm from her mother's grip as she stared at her in astonishment.

"Mother, Edmund was going to rape me. The dragon saved me from him. He is the one who is lying."

Mother stared at Keira for a moment, her eyes narrowing. "Why are you doing this? You've known Edmund all your life! And you're going to be his wife! But instead of standing by him, you defend the actions of a hideous monster!" She gave Keira an angry look before turning on her heel and storming away. Keira watched in shock as angry tears gathered, but a moment later she was running after the retreating figure.

"Mother, stop!" she shouted. "Why would I lie about Edmund? And why would the dragon have brought me back if he wanted to hurt me?"

Her mother stopped her marching and twirled around to face Keira once more.

"I don't know why you would lie about Edmund," she said. "Perhaps he said something to upset you, and you want vengeance." Keira drew back in disbelief. "And as for the dragon," Mother continued, "who knows what evil motives drive its actions." She glared at Keira for a long moment, then spun around and marched off once more. Running after her again, Keira caught up as they neared the house.

"Mother, please," she begged. "You have to believe me."

"Keira, I don't know what has gotten into you," Mother said, "but dragons are hideous, evil monsters! The spawn of hell!" She spat out the words, and Keira instinctively took a step back as Mother continued. "Perhaps the dragon did rescue you from Edmund's advances, but the question is why? Dragons are crafty and shrewd, so why would a man-eating beast choose to save a pretty girl and bring her back? And as for Edmund, I've known him since he was a babe in his mother's arms. Perhaps he behaved rashly, but his intentions are never dishonorable. Yet you're asking me to believe that Edmund is bad, while a dragon is good. That would be like asking me to say that night is day and day is night – that fish live in nests while birds dive to the depths of the lakes. These things are impossible, Keira, as impossible as a noble dragon!

Keira's mother yelled the last word as Father rounded the corner, Anna close on his heels. He grabbed Keira by the hands.

"Keira! Thank God you're safe," he said. "We've been so worried. When Edmund said that you'd been taken by the dragon we feared the worst. How did you manage to escape?" He lifted his hand to his daughter's cheek. "The dragon has hurt you."

"No, Father," Keira replied wearily. "Those scratches were inflicted by Edmund, not the dragon. The dragon saved me from Edmund when he was attacking me."

"Why am I not surprised?" Anna said, and Keira looked at her in astonishment.

"What does that mean?" Mother asked sharply.

"Edmund's only charming when he chooses to be. I've heard how he speaks to Keira."

Keira smiled at Anna gratefully then turned back to Father. "Please, Father, you must believe me when I say that the dragon did nothing to hurt me, and was the means of my rescue."

Father glanced quickly at his wife, who shrugged, hands upraised to indicate her incomprehension, before answering. "Keira, dragons are not good creatures. They are wild beasts that savagely hunt people and eat them. This is not the first dragon to have lived near the village, and you know the story about the last one. It burned down half the village, killing many in the process." He laid his hands on his daughter's shoulders and waited for her to meet his gaze before continuing. "Keira, I don't know what happened between you and Edmund, but if you persist in saying that he hurt you while the dragon rescued you, there will be repercussions. The reeve won't let your accusations lie unanswered. And since it's your word against Edmund's … well, you won't win yourself any friends. Half the village is indebted to the reeve. They cannot afford to have him as an enemy."

"I know, Father, but Edmund did try to rob me of my maidenhood. And I cannot let people think badly of the dragon."

"Clearly, her wits have been addled," said Mother. "She's been going on like this since she returned."

"The important thing is that she's returned to us safely," said Father, turning to his wife. "She's been through a trying ordeal, and probably needs to rest. She should go inside, out of the sun, and have a strong drink before lying down for a while."

"I'm fine," Keira insisted, but Anna linked her arm

through her sister's and drew her away.

"Come, Keira. A little wine will help to settle your nerves," she said. She led her sister towards the house, lowering her voice as she did so. "Nothing you say is going to convince them that the dragon meant you no harm. Just leave them be."

"But Anna, I can't let them think that," Keira said. "The dragon really did save me. He really is a good dragon."

Anna rolled her eyes. "There's no such thing as a good dragon, Keira. I believe you when you say that Edmund meant to hurt you, but you can't say that the dragon isn't dangerous." Keira opened her mouth in objection, but Anna quickly raised her hand to silence her. "I know what you're going to say, Keira, but there's no point. Clearly your dragon decided to let you live, but that's no reason to think it won't hurt others, or try to burn down the village one day. Instead of helping people, you could land up helping the dragon destroy us."

"No," Keira said, shaking her head. She pulled her arm from Anna's and stepped into the house. Suddenly, retreating to her room where she could be alone seemed very appealing. She hurried up the stairs and closed the door behind her, before sinking to her bed. She closed her eyes, remembering the burning touch of a dragon as his lips seared hers.

CHAPTER TEN

The next day was market day, and Keira sat at the table, her regular smile missing as a cloud of dejection settled over her. Her mother had been aloof that morning, and the merchants at the other tables were pointedly ignoring her, looking away when she smiled and waved in greeting.

It hadn't taken long for the villagers to hear that Keira had been returned, unharmed, by the dragon. At first they were incredulous, but as she continued to insist that the dragon was not to be feared, and was, in fact, a good dragon, her neighbors' incredulity turned to anger, and then to downright hostility. It seemed that Aaron was right about changing people's beliefs, she thought dejectedly.

Anna was sitting at the table with Keira, determined to be a friendly face for her sister through the long day. Keira was surprised at Anna's unexpected loyalty. When she commented on it, Anna had raised her eyebrows. "You're my sister! I'm the only one who can be mean to you," she'd said. Keira smiled, grateful to have someone at her side.

The sounds of the market grew louder as merchants called out to potential shoppers, but Keira just stared at the hands in her lap. A shadow fell over the table, but she kept her eyes averted, unwilling to read the hostility in yet another person's expression, as she listened to her sister's voice of admonishment.

"Have you come to gloat over my sister, like everyone else, milord?" Anna hissed.

Keira brought her head up in astonishment, meeting the golden brown eyes that gazed at her in question. "Keira? What's happened?" Aaron asked softly.

Keira opened her mouth to answer, but Anna was quicker. "You mean you haven't heard?" Anna snorted. "Keira was taken by the dragon yesterday – it rescued her from Edmund, but he's saying he tried to save her from the dragon. Of course, no-one believes Edmund did anything wrong, and they're saying that Keira is siding with the dragon over her own friends and neighbors!"

"Keira, is this true?" Aaron asked. She nodded, and his voice grew harder. "What about your parents, what do they say?"

"My mother doesn't believe me," Keira said.

"She believes Edmund instead," Anna chimed in angrily. "She's telling everyone that somehow the dragon has affected Keira's mind. Everyone knows that dragons are man-eating monsters, so why would a dragon return a maid unharmed? And of course, there are no other witnesses to verify Keira's story."

Aaron watched Keira as Anna spoke, his eyes narrowing in fury as he heard her answer. His fists clenched at his sides as his eyes started to blaze with open flames, while gold shimmered just below the surface of his skin.

"Aaron," Keira said softly, shaking her head.

He glared at her for a moment, but then his expression softened as a long stream of hot air escaped his lips. He turned to Anna, a hard smile on his face.

"On the contrary," he said, "I can provide testimony to the occurrences of yesterday. I was walking near a small lake yesterday morning when I heard voices close by. I recognized

Edmund's straight away. A girl screamed, begging him to stop what he was doing." His voice rose as he spoke, his words carrying through the market as they were quickly relayed from one merchant to another. "It was Keira, and I ran towards the sounds, but before I reached the scene, the dragon swooped down and grabbed her. It was clear from Keira's pleading that Edmund's intentions were not honorable."

"Why should we believe you, a stranger in our village?" asked one of the merchants who had edged closer to hear Aaron's words.

"The fact that I am a stranger to these parts makes me an impartial observer," rejoined Aaron tightly. The group of people around the wood carver's stall was growing, and some of the listeners shuffled as they considered Aaron's response.

"Edmund was probably just having some harmless fun and got carried away," said another merchant.

Aaron shook his head. "Are you so anxious to think badly of the dragon that you're prepared to overlook what Keira endured at Edmund's hands?"

Another voice piped up. "We should give Edmund the chance to answer these charges before we pass any judgment. I'm sure it was just a misunderstanding."

Cries of "yes" ran through the crowd, but before matters went any further the reeve pushed his way through the gathering, his white reeve stick clenched tightly in his fist. He glared at Keira for a moment before turning towards the throng. He waited in silence as those gathered turned their attention to him.

"You, Daniel Draper," he said, pointing at one of the merchants near the front of the crowd, "what's going on here?"

Daniel Draper glanced around nervously and cleared his throat. "Um, Reeve Hobbes, this man here," he said, waving in Aaron's direction, "says he heard Keira screaming in distress just before the dragon snatched her yesterday."

The reeve turned to Aaron with a frown. "Is this true?"

"It is," Aaron said, his expression like steel.

The reeve turned back to Daniel. "Pray, continue."

"We thought that Edmund should have an opportunity to defend himself."

The reeve stared at the merchant, his eyes narrowed in consideration, then looked out over the crowd with a nod. "Indeed, he should. We'll have a meeting at the town hall this evening at sundown. You," he said, turning back to Aaron, "will be present to give your version of events, I'm sure?"

Aaron met his gaze and inclined his head. "Of course."

The two men glared at each other for a moment before the reeve turned back to the crowd.

"Everyone, clear out and get back to work."

Keira and Anna had been quiet as the events unfolded before them, but as the crowd slowly dispersed, Keira rose and leaned towards Aaron.

"What are you doing?" she demanded softly.

Aaron met her glare with eyebrows raised. "Just telling them the truth, my sweet."

"You're making enemies," she said, dropping her voice lower. "You will have the whole village against you."

Aaron leaned his hands against the table, bringing his face close to hers.

"I really don't care what this village thinks of me," he said, his voice hard and low, "but I do care what they think of you, and I'm not going to sit back and let them spread lies about you." His voice softened as he looked into her eyes. "Do you really think I'd stand back and let them make these accusations against you, and not do anything about it? Do you not understand what I feel for you?"

His eyes started to brighten as he looked at her, and Keira caught her breath, her own expression softening in response.

"Thank you," she whispered.

"The pleasure is all mine."

"Ahem." The sound of Anna clearing her throat made

Keira jump. "Mother's headed this way."

Keira returned her gaze to Aaron, still leaning on the table, and his eyes held hers for another moment before he pushed himself to his full height and took a slow step back.

When Mother appeared a moment later, she glanced between her daughters before turning to Aaron.

"I heard there was some sort of commotion, daughter," she said, addressing Keira, but continuing to watch the man before her.

Keira remained silent, and Anna answered. "Yes, Mother. Milord Drake had some information about Keira's abduction yesterday. It seems he heard Keira screaming just before the dragon snatched her."

"Is this true?" asked Mother, her eyes never shifting from Aaron. He met her gaze steadily.

"Yes, it is true," he said. "I heard her begging Edmund to stop what he was doing, just before the dragon rescued her."

"You're a stranger in these parts," Mother said. "For all we know you're in league with the dragon. They are not kind and sweet, but rather, cruel monsters that feast on humans." Her eyes narrowed. "Edmund's mother was my closest friend before she died, and I've watched her boys grow up. You expect me to believe that he would knowingly hurt Keira, but that is impossible." Mother placed her hands on her hips. "I don't know what your purpose is in spreading these lies, but I do know that dragons are wicked beasts, while Edmund is a good man."

Aaron's eyebrows shot up in surprise. "What about your daughter, Madam Carver?" he said. "Is she not a good woman? Should she not merit more of your concern than that worthless boy?"

"How dare you?" Mother said. "Do not presume to question my relationship with my daughter. You! A stranger! Now, unless you have business here, I suggest you leave."

"You'll not get rid of me that easily, Madam Carver. I'll leave now, because I can see that this is distressing your daughter, but I won't go far."

He glanced at Keira as he said these words. Her features were pale and her hands trembled, but she held herself erect as her parent finished her rant. The tightness around his eyes softened as he looked at her, his eyes becoming more golden.

"Keira," he said softly. He gazed at for a moment before he turned and walked away.

"That man is infatuated with you, Keira, so it's clear he cannot be trusted," Mother said.

Keira watched him retreat and knew he had heard Mother's words when his shoulders stiffened and his hands curled into fists. He paused for a moment before continuing on his way, and Keira breathed a sigh of relief, glad that further confrontation was avoided, even if it was to be only a temporary respite.

CHAPTER ELEVEN

The small village hall was filled to overflowing by the time the sun dropped behind the mountains. People are drawn to a scandal, and they are getting it here aplenty, thought Keira bitterly. She wished she could climb into bed, pull the covers over her head, and wake up to find that this had all been a terrible dream. Except, was it so terrible? The events at the lake had brought Aaron to her, and Keira could not regret that.

She glanced around, wondering if Aaron had arrived yet, but a quick sweep of the small hall brought no sight of him. Next to her, Keira's mother sat stiffly on the long, wooden bench, looking straight ahead. As Keira looked at her, a familiar numbness settled over her heart. Keira was the oldest, the firstborn, and she knew that her mother had been happy with her once, when motherhood was still full of promise. But while Mary Hobbes had borne four sons, Mother had lost four, one after the other. And each time Mother had buried one of her children, she'd buried a little piece of her heart along with them. Anna was the answer to all Mother's prayers – the child that survived infancy when the previous babies had succumbed to various childhood ailments. And even though she wasn't the longed-for boy, Anna was Mother's miracle child. By the time Anna was a toddler, Keira knew that the affection her mother had once had for her had been transferred to Anna. It was a tough lesson for a girl of eight, but Keira was filled with natural optimism, and it never occurred to her to be jealous of her little sister. Instead, she shouldered the additional burden of care that Mother placed on her small shoulders without complaining. But her heart ached for a mother's soothing love to heal it.

Soft murmurings and the sound of shuffling feet caught Keira's attention, and she turned to see the reeve amble through the crowd, passing the villagers with a wave and a friendly word. Edmund walked behind him, flashing a charming smile at the crowd as he hobbled along with a crutch for support. His leg was swathed with bandages, and a sling kept his arm in place. Cuts and bruises marred his handsome face, but did not detract from his good looks. His eye fell on Keira, and for a moment the smile was replaced with a scowl, but it was quickly wiped away. Keira shivered. Edmund would never forgive her for this latest insult.

The reeve reached the front of the room and turned to face the crowd with a smile. His gaze fell on Mother, and he nodded at her sympathetically, before his gaze moved on to look at Keira and the smile became a little more brittle. He turned back to the crowd.

"Thank you, friends and neighbors, for joining us tonight. There has been much speculation about what happened yesterday at the lake between my son and Mistress Keira. There seems to be no doubt that Edmund and Keira met there, perhaps by design. There also seems to be no doubt that Mistress Keira was removed from the lake by the dragon that has been plaguing our village, and returned, unharmed, quite a few hours later." He paused a moment, allowing this to sink in. "Mistress Keira, for reasons of her own, has decided to level the most heinous accusations against my son.

Now, I think we all know that Edmund is an upstanding and honorable member of our community, and these accusations stretch our incredulity. Even though he is my son, you also know that, as your reeve, I hold myself to the highest standards when judging a person's character, and would not allow the prejudice of a parent to sway my objectivity.

"Of course, Mistress Keira is a young woman; friendly and amiable, to be sure, but, like all women, prone to excitability and nervous emotion. You all know what I'm talking about," he continued. "How many of you have come home to your wives fussing and fuming over some trivial incident that she's blown up to gigantic proportions?" There were a few snickers around the hall as the women glared at the reeve. He raised his hands as he continued. "And if it hadn't been for the interference of a stranger, we would be able to forgive her and move on to other matters. However, a stranger did interfere, and now we are forced to give up precious time to sort out the facts in this matter, and absolve Edmund of wrongdoing." He turned to Edmund. "Would you like to tell us what actually happened?"

Edmund hobbled forward with a grimace. Beside her, Keira felt her mother tense in sympathy. He glanced around the crowd. "Many of you know Keira and I are intended for each other," he began. "Although we haven't yet named a day, we are, er, eager to spend time together. She was pleased to meet at the lake that morning – in fact, she may have even suggested it. Of course, I was quite happy to oblige." Keira listened in mounting anger as a few laughs ran through the crowd. He gave a contrite smile. "She was eager at first, allowing me to get close, but then began to play coy and tried to push me away. She wanted me to stop touching her, but, well, you know how it is. It isn't always so easy to stop." His eyes settled on Keira, taunting her, and she leapt to her feet, trembling with rage at his insinuations.

"No," she shouted, but her voice was drowned out by another that rang out from the back of the room.

"It seems that your professed affection for Mistress Keira does not prevent you from casting her in the light of a coquette." Keira turned to see Aaron striding down the aisle. He was strikingly dressed in a gold silk shirt worn beneath a red velvet doublet, gold silk hose and long leather boots. Over his shoulders he wore a woolen coat of radiant scarlet lined with blue silk, clasped together over his chest with a gold brooch of a dragon, inlaid with precious stones. Murmurs rippled through the crowd as the villagers took in his splendid raiment, far more spectacular than the reeve had ever worn. "It does make me question how sincere you'll be when you give your vow to love and protect her. After all," he continued, "will you protect her from yourself?" He looked out over the crowd. "Perhaps we should give Mistress Keira the opportunity to give her version of events."

Keira gasped in surprise – women were never invited to speak for themselves, but no sooner had he said the words than the reeve quickly dismissed the suggestion.

"Now, milord, I don't think that's necessary. She's just a woman, after all, but if there are any men who would like to speak on her behalf …" The reeve looked out over the assembly for a brief moment, then turned back to Aaron. "Perhaps you'd like to speak for her?" he asked graciously.

Aaron gave the reeve a derisive look and turned to the audience once more.

"I was walking in the woods yesterday morning when I heard Mistress Keira crying, begging Edmund to let her go. It was clear from her pleas that she was very much afraid. I hurried towards the lake to lend my aid, but before I reached her, the dragon snatched her in his claws, rescuing her from her persecutor." He stopped and looked out over the crowd. "Do you know that dragons can smell fear? That the dragon would've known that Mistress Keira was in a situation not of her own choosing?"

"You're lying," Edmund snarled. "You weren't there. I would've seen you if you were."

"Of course you didn't see me," Aaron replied, unperturbed. "You were lying on the ground surrounded by flames. When I saw that the dragon had already dealt you a fitting punishment, I left you to your own devices."

"So you left me to die?"

"Well, clearly you didn't die," was Aaron's reply, "so any interference by me was unnecessary."

Before Edmund had a chance to respond, a voice rose from the center of the room.

"You live in Storbrook Castle." Keira looked back to see Widower Brown pushing his way forward. He shook his finger at Aaron as he spoke. "We all know that the dragon has his lair around there. It's even been said that the dragon comes and goes as it pleases. You're probably in league with that monster. For all we know, the dragon brought the girl back to you so that you could ravish her."

"Yes!" Will Hunter shouted. "How else do you know that dragons smell fear?"

"You're in league with the dragon," yelled Jem Young.

"You don't belong here," shouted someone else. Around the room a babble was starting to grow.

"Silence!" ordered Aaron, his voice rising above the din. The word rang out with an air of command and authority, and a hush fell over the room as everyone turned to face him once more.

"I have had business dealings with many of you. I've bought your wares, traded with you for your livestock and bartered with you for food for my pantry." He paused and allowed his gaze to slowly sweep across the room, his eyes lingering on people he knew before; they looked down in embarrassment. "Have I ever been dishonest in my business dealings? Ever given any of you cause to question my honor? Have I ever underpaid you, or driven too hard a bargain?" Aaron paused for a moment, his eyes sweeping across the room. "No!" Aaron shook his hand in emphasis. "Yet you refuse to listen to me because I'm a stranger to these parts.

You imagine there exists some alliance between me and this dragon that has taken up residence in the surrounding mountains." Aaron's hand swept across the room as he continued. "Have any of you actually seen the dragon's lair? Can any of you say for certain that it's below Storbrook Castle, the home of my ancestors? And what has this dragon done that has given you cause for concern? Has he stolen your property? Killed your daughters? Burned your houses? No! But when the dragon saves one of your own, you are ready to assume the worst."

"We all know what happened the last time a dragon took up residence around here," Jem shouted. "It seemed friendly enough at first, but in the end it burned down half our village."

"I've heard of this dragon," said Aaron, his voice dropping so people in the back had to strain to hear him. "But I've also heard that it was sorely provoked when one of the villagers killed a woman when she was seen in its presence."

"The dragon was abducting her," Edmund shouted. "It would have killed her."

"Indeed?" Aaron said. "The story I heard was that the lady was killed at the hands of a villager, despite the dragon's efforts to save her." He turned to face the reeve as he spoke. Reeve Hobbes met his gaze for an uncomfortable moment, before dropping his eyes to the ground. Aaron looked at the crowd. "However, I'm not here to debate what happened more than seventy years ago, and only wish to suggest that the dragon then may have had his reasons for attacking the village. Regardless, the dragon who lives here now did rescue Keira from her attacker, as I can attest."

There were some murmurs around the hall, but the hecklers had been silenced. The reeve stepped forward.

"Well, friends, you've heard what Master Drake, a stranger to our village, and maybe even an associate of the dragon, has had to say. And you've heard Edmund relate the events as they unfolded. I will leave you to decide who to believe, but for myself, I know that I will place my trust in someone I know. I can only urge you to do the same." He motioned to Edmund and headed out of the room, as his son limped out behind him.

As they left, others in the room stood up and began to take their leave as well. The crowd was hushed, but as the noise of departure grew, so too did the sound of voices. Aaron grabbed Keira by the hand and hauled her to her feet.

"You should go home," Aaron said. "It would only take one ill-considered comment to get the crowd going again." He turned towards Keira's father, his expression grim. "Get your daughter home while it's still safe."

Father gazed at Aaron for a moment before nodding his head in acceptance. "Thank you for coming forward to defend my daughter's honor," he said softly.

"Since there seems to be a dearth of supporters willing to speak in your daughter's defense, it was the least I could do, especially since I related nothing but the truth." His eyes regarded Mother as he said the words, his features hard. Father looked down in embarrassment, but Aaron had already returned his gaze to Keira. She stepped around him, and he turned to face her.

"Thank you," she whispered fervently. "But if they turn against you, I'll hold myself responsible."

"No!" His response was vehement. "This was my fault. I'm so sorry that you have been placed in this position."

Keira placed her hand on his arm and gazed into his eyes. "I'm so glad it was you who saved me," she murmured. "I cannot regret that." She smiled up at him before continuing. "Meet me by the river near the old mill tomorrow morning. I'll be there as early as I can, but if I'm not, it's only because I couldn't get away." She gave him one last, longing look, then turned and headed for the exit.

CHAPTER TWELVE

Keira was up before the first cock announced the new day, slipping out of the house in the darkness and rushing towards the river. Aaron was waiting for her in the shadows around the old mill, where the light of the early morning sun glanced off the stones and turned them to glowing amber. She rushed into his outstretched arms, reveling in his warmth as he drew her close and kissed her with a savage intensity that took her breath away but left her gasping for more. His eyes blazed gold as he stared at her, his hand trailing over her face and along her neck before slipping down her back to draw her closer to him. He kissed her again, and this time he took his time exploring her in a leisurely but thorough manner, his strong arms holding her upright when her trembling legs threatened to give way. He pulled away and drew her down to the ground, wrapping his arm around her while he leaned against the weathered stone of the abandoned building. The dew had made the ground damp, but Aaron's unusual heat quickly worked its way through her chilled skin.

"Aaron, what do you know about the other dragon?" Keira asked, leaning her head against shoulder.

Aaron was silent for a while, and Keira wondered whether

he was even going to answer her, but when he finally did, it was with careful consideration of each word.

"Keira, in order for me to answer that question, I think I need to tell you about my people, and where we come from." He drew in a deep breath, before releasing it in a long stream of hot air that tickled Keira's ear.

"There weren't always dragons," he said. "We are creatures under a curse. It happened a very long time ago, so long ago we've lost count of the passing years, but we haven't forgotten how it all started. A small tribe of my ancestors crossed over plains and hills to make a new home for themselves in the mountains. They were a tough and wiry people, well prepared for the formidable challenges life in the mountains would present. What they weren't prepared for was the animosity of the people who lived in the nearest village. It wasn't a problem at first, and the tribesmen traded with the villagers for food and produce, but as time went on, the villagers grew jealous. The tribe were skilled craftsman, and they mined the mountain for precious metals, using it to create jewelry of outstanding beauty, plates etched with intricate designs, and vases of great value. Word of their fine craftsmanship soon spread, and people came from far and wide to seek them out and buy their wares.

"Meanwhile, the people in the village struggled for their meagre existence, despite the new influx of trade. When they saw the wealth of the miners, they grew angry. They inflated their prices for basic goods and services, but rather than pay the exorbitant amounts, the tribe took their trade to the next town. At that, the villagers were furious, and they decided to rid themselves of the miners. They thought that if they made life unpleasant enough, the miners would leave, so they taunted and mocked them whenever they came into the village. When these insults were ignored, they became violent. They manhandled the women, until they were too afraid to travel anywhere near the village; they beat up the men, unless they traveled in groups. The miners started to avoid the village altogether, but that just incensed the villagers even further. Things came to a head when two children disappeared. Their dead bodies were discovered two weeks later." Aaron paused as he stroked Keira's arm absentmindedly.

"That's terrible," she said.

"The villagers grew bolder and started harassing the traders and merchants that traveled through the village to buy the miners' wares, until they, too, began to stay away. In their jealousy, the villagers were destroying their very livelihood! There were those amongst the miners who were ready to arm themselves and fight the villagers – even kill them if necessary – but the tribe elders sought a different solution. They pleaded with the Creator to help them, and he heard their plea. He gave them the ability to transform themselves so that they could travel far and wide to sell their wares, and natural armor to protect them from those who would harm them. But the Creator warned the miners never to use their great strength in anger. They must never seek revenge against the villagers, and must only use their new strength and power to protect themselves, never to hurt the innocent.

"The miners were still human, but they had been given the ability to take on dragon form. It didn't take long for the villagers to realize that they were now fighting a far more formidable foe, creatures that could kill them in an instant. They repented of their terrible deeds, and pleaded with the mountain people to leave them in peace.

"For many years," he continued, "the miners and villagers did live in peace, and the time came when the mountain people no longer needed to take on their dragon forms. But power is a difficult thing to surrender, and the miners continued to transform. Then one day the unthinkable happened."

"What happened?" Keira asked softly when Aaron fell silent. He drew in a deep breath. "Even though many years had passed, hatred burned in the hearts of some of the miners towards the villagers for what they'd done. One day, a group of mountain men took on their dragon forms and attacked the village, killing men, women and children, before looting their houses and heading back to the mountains with their plunder. The Creator was enraged with the miners, and as punishment he took away their humanity, making them fully dragon. They could still take on human form, but only for a few days, or they would weaken to the point of death.

"Because they had killed the people of the village, they were forced to feed on the dead. Dragons have been predators ever since, hunting humans in order to survive. The Creator also cursed the dragon women with childlessness, because they had done nothing to stop their men from attacking the village. So only a human woman can bear a dragon child."

"Oh, Aaron," Keira whispered, gently placing her hand on Aaron's arm. "I'm so sorry."

"Sshh," he replied, smiling down at her. "Don't be sad. I do not regret what I am. And I would never have found you if I were not a dragon.

"Like the men of old, dragons have extraordinarily long lives," Aaron continued. "The Creator wanted to give them plenty of time to repent of their wicked actions, and indeed they soon realized how wrong they'd been to take the lives of the villagers. But the curse remained, and the hearts of many dragons hardened. They abandoned their human natures completely and embraced evil, quickly becoming the monsters they are known to be."

"Dragons are not monsters, Aaron," Keira protested, shaking her head. Aaron smiled bleakly before continuing.

"You know the stories of dragons abducting beautiful maidens? In days gone by, many dragon men abducted young women in order to mate with them, so they could bear a dragon child, but once the child was old enough it was taken from the mother, who was then abandoned, or worse. The dragon children were raised by dragons who no longer retained any humanity, and the children learnt nothing about love, kindness towards others or goodness."

"But that's not you!" exclaimed Keira. "You haven't done those things."

"Are you so sure, my sweet?" asked Aaron softly. "Do you know me so well that you can be certain I haven't?"

Keira felt ill, but she was emphatic in her response. "Yes," she said. "I may not have known you for long, but you're a good man, Aaron, and I refuse to believe that you've done such dreadful things." She looked at Aaron steadily as she spoke, willing him to see her belief in him.

"I haven't abducted any maidens, nor got them with child," he said. "And I believe that it is possible for a dragon man to fall in love with a human woman, choosing to spend his life with her and committing himself to her happiness. In fact, the dragon who lived in these mountains before was one of those. He was my father, and the woman that was killed was my mother."

Keira stared at Aaron. "Your mother?"

Aaron nodded, his smile grim as he continued his story.

"My father was living at Storbrook Castle when he met my mother," he said. "Her name was Eleanor, and she came from your village, the only child of elderly parents. She and my father fell in love and were married, but there was a young man in the village who also loved Eleanor. He was awkward, often teased because he stuttered and was a little slow. My mother was one of the few people who was kind to him, and somehow he convinced himself that my mother returned his love. His name was Arnold Hobbes."

Keira's eyes widened in surprise. "Like Reeve Hobbes?"

"Yes, Reeve Hobbes is his descendant." Aaron smiled at her look of shock before continuing.

"He eventually married, but always pined for Eleanor, certain that she would've learned to love him if only my father had never come along. My mother visited the village regularly, my father carrying her on his back and landing outside the village before changing form. But he grew careless, and one day he landed too close to the village. Close enough that Arnold saw my mother with the dragon. He saw my mother smile at him, and touch him. He did not know that the dragon and Eleanor's human husband were one and the same, but still, I can only suppose that a jealousy so fierce flared up in him, because he grabbed a branch lying on the ground and ran towards her, brandishing the branch. I'm not sure if he was aiming for my mother or my father, but my father quickly swung my mother away and placed himself between her and Arnold. He was still running at full speed towards them when she again stepped into Arnold's path." Aaron shook his head in disbelief.

"I cannot imagine why she did it," he said, "perhaps she thought she could reason with Arnold – but that action sealed her fate. Arnold didn't pause, and the blow he dealt to her head proved to be fatal. I know all of this because I came upon the scene as Arnold was bearing down on my parents. I was just a young dragon of thirty-two years and had come into the village with them, but had landed further afield.

"My father fell beside my mother, his claws ripping open the soft skin on his chest, drawing his blood. Dragon's blood is very powerful, and can heal many wounds, but the blow my mother sustained was fatal. She died before his blood was even on her lips." Aaron drew in a deep breath, his eyes far away. "I can still remember the roar of utter anguish that poured from him when he realized she was dead. The flames rolled non-stop from his mouth, setting everything around him alight."

Aaron paused for a moment, his voice mirroring the anguish of those memories while his face reflected his pain. "In those few moments Arnold collected his wits enough to realize that he could not defend himself against a dragon, and he ran back to the village shouting that the dragon had killed my mother. When the villagers came out, armed with whatever weapons they could find, my father lost his mind. The villagers should not have been able to defeat him, but in his anguish he was an easy target. He did nothing to defend himself. Instead he roared out his pain, burning down half the village in the process. The villagers attacked him with whatever they could find – axes, rakes, pitchforks. A few had spears, which they drove into his underbelly, again and again. The villagers were triumphant as they killed my father, slowly and painfully. They chose to forget that my father had never once before used his strength against the village." Aaron's forehead furrowed in anger, and his voice was hard.

"Of course, Arnold told everyone that it was the dragon that'd killed my mother, while he'd been trying to save her. He proclaimed far and wide that he'd attacked the dragon, weakening him, before he sounded the alarm in the village. How quickly people believe what they want to believe! Arnold, who'd been weak and cowardly all his life, was lauded as a hero, while my father was vilified and slandered as a monster."

Aaron stopped and passed a hand over his eyes. Keira could feel the tension building in the arms still holding her as he remembered the events of that day. Leaning forward, she gently pulled his hand away from his face, and held it in her own as she looked deep into his eyes. Aaron stared at her for a moment, then buried his hand in the hair at her neck and pulled her lips to his. His touch was rough, and his kiss was fierce and savage. Keira stiffened in momentary shock, then wrapped her arms around his neck and pulled him closer, opening her mouth to him and boldly exploring his with her tongue. She knew, instinctively, that his kiss was born of a primitive, physical need, and when he groaned at her response, she slid one hand down his back to pull him closer still. His hands were all over her – in her hair, on her back, sliding down her arm – and when he lifted her onto his lap, her body molded to his. It was Aaron who finally broke the kiss, leaving Keira panting for breath, as he rested his forehead against hers.

"Ah, Keira," he whispered, "I want you so much. You've

touched me in a way I never thought possible. You've given me something to live for – something better than the anger that has consumed me for so many years. I was so angry when my parents died, that I chose to deny my human nature. I hated all humanity for a long time, thinking that all humans were equally evil, and therefore equally responsible for my parents' deaths. For years I refused to take on human form. I could feel the monster growing in me, and I gave myself over to the beast, glad of the darkness that I could feel spreading through my being. So little of my humanity still remained." Aaron stopped for a moment, before adding in a whisper, "My sweet Keira, you said I wasn't a monster, but if I told you some of the things I did, you'd hate me forever."

"Never," Keira replied, her voice just as low. "I may hate some of the things you did, but I could never hate you. Don't you know that I love you?"

"Keira," he whispered, lifting his face and gazing into her eyes. "As I love you." His eyes were a bright, burning gold, the light reflecting onto her skin, bathing her face in a golden glow. "When I came to Storbrook, it was to face my memories. I'd become almost a total monster, with only the barest shreds of my humanity remaining as I raged against all humans, whether they were man, woman or child – but somehow, a few years ago, I started to remember. Not the pain of my parents' death, but the joy of their living. They'd lived fully and loved completely. In my anger, I had focused only on the pain, forgetting the lessons of joy. Slowly I began to realize that I was shaming their memory by turning my back on my humanity, and so I started looking for good amongst humans." Aaron paused as he pushed a loose lock of hair behind Keira's ear, his hand lingering on her neck.

"And to my surprise, when I started to open my eyes to the world around me, I found what I was looking for. I realized that the wicked actions of some could not be held against all. And that I needed to find the humanity in myself once again if I was ever to have a hope of happiness. It has been a slow and painful journey, and it brought me to the place where I knew both pain and joy. I came, intending to stay for a short while – just long enough to deal with the memories captured in the very walls of Storbrook. I didn't plan to come into the village, or seek out the people here, and I was already preparing to leave when I first saw you. The only reason I came to the market that day was to find you, because I was fascinated by your courage in the face of potential danger. I had to learn more about this remarkable woman, and not much time passed before I was thoroughly captivated, my heart ensnared."

Aaron bent down and kissed her, his grip tightening as her hands made their way up his back and brushed against the ridges where his wings would emerge before winding into his hair. The brush of his tongue against hers sent shivers down her spine, and when he moved his lips away from hers, they trailed along her jaw and down to her shoulder. A faint rustling sound came from a clump of nearby bushes, and Aaron lifted his head, before sighing in frustration.

"Your sister is here, my sweet," he whispered into her hair.

"How –" she started, but he answered before she finished.

"I can smell her scent. Nose of a dragon," he said, tapping the side of his nose with a finger. "You smell like summer – the scent of jasmine wafting through the warm air." His breath was warm against her neck. "I get very distracted when I'm with you, but I believe Anna has been eavesdropping." He sighed in frustration, then rose to his feet, pulling Keira along with him.

CHAPTER THIRTEEN

Keira stared at Aaron as she rose to her feet, her mind reeling at what he'd just revealed. He could smell her! There was another rustling, and she turned towards the bushes near the old mill wheel.

"Anna!" Keira said. "Come here!" She watched as Anna emerged. "What are you doing here?"

"I heard you tell him," Anna said, nodding in Aaron's direction, "to meet you at the river, so I sneaked out after you left this morning."

"You were spying on me?" Keira choked. "How much did you hear?"

"Enough!" Anna thrust her chin out, her stance openly defiant. A look of horror crossed Keira's face.

"You cannot tell anyone."

"She won't," Aaron said. He grinned at Anna. "If she does, I'll have her for dinner."

Anna gulped, turning pale as Keira turned to Aaron, shock written over her face.

"You wouldn't," she gasped.

"Oh yes, I'll make it swift. She won't feel a thing." He smiled teasingly at Keira, before bending down and whispering softly in her ear. "I try to limit my human diet as much as possible, so your sister has nothing to fear from me." He turned back to Anna, who was looking decidedly white, and she took a deep breath before bravely responding.

"I won't say anything on one condition," she said. Her voice was trembling, but she met Aaron's gaze boldly. He lifted one eyebrow enquiringly. "When you take Keira away from here, take me with you."

"Anna!"

Keira's voice was heavy with admonishment, but Anna ignored her, her attention fixed on Aaron.

"Why?" he asked.

"Because I need to get away from this village," Anna said. "And away from Mother. What do you think will happen when Keira leaves with you? Mother will be certain to shackle me to any man who offers. And Edmund might turn his attention to me."

Aaron nodded in agreement, but his expression was skeptical. "Do you think you could stop behaving like a spoiled child, and start behaving like a woman?"

"Yes." Anna held his gaze as she continued. "I know I shouldn't have been spying, but I was desperate."

"Well, it's up to Keira."

Anna and Aaron both turned to look at Keira, but her mind was having difficulty in understanding the conversation.

"Anna," she said at last. "Aaron's not taking me anywhere."

"Oh, I think he is," was Anna's smug response.

Aaron sighed. "Keira, Anna's untimely arrival forestalled me, but there is something I would ask you."

He glanced at Anna, then taking Keira's hand, drew her around the corner of the old mill house. When they were out of Anna's sight, Aaron grabbed Keira's other hand then dropped down to one knee.

"My sweet Keira, I have loved you from the first time I

saw you. Will you take this dragon as your husband?"

Keira stared at Aaron incredulously, before a radiant smile replaced the expression.

"Yes," she whispered. "Yes, I'd be honored to be your wife, Aaron Drake."

Aaron's expression was exultant as he stood up and wrapped his arms around her, drawing her into a passionate embrace. His wings broke out behind him, unfurling and wrapping around them, hiding them from the world in their own private sanctuary.

Keira smiled to herself later that day as she ambled around the garden with a pair of shears, deadheading the bushes of bright summer blooms. High above her the form of a mighty beast was circling slowly in the air, creating a shadow on the ground as his powerful body passed in front of the sun. Keira pulled herself upright and scanned the sky, a hand held across her forehead to shade her eyes. She smiled when she saw the dragon gliding through the air, his face turned downward. From so far below Keira could not make out the dragon's features, but she knew that Aaron's sharp eyes could see her every expression and could read the joy written clearly over her face. Her smile deepened as she thought of her meeting with Aaron that morning. She still could not quite believe that Aaron wanted to marry her, a simple country girl! Aaron had wanted to go talk to her parents right away, but Keira suggested that they wait a few weeks.

"Why?" Aaron had demanded.

"Well, for one thing, it will cast doubt on your testimony," she said. "Mother already thinks you're lying, and this will only serve to strengthen that belief. I cannot bear the thought of people doubting your honor."

"I really couldn't care less what people think of me, Keira, and nor should you." But when Aaron saw the look of concern on Keira's face, he growled in frustration, pushing his hand through his tawny hair as he did so.

"Keira, I have waited a very long time to find you, and the idea of skulking around in order to spend time with you does not sit well with me. Do you really think a few more weeks will change your parents' attitude towards me?"

"Maybe not," she said, "but I do know that this news will not be favorably received today, especially by my mother. Does a few more weeks really matter when we have the rest of our lives?"

"Very well," he reluctantly agreed. "I'll give you two weeks, no more, and your parents will have one week to get used to the idea of having me for a son-in-law, because I'll be waiting at the church door to marry you three weeks from today."

The thought of Aaron being impatient to marry her made Keira laugh as joy bubbled up from deep inside her. Three weeks! That didn't give her much time to finish her wedding chest. She hadn't put much effort into it lately, dismayed as she had been with her potential suitors, but now she wished she'd spent more time filling the chest. And she certainly didn't have a gown good enough to be married in. When she had mentioned this to Aaron, however, he'd laughed off her concerns.

"Keira, you don't need to bring anything with you when we get married," he said. "I am not a young groom leaving his parents' home for the first time."

"Yes, because you're already ancient," Keira teased. "And I thought Widower Brown was old!"

Aaron had laughed before continuing. "Storbrook has anything we need and more," he said, "as do all my other homes. I already have all manner of linens and quilts. And I'll ensure you have a wardrobe filled with gowns made from the finest silks and velvets the world can offer, in the brightest hues imaginable. All that is needed is you, my sweet. And as for a wedding gown, I don't mind if you marry me in rags."

Of course, Aaron might not mind her in rags, Keira

thought sardonically, but she wasn't about to get married in any old gown. She might not be able to afford silks and velvets, but her mother had already set aside some fine linen for a wedding gown, in a dark, traditional blue. Her mother would probably be suspicious, but Keira intended to start working on a gown that very evening.

The dragon continued to circle high in the sky as Keira pulled herself from her musings, and she glanced up once more, laughing as he dipped and dived. Hearing her laughter, the dragon swooped down towards her, his wings creating a huge shadow over Keira as she watched him. He swung back towards the clouds as flames poured from his open mouth. She smiled once more, then turned her back to him and stooped down to snip another dead bloom. The door to the cottage opened and she spun around, suddenly concerned that her mother had seen the dragon's display, but it was only Anna.

"Show-off," Anna mumbled, glancing at the dragon now high up in the air. A sound that sounded suspiciously like laughter floated down to them before the dragon turned towards the mountains and flew out of sight.

"I can't believe you're making me wait a whole month before allowing me to join you and Aaron," she grumbled as she sat down on the ground near where Keira stood.

"The wait will do you good, Anna," Keira replied, a little more sharply than she intended. Softening her tone, she added, "Besides, a month will pass by quickly."

Keira and Aaron had agreed that Anna could come and live with them after they were married, on the condition that not a single clue about Aaron's true nature fell from her lips. Aaron hinted at dire repercussions if she broke her word, but Keira was confident that they could trust Anna, since it was in her own best interests to comply. She held the shears out to Anna, who stared at them for a moment before taking them from Keira's hands and rising to her feet.

"You're going to do all you can to teach me some

responsibility before you leave, aren't you, dear sister?" Anna asked wryly.

"A few lessons won't go astray, Anna," replied Keira with a grin. "You can use the next few weeks to prove to me that I haven't made a mistake in agreeing that you can come live with us."

Keira headed back to the house, leaving Anna in the warm sunshine with shears in hand.

CHAPTER FOURTEEN

Market day arrived once again, and Keira wondered what kind of reception she would receive from the villagers. She had avoided going into the village since the meeting at the town hall, not certain that she would be welcome. She also begged Aaron to stay away, certain that his presence would arouse the villagers' suspicions as to his motives in supporting her, but he refused.

"People will know soon enough, Keira," was his response. "I have made concessions with regards to your family, but I refuse to stay away from the village to avoid rumors. If I cannot openly court my future wife, I will at least take every opportunity I can to be in her presence."

Despite Keira's fears, she was secretly pleased that Aaron had resisted her urgings. She too wanted to see as much of him as possible, even if it was only from a distance.

As Keira had suspected, most of the merchants turned away from her as she took her place at the stall, but there were some who greeted her with a smile and a nod, including Madam Draper and Madam Hunter. Although the support was muted, Keira was relieved to find she wasn't completely isolated.

She took her place behind the table, next to Anna, who had astounded her mother when she announced she would help Keira at the market that day. Keira had raised her eyebrows at her sister in silence, and Anna shrugged her shoulders, a wry smile playing on her lips.

"Just proving my worth," was her only comment.

It was midmorning when Keira saw Aaron striding through the market, dressed as befitted a gentleman. She watched in amusement as he stopped to chat with blushing girls helping their parents at their stalls. Clearly, they weren't concerned about the reeve's opinion of Aaron! She could almost hear them sigh as he greeted them with a courtly bow and a smile: "Mistress Gwyneth, isn't this a fine morning?" "Mistress Jane, you're looking lovely today."

As Aaron made his way along the path, he looked up and caught Keira's glance, before he turned his attention to another girl, who stared boldly at him from behind the table she was tending. "Mistress Sarah, I trust you're enjoying this beautiful day."

Sarah smiled at him coyly, but he quickly turned away and headed towards Keira. He stopped a few feet away, his eyes sweeping over her form in bold perusal.

"Mistress Keira! You're quite radiant this morning."

"Why, thank you, milord," Keira responded with a grin. "Although I must confess I'm not sure I trust your easy compliments – they seem to fall from your lips without much thought. Still, if you do see something different about me, I expect it's due to the fine weather we're having."

"Really, Mistress Keira? You wound me to the quick," he said. "First you rudely refute my kind comments regarding your radiance, and then you tell me it's due to the weather, when I was certain that I had stumbled upon some profound reason for your sparkle this morning."

Keira smiled in response, but the look in his eyes made her catch her breath. His gaze held hers, the color turning to a glowing gold. It wasn't until Anna cleared her throat, shoving her elbow into Keira's side, that the spell was broken.

Aaron glanced across at Keira's sister, his eyebrows going up as he scrutinized her.

"Anna, what a surprise," he teased. "Have you developed a sudden liking for work, or a newfound desire to be with your sister?"

"Hmph," was Anna's only response, but before she looked away, Keira caught a glimpse of a smile. Aaron turned his attention back to Keira as he leaned forward over the table, bringing his face close to hers.

"You really are radiant this morning, my sweet. Like a beautiful rose shimmering with dew in the early morning light." He breathed in deeply before adding, "And you smell like a summer dawn, too, with the hint of jasmine floating on a warm breeze." She blushed. "Meet me at the lake tomorrow morning," he whispered.

"At the lake?" Her tone was bemused, the memories of her last experience at the lake clouding her expression.

"It's further away," Aaron responded, "and I want some time alone with you." Aaron glanced at Anna as he said this, but she was studiously ignoring the conversation. "We won't be staying there, so no one can spy on us."

"Oh!" Keira said. The word came out slowly as his meaning became clear. Keira glanced at her sister, who was now studying her nails, before smiling up at Aaron. "I'll be there as soon as I can."

The next morning Keira woke early and pulled on her kirtle and shawl as quietly as possible, careful not to wake Anna. She slipped out of the house a few moments later and headed towards the lake. The early morning mist hung on the ground, making it difficult to see more than a few feet ahead of her, but Keira's step was sure. She'd walked this same path many times before, and she knew each twist and turn.

The sun was just starting to appear behind the mountains

when Keira arrived at the clearing surrounding the lake. It was impossible to miss the huge dragon crouching low on the ground as he waited beyond the trees. His wings were folded against his back, and as Keira moved into the clearing, he inhaled deeply, breathing in her scent. The sight of the enormous beast made Keira stop in her tracks, her pulse suddenly racing as a tremor of fear spread through her.

She pushed the feeling away, mentally chiding herself, but seeing Aaron in his true form, as a beast, suddenly filled her with dread as she realized the enormity of the commitment she had entered into. She was marrying a dragon! Aaron's nostrils flared as he watched her.

"Keira," he said softly, his warm breath caressing her face. "Please don't be frightened. I haven't changed. It's still me – the same creature that you know, and that loves you. You know I would never, ever do anything to hurt you."

Keira closed her eyes as he spoke and his familiar voice washed over her. Suddenly her fears seemed foolish, and she opened her eyes with a smile.

"I know," she said as she stepped forward. She reached up her hand and gently placed it against Aaron's cheek as she looked into his glowing eyes. "I love you," she whispered.

He gazed at her for a long moment before lifting his head and stretching his neck to its full length.

"Come on," he said, "up you go." This time Keira was ready when he wrapped his tail around her, and she steadied herself as he lifted her onto his back. Inching forward until she lay along his neck, she wrapped her arms around him as he lifted himself into the cool morning air.

Aaron flew in silence, the movement of his strong wings making the air pulse around them. The sun was almost above the mountains when he started dropping, circling around in slow, leisurely sweeps.

"Look down, Keira. That's Storbrook."

Holding on tightly around his neck, Keira inched her head over to one side of his massive body. She gasped when she saw the castle laid out below her. Instead of the dark, forbidding structure she had imagined from childhood tales, Storbrook Castle seemed to shimmer with light as the early rays of sun glittered against the light yellow stone of the building. It was so huge that Keira wondered how long it would take to walk from one end to the other. The castle had been built on top of a mountain, completely covering the entire surface, the sheer rock at the top of the mountain merging with the tall stone walls that surrounded the castle. Within the walls stood the main building, the donjon, which soared to heights far above the castle walls. The back half of the building formed part of the wall, and reached another twenty feet higher than the front, and along this section were turrets that soared so high that Keira was certain she could reach out and touch them as they flew past. Along the back wall were enormous arched windows, open to the elements. Large enough for a dragon to fly in or out of, Keira realized.

There were other buildings within the castle walls – workshops, stables, a chapel and a priest house, and she could see people moving around the massive courtyard, going about their daily duties. A walled garden stood adjacent to the donjon, which Keira supposed was a kitchen garden, while beyond that was a pleasure garden, bright hues competing with the greens of the trees and lawn. A path wound up the mountain, leading to a huge gate with a portcullis covering the entrance. As Keira looked, Aaron circled around the castle, dropping lower with each turn to give her a better view, before finally heading back up to the clouds.

"We're not going to the castle?" asked Keira.

"Not today, my sweet. There are too many people at Storbrook, and I want you all to myself."

"You didn't show me the caves beneath the castle," Keira said. "Someone told me that the dragon's lair would be dark, malodorous and filled with bones." Keira felt the laughter rumbling in his chest before he responded.

"I don't want to scare you away," he said. "I'll show you my filthy lair as soon as you're mine. That way, if you try to run away screaming, I can lock you in a tower."

A few minutes later, Aaron began to lose height once more. He came to a stop at the top of a mountain, above a waterfall thundering to the depths below them. The sun catching the water spray sent bright rays of color shooting through the early morning air, and Keira gasped.

"Look Aaron," she whispered, afraid to break the peace of the morning. "It's so beautiful." She slid off his broad back and turned towards him with a smile.

"That's why I brought you here," he said.

She turned back to look once more at the shimmering colors, but in the next moment they were muted by a sudden flash of light that radiated out from behind her. A moment later Aaron laid his hands on her shoulders. She could feel his warm breath tickling her nape as he gently pushed his fingers into her hair, allowing it to fall softly over his hands, before running them down her arms and drawing her closer. With his arms wrapped around her she leaned against his bare chest.

"Fancy flying over a waterfall, my sweet?" he asked. Twisting herself around, Keira looked up at him, her expression dubious.

"Flying over a waterfall?" she repeated. "Are you going to throw us over the edge?"

"Are you doubting my flying abilities?" he asked in amusement. "There's a small ledge about halfway down where we can sit behind the waterfall. I thought we could spend some time talking down there."

"A ledge?"

"Yes," he said. "Come along. You know I won't let you fall. Wrap your arms around me, and I'll fly us down."

Keira wrapped her arms around his neck and tightly clasped her hands, and Aaron looked at her with a grin before unfurling his wings. Even though she had seen them before,

Keira watched in amazement as they spread out behind his back, the light glimmering against their smooth surface, aware once again of the awesome power of the man holding her in his arms. He wrapped his arms tighter around her as he beat his wings against the air, bearing them over the edge of the waterfall. Keira buried her head into his shoulder, then lifted it slowly when she heard his voice in her ear.

"Look, Keira," he said. "I'm going very slowly. There's nothing to be afraid of."

Cautiously, she looked over Aaron's shoulder, and her eyes widened when she saw that they were barely moving. His wings beat languorously through the air, keeping them aloft, as he slowly moved down the length of the waterfall, spray from the water covering them in a fine mist.

He had flown about halfway down when he brought them over to the side of the waterfall and landed them onto a small ledge that led behind the thunderous falls. The water fell clear of the ledge by a few feet, and Aaron sat down at the edge, his legs dangling in the air. Pulling Keira down next to him, he wrapped his arms around her as they sat, and she leaned her weight against his side. The water was like a curtain, hiding them from the world behind a rushing, sparkling screen. The sun was starting to climb higher, and Keira could see the light sparkling off drops of water that cascaded down the mountain. Each droplet seemed to take on a life of its own as it twisted and turned its way down past the ledge to join the rest of the water crashing hundreds of feet below them.

"What are you thinking?" asked Aaron.

"I was wondering about the journey each drop of water makes as it goes tumbling down the waterfall," replied Keira, her tone contemplative. "Will it travel through many distant lands? And what creatures will it meet on its journey? Where will it finally end up?" She glanced at Aaron, and blushed when she saw he was watching her intently. "I'm sorry, I'm being absurd!"

"No," replied Aaron emphatically. "Never apologize for your thoughts, my sweet. I love the fact that you're so curious. Maybe one day we can follow those water droplets and discover where the river takes them."

"Really, Aaron?" she said, her eyes sparkling. "Do you mean it? I'd love to see distant lands. And the oceans! Are there really huge creatures that live in the depths? And rivers so wide you have to take a boat to get across them? And cities – I've heard that hundreds of people live in the big cities! With enormous churches and glass in the windows."

Aaron laughed at her excitement, and caught her hands in his own. "I will show you all those things and more, Keira. I give you my word, and the word of a dragon can never be broken."

"Really, Aaron?"

"Yes, really."

"Oh, Aaron, never in my wildest dreams did I ever think someone like you would want to marry someone like me. I thought the best I could hope for was Edmund Hobbes, but then you came along and fell in love with me!" Her voice was full of wonder. "I don't know what I did to deserve you, but you're a gift sent by God."

"Keira," Aaron said, shifting himself around so that he could look Keira full in the face, "it isn't a wonder that I fell in love with you. The wonder is that you fell in love with me – a beast. It is me who has received the gift, and I'll spend every day of the rest of my life proving myself to be worthy of you."

"You're no beast, Aaron, and you don't need to prove yourself worthy – you already are. And I love you. Maybe we've both been given a gift – the gift of each other."

Aaron smiled. "I think you're right," he murmured into her ear before he brushed his lips across her cheek and kissed her.

CHAPTER FIFTEEN

A fine mist covered Keira as she sat with Aaron behind the waterfall, her legs dangling over the edge of the ledge as she leaned against him. His skin was steaming as the moisture came in contact with his heat.

"Aaron?" said Keira.

"Hmm?"

"I was wondering about the wedding ceremony," she said. "Does the priest know what you are?"

"No."

"So he believes you're just like any other man?"

"Yes."

"So there isn't anything different that happens because you're not ... human?"

Keira had been gazing at the stream of water rushing before them as she spoke, but when Aaron didn't reply, she turned to look at him. His eyes were narrowed and jaw clenched as he looked out at the water.

"Aaron? What's wrong?"

He let out a sigh as he turned to her. "There's something I need to tell you, Keira," he said. "I should have told you before, but I didn't know how you'd react."

"What is it?" A sense of foreboding passed through her, making her voice sound high and thin. "Can't you marry me?" He didn't reply. "Are you already married?"

"Goodness, Keira," he said. "What do you think of me? Of course I mean to marry you." He had been leaning back on one hand, but he straightened himself and turned to her with a glare. "And I don't have a wife hidden away. What kind of man do you think I am?"

"How would I know?" she snapped. "You're not a man, you're a dragon." The words were barely out of her mouth when she wished she could take them back. His mouth curled sardonically as he looked away.

"I'm sorry, Aaron," she said, touching his arm tentatively. "I didn't mean it like that. But please tell me what's going on. You're making me nervous."

"No," he said, his expression softening as he turned back to her, "I'm the one who should apologize. You're right, of course, I am a dragon, not a man. And I should never have hidden anything from you." He took her hand in his as he continued. "The thing is, Keira, for a dragon marriage to be recognized, there needs to be a dragon ceremony as well. We'll still have a regular human ceremony, at the church with a priest, but later, at Storbrook, we'll have a dragon binding ceremony."

"A dragon binding ceremony?" she said. "What's that?"

"Well," he replied slowly, "it's more of a blood binding, actually."

"You mean like pagan ceremonies?" Relief crept into her voice. She'd heard of people who still had a pagan blood binding after getting married by the priest. The bride and groom would each cut their wrist, then hold them together so that the blood could mingle.

"A little like that. But instead of putting our bloodied wrists together, we'll drink each other's blood."

"Drink each other's blood?" She stared at Aaron in

horror. "I must drink your blood?" Surely he didn't mean that!

"Yes."

"You want to make me into a monster?"

"No! Of course not!" Aaron frowned. "Drinking each other's blood will bind us together in a way that two humans can never be bound. Your blood will run through my veins, and mine through yours. For as long as we live, nothing can separate us. But you won't turn into a dragon, although my blood will affect you. It's very powerful, so once you drink it, you'll be stronger. You'll heal faster, and be less susceptible to disease. Your senses will be more acute, and my transformations will no longer damage your eyes. And you will also live longer."

"Live longer?"

"Yes," he said. "Each time you drink my blood, years are added to your life. Human mates usually drink their dragon's blood on a regular basis, so they'll live as long as their mates."

She stared at the sheet of water rushing before her. "How?" she asked. "How does it happen?"

"I'll cut you here," he said, trailing a finger over her wrist, "and you blood will be spilt into a cup. When there's enough, the cup will be given to me to drink. Then you'll cut me here," he continued, placing his hand over his heart, "and drink my blood."

Keira could not mask a look of revulsion. "Will you be in human form?" she asked. "Or a dragon?"

"A dragon." He paused. "Do you still want to marry me?" he asked softly.

She looked away. "I want to go home," she said.

He nodded and rose to his feet, then held out a hand to help her up. She ignored it and instead used a rock to steady herself. He leapt off the ledge, through the curtain of water, and the light of his transformation shimmered through the drops. His tail snaked around her a moment later, and he placed her on his back. She sat stiff and silent as Aaron flew her back to the village, and when he landed, she slipped off his back without a word.

"Keira," he said as she started walking away. She stopped, but didn't turn. "I'm sorry I didn't tell you sooner. I know that what I'm asking you to do revolts you, but it will not turn you into a monster. I'd never do anything to change you. I love you." She began to walk away. "I'll be at the lake every morning, waiting for you," he said.

Keira stumbled away, not noticing the surrounding woods. The man she loved wanted her to drink his blood – only savages and monsters did that! And to make matters worse, he'd kept this from her. How could she agree to marry him, now? What other terrible secrets had he hid from her?

She'd reached the end of the forest and was crossing the field towards their house when her mother came rushing out.

"Keira!"

Keira flinched at Mother's harsh tone. "Where have you been?" Mother said. "Wasting away the hours when there's work to be done."

Keira turned away, but not before a single, unbidden tear slid down her cheek. Mother's face softened, and she took a step towards her daughter.

"Oh, Keira," Mother said. "Have you been fighting with Edmund again?"

Keira looked at her mother in shock. "Edmund?" she repeated. "I want nothing to do with Edmund. Why can't you understand that, Mother?"

"Keira!" Her tone sharpened again. "What has gotten into you? Ever since Milord Drake arrived in the village, you've been acting strangely. A man like that is not to be trusted. Besides, what do you think you could offer him, a simple girl like you?"

Keira stared at her mother, astounded at her outburst. "What do you have against him, Mother?"

"What do I have against him? I'll tell you." Mother made a wild gesture towards the mountains. "He lives in Storbrook

Castle, that's what. Everyone knows that the dragon lives beneath the castle, so he must be in league with that monster. And anyone in league with the dragon is not welcome here."

"The dragon has done nothing to harm us, Mother," Keira replied heatedly, not bothering to refute her mother's assumptions.

"That's what people said about the last dragon that decided to live in these mountains," Mother said, "until he burnt down half the village and killed our men."

"Maybe the last dragon was provoked."

"The last dragon killed my grandfather, Keira, leaving behind a widow with three young children to raise on her own. So tell me that you'll stay away from Aaron Drake."

"I cannot do that, Mother," she flung back, before storming towards the house. Her words caught her off guard – had she really just said that? She wasn't even sure that she wanted to see Aaron again.

Before reaching the house, Keira heard Father's heavy footsteps rounding the corner. She avoided his gaze, but slowed down when she heard him addressing Mother.

"Leave her be, Jenny," he said. "She's no longer a child, and we'll not force her into a marriage she considers abhorrent. Despite your reservations about Milord Drake, he may prove to be a man of worth and honor." Keira held her breath as she waited to hear Mother's response.

"I only want what's best for her, but I've lost her." Mother finally said. "She sees me as the enemy."

Keira could imagine Father taking Mother into his arms.

"Sshh," he said. "I know you love her. Perhaps if you just listened, instead of railing against her, she'd know it too."

As the sun rode through the sky, Keira threw herself into the task of mending, seeking distraction from the chaotic thoughts whirling through her mind; but when she lay down that night, her mind refused to be quiet. Simmering just beneath the surface were a thousand conflicting emotions: anger, horror, hurt, disgust, shock, awe, love. She thought again about what he expected her to do – how could she ever drink someone's blood? Just the thought of it made her feel sick to the stomach.

She looked at her wrist where Aaron had said he would cut her, her finger tracing the purple vein running just below her skin. On an impulse, she grabbed a knife and scored her skin over the vein so the blood welled up on her wrist. Tentatively, she placed her mouth over the wound and sucked the blood from her arm. It had a faintly metallic taste that she didn't find completely unpleasant. She blew out the candle at her bedside and closed her eyes. In her dreams, the rivers had turned to blood, and she tossed and turned restlessly as she sought just one spring of fresh water to quench her thirsty soul.

Keira's first thoughts on waking were of Aaron, and she smiled, only half conscious, before she remembered the conversation of the previous day. She rolled onto her back as she played it through in her mind. Aaron wanted her to drink his blood. And he'd kept that information from her when he'd asked her to marry him. She covered her face with her hands as it occurred to her that her reaction was the very reason Aaron had been reluctant to tell her about the blood binding ceremony. Still, the idea of drinking his blood was by no means pleasant. He'd said that other human mates drank their dragon's blood regularly, but if she only had to do it once, could she?

Keira pushed herself out of her bed and glanced at Anna's sleeping form. She knew Anna could spend the entire day in bed, given half a chance. Creeping to her sister's side of the room, she pulled the covers down with a hard jerk, making Anna jump up in fright. She grabbed the covers and slumped back on the bed, glaring at her sister. Keira laughed and pulled on her clothes, then headed into the kitchen to start the fire. Mary hadn't arrived yet, and the house was cold. She raked out the cinders and carefully added fresh wood from the stack against the wall. The spluttering sparks made her think of Aaron, and how he could get the flames roaring with a mere breath. Of course, he was a dragon, not human. Her smile slipped a little as she considered that. He had never been human, and never would be. She could never expect him to act totally human. She already loved the man within the dragon, but could she love the dragon within the man? Could she bind herself to a beast, and be willing to suffer the consequences?

The thoughts niggled throughout the day as she plied a needle through her father's torn tunic, and later when she walked to the miller's to place the weekly order of ground wheat. Her mother had been right when she said that dragons were not gentle creatures – they were wild and primal. The most powerful of all beasts. How could she take such a creature into her arms and into her heart? Could a dragon ever be tamed?

Keira's head was pounding when she finally fell into bed that evening, as the questions continued to swirl through her mind. She didn't have many answers, but there was one thing she knew. She loved Aaron. And maybe the love between a human and a dragon was enough to withstand the wildest and most primal instincts.

Keira was up early the next morning, once again creeping out of the house before the birds had taken up their chorus. She raced towards the lake, only slowing down as she drew near the clearing. She stopped a few feet away and took a deep breath, then rounded the last tree.

As promised, Aaron was waiting. As usual when she met him alone, he was wearing a loose pair of trousers, but this time a tunic covered his bare chest. His eyes lit up when he saw her, but he approached her warily, his hands held tightly at his sides. He stopped a few feet away, waiting in silence.

"Tell me," she said, "in detail, exactly what happens at the binding ceremony. Will there be other dragons there?"

"Yes," he replied, "my clan will all be invited."

"Dragons have clans?"

"Yes," he replied.

"And will your clan leader be there?"

"Keira." He took another step towards her but stopped when she raised her eyebrows. "There is something more you need to know." He glanced into the distance, towards Storbrook, then brought his eyes back to hers.

"I am the clan leader," he said. "The clan serves me and follows my bidding."

Keira nodded. That seemed right to her. "And what do they call you?"

"I'm the dragon master. They call me Master."

"I see. And will anyone else will be involved with the ceremony?"

"One of the elders will lead it."

"Elder?"

"Yes," he said, "my uncle."

"And all the dragons at the ceremony will be there as ... dragons?"

"No, they wouldn't all fit in the room if they were there as dragons." He smiled wryly. "They will be in human form. And there will be humans there as well. Many of the dragons are married to human mates."

Keira nodded slowly as she took this in. "And what else will happen at this ceremony?"

"Once the blood binding is done, there'll be feasting."

"Feasting? Will you be serving roast pig or roast human?"

He closed his eyes and drew in a deep breath. "Keira, there won't be humans on the menu, but ..." He paused, clearly uncomfortable.

"Yes?" she prompted. Aaron's face was tense, but he met her enquiring gaze steadily.

"Keira, I'm a dragon, you know that. And dragons live under a curse. To ensure our survival, we need to eat some human flesh. Not often, and not for pleasure. We eat the flesh of animals as much as we're able. But there are times

107

when we need to feed on humans, or else face death."

The color drained from Keira's face as she took a step back.

"Keira," Aaron entreated, "you know I don't go abducting maidens from the countryside. The humans are prisoners, men already condemned to die. We offer them the choice – if they choose to be killed by a dragon, we provide for their families. Many prefer this way over the noose, and it is very quick – the men do not feel a lot of pain."

Keira turned away, her face a mask of horror. She knew Aaron was a dragon, and she knew what dragons ate, but somehow she hadn't connected them in her mind. He was a beast, a hunter that preyed on her own kind. Wild and primal.

She either had to accept all of him, or nothing at all. The thought of losing him, the man who had captured her heart, made her chest tighten in pain. She took a deep breath, then turned slowly around to face him. His expression was strained as he stared at her, unmoving.

"Very well," she said.

"Very well?" he asked, his voice cracking.

"Yes," she said, a slight smile hovering around her lips. "Very well."

He took a step towards her, then paused. "Very well?" he repeated again, the question still heavy in his voice.

"Yes," she said. "I love you, Aaron Drake."

The words were barely out of her mouth when he pulled her into his arms, his mouth covering hers as he kissed her passionately.

"Are you sure?" he asked, when he lifted his head.

"Yes," she whispered, her hands pulling him closer as she wound them around his neck. He wrapped his arms tighter around her, the heat of his body searing through her clothes, reaching the very center of her being. Aaron's lips moved along her neck, leaving a burning trail. "We should go tell my parents," she said.

He drew back in surprise. "I thought you wanted to wait."

"Well," she said, "I've already accepted the beast. What's the point in waiting?"

His expression was exultant as he bent his head down to claim her lips once more.

CHAPTER SIXTEEN

Keira sat on a stool in the kitchen, shelling peas, as Mary stirred a pot over the fire. The task was mindless, and her thoughts wandered to her meeting that morning with Aaron, lingering on his warm embrace and passionate kisses. She didn't notice when Anna walked into the room.

"You were gone early this morning," she teased. "I hope you enjoyed your walk." A faint blush stained Keira's cheeks but she just smiled as she remembered how Aaron had walked with her to the edge of the forest before leaving her with a kiss.

"I'll come around later this morning, suitably dressed," he'd said, glancing down at his loose clothing.

"I don't mind you dressed like this," she murmured, "but we don't want to give my mother further reason to hate you."

Keira had told Aaron how her great-grandfather had died, killed by Aaron's own father, the dragon. He listened in silence, staring off into the distance as she related her mother's words.

"I'm so sorry, Keira," he finally said. "I've only ever considered the hurt my family suffered that day, without pausing to consider that others suffered just as much as we

110

did."

"It's not your fault, Aaron," Keira responded, but Aaron was already shaking his head.

"It may not have been my fault," he said, "but I blamed the humans of the village for what happened, and hated all humanity because of it." He turned to look at her. "I have to take responsibility for that," he said. "I refused to see it wasn't only my parents that suffered that day, but the humans as well, and for that I am so sorry." He lifted his hand to her face and traced his finger down her cheek. "The healing starts with us, my sweet. Your mother may never understand that she need not fear this dragon, and that there will always be humans who will cause pain; but between this dragon and this human, we will start afresh."

Keira replaced the full bowl of peas with an empty one. What was taking Aaron so long, she wondered? The thought of her mother's reaction to the news of their betrothal was far more terrifying than any dragon, and she longed to get it over with.

It was already late morning when she saw Aaron through the open door, striding towards their house. She left the bowl on the ground and hurried down the path to greet him. He smiled when he saw her, offering a courtly bow in greeting.

She dropped a shallow curtsey. "Milord," she said, "please come inside."

"Wait!" He grabbed her hand, pulling her to a halt. "There's a reason I'm arriving so late. When I left you this morning, I went into town in the hopes that an item I ordered was ready for delivery. I placed the order a week ago, from a dragon goldsmith, when you first agreed to marry me."

He reached into the purse that hung at his side and pulled out a ring, a crimson ruby glittering in a dainty setting of gold. Keira stared at it for a moment before looking up at Aaron.

"You can't possibly mean me to have that," she whispered.

"Why not?" he asked in surprise.

"It must cost a whole year's wages! I've never even seen something of such value, never mind worn something like that."

"Keira, this ring is yours, to be worn on your hand as a reminder of the love I have for you. There is nothing in this world that would match the value you have for me. Compared to you, this is a mere trinket." As he spoke, Aaron pulled her hand into his own, and slid the ring onto her finger. Keira twisted her hand, letting the sunlight catch the gem, then looked at Aaron.

"I have nothing to give you," she said.

"You've given me your love. I need nothing else. Now come, let's go face your mother." He lifted her hand to his lips and gently kissed her fingers, then gestured for her to lead the way.

A short while later, Aaron sat on the bench in the parlor, while Keira's parents sat across from him on hard-backed chairs. Keira stood outside the room, her back pressed against the passage wall as she listened in.

"Master Carver," he said, "Madam, I'm sure you have guessed my reason for coming to see you today."

Aaron paused, waiting for them to respond, but when they didn't, he continued.

"I intend to wed your daughter, Master Carver."

Keira peeked around the door to see her mother stiffen at Aaron's words.

"I am fully aware of the animosity you bear towards me, Madam," he went on, "but let me assure you that that will not deter me in my goal of having your daughter as my wife. I love her, and will see to it that she has all the comforts money can buy. For her sake, I'll also ensure that her family is well looked after."

Keira's mother stared at Aaron for a moment in silence, then turned her attention towards the doorway. "Keira!" she called, her voice sharp.

Keira smoothed down her skirts nervously and stepped into the room. She glanced at Aaron before turning her attention to her parents.

"Yes, Mother," she said.

"This man," said her mother, nodding towards Aaron, "says he intends to marry you. What say you to this?"

Keira glanced at Aaron again and his warm smile lent her strength.

"I say that I would be happy to marry him, Mother. I love him."

Keira could see the astonishment skip across her mother's face, but it was her father who spoke next.

"Well, then, it's all settled," he said as Mother gaped in shock. "We'll post the announcement of your wedding. Have you named the date?"

"Two weeks from today," was Aaron's immediate reply.

"Very well," Father said. "I'll leave you to make arrangements with the priest. We'll provide the wedding fare, and let the village musicians know to ready their instruments."

At this, Keira's father stood, signaling the end of the visit. He held his hand out to Aaron, who quickly stood and shook the extended hard warmly.

"Thank you, Master Carver. Madam." Aaron nodded at Keira's mother, still sitting on her stool, as she stared dazedly back at him. Keira followed Aaron to the door as he laced his fingers in hers.

"That wasn't so bad," he whispered. "Your father is definitely starting to grow on me." He bent down and grazed her lips with a kiss before turning away with a grin.

As Keira re-entered the house, she watched from the entryway as her mother rounded on her husband in the parlor. "How could you allow this?"

"Jenny, did you not see how they looked at each other?" he said. "It's clear that Aaron Drake loves our daughter, and that she returns his love. If we prevent this marriage, the best outcome we can hope for is that our daughter stays at home until we force her into an unhappy union, and then spends the rest of her life hating us." He grabbed his wife by the shoulders, forcing her to look up at him. "The more likely outcome will be that she runs off with him, and we never see her again. I suggest that you give in with good grace, rather than pushing her even further away." He dropped his hands and took a step back, and Mother's shoulders slumped.

"I suppose you're right," she said.

Keira quietly slipped back out of the house as she reflected on what Father had said. He'd never been a man of many words, but when he did say something, it was usually with great insight. She only hoped Mother would give heed to his wisdom.

That evening Mother sat down opposite Keira as she sewed in the candlelight, her partly finished wedding gown spread over her lap.

"There is still much for you to finish if you are to be ready by your wedding day," Mother told her. "Why don't I sew the sleeves while you work on the hem?"

Keira glanced at her mother in surprise before handing over the unfinished sleeves. Father, writing his daily accounts at a small desk in the corner, looked up with a smile, before returning his attention to the pages before him.

The next morning was market day, and Keira took up her place at the table in her own private world of happiness. Anna had joined her at first, helping her arrange the pieces, but had disappeared with Sarah Draper more than an hour before, and had not returned. Mother slipped behind the table.

"Go have your dinner, daughter," she said. Keira nodded and made her way through the throngs of shoppers shoving their way through the narrow spaces of the market.

"Good morning," she heard a voice say in her ear. She shivered slightly as she turned to look into Aaron's golden eyes.

"Good morning," she said. He held out his arm for her, and she slipped her hand into the crook. His skin was warm, and she leaned closer to him as they walked.

"Are you going for your morning repast?" he asked.

"I am. Have you eaten?"

He leaned a little closer. "I have. I hunted early this morning, before the sun had even risen." She glanced at him, and saw his eyes were burning brighter than usual. "I want to make sure I have all the strength I need to satisfy my beautiful bride."

She stared at him, not sure if she should be amused or affronted, but when he pulled her into an alley and dropped his lips to hers, all thought fled from her mind as she wrapped her arms around him. He pulled away a moment later with a look of regret.

"Soon I can hold you in my arms the whole day if I choose, and kiss you until you can no longer stand, but I have to control myself a little longer." He pulled her hand back into his arm. "Come, my sweet, I'll walk you home."

They walked along the lane and past the church, in the direction of the Carvers' home, until they reached the fork in the road. "Goodbye," Aaron said. He touched her face with his fingers, lingering a moment on her lips, then kissed her forehead. "I'll see you soon."

Keira turned towards the house, pausing once to turn and smile at Aaron, before hurrying to the door. It had been left open to allow the bright, summer sunshine in, and as she approached, she heard the sound of voices.

"You've betrayed me, Richard!" It was the reeve, his voice raised in anger. "After all the years we've known each other, how could you do this?"

"It has nothing to do with you, Matthew." Father's voice was calm. "This is a private, family matter."

"Of course it concerns me! Your daughter and Edmund have been intended for each other since they were both in the cradle."

"You know as well as I do that there's nothing more to it than the wishful thinking of two women."

"You've spoilt your daughter, Richard, letting her believe she can marry whom she chooses, and do as she wishes."

"You would have been much sterner, I know," Father said. His voice was mild, but Keira heard an undercurrent of anger. "You'd expect her to obey unquestioningly, as you did your wife. However, I believe that both my daughters are quite capable of making their own choices, and living with the consequences, whatever they may be."

"Well, the consequences of this union will be disastrous, mark my words! Aaron Drake is a dangerous man. He's already stirred up trouble in the village, and tried to make my son look like a fool. What troubles me even more, however, is his connection with the dragon."

"I'm not sure I follow," Father said.

"When did the dragon return to these mountains, Richard? Nine months ago? And not long afterward, Aaron Drake moves into Storbrook. Whenever there's a dragon in the mountain, there's a Drake at Storbrook."

There was a moment of silence. "You know I'm right, Richard!" Keira heard a note of triumph in the reeve's voice, and her heart sank.

"Perhaps there is some connection," Father said, his voice contemplative, "but what of it? The dragon has made no threat."

"Not yet! But it will. And Drake will be behind it. We need to get rid of him. And you must lead the charge by refusing your daughter's hand."

Another long silence filled the air, and Keira could imagine her father pacing the room as he considered the reeve's words.

"Well, here's the thing," he finally said, "I've already given my consent, and I'm not a man to go back on my word."

"That's preposterous," the reeve shouted. "Your actions

could put the whole village at risk."

"I don't believe so," Father said. "Everything I've seen of Aaron Drake so far makes me believe he's a good man. Besides," he added with a note of humor, "if I deny him Keira's hand now, perhaps he'll set the dragon on us!"

"You're making a big mistake, Richard Carver," snarled the reeve. "There are few in the village who take your side, and the day will come when we rise up against this threat and ensure it is eliminated once and for all!"

His footsteps grew suddenly louder, and Keira ran down the side of the house and around the corner. She peeked around to see him storm from the door, Father a step behind. He stood at the doorway and watched as the reeve strode away, hitting his reeve stick against his thigh as he walked. The reeve reached the lane, and Father glanced at where Keira was hiding.

"You can come out now," he called.

Keira rounded the corner with a blush. "You knew I was there."

"I saw you through the window. You heard all of that, I suppose?"

"Yes," she said, and he nodded.

"The reeve's right, you know," he said, "there is something between Drake and the dragon. But I do not agree that we are in danger from either."

"Why not?" she asked.

He glanced at her, then looked up at the mountains. "Like you, I've watched the dragon. It's not like other animals; it comes to the village because it's curious. And we cannot overlook the fact that the creature has compensated for the loss of any animals it's taken. In fact, I believe the dragon has superior intellect and wit."

"And Aaron?"

"I don't understand the nature of the relationship between him and the dragon, but I'm not concerned. Curious, but not concerned."

"So when you said you could not rescind your word?"

"That's true, of course, but I have no qualms about giving you to Aaron. I believe he'll make a good husband. Better than most, in fact."

"Edmund?"

Father gave a wry smile. "Your mother's always had a soft spot for that boy. If his mother had lived, he may have turned out differently. But maybe not. She'd lost the will to live by then, unable to stand up to Matthew. Of course, she never spoke of such things, not even to your mother, but I could see the defeat in her shoulders whenever she came around. I would not wish that for you."

"But why don't others see it?"

"Reeve Hobbes and his son are skilled at hiding behind a show of friendliness and benevolence. But Matthew and I are of an age, and when we were young, we were good friends. It was only later that I saw glimpses of the true man. Even then, it wasn't until Mary died that I fully understood how much cruelty was hidden beneath his pleasant exterior."

"Edmund's already hurt me," Keira said. "He may try to hurt Anna as well."

Father nodded slowly. "I'm sorry I didn't protect you better, Keira. But I think your fears for Anna are unfounded. It was you that Edmund was promised to. You are the prize that has now been snatched away. But Aaron will keep you safe."

"I know, Father."

"Your mother's probably wondering where you've got to," Father said. "Eat your dinner and get back to the stall. There ae some pieces there that Master Drake may be interested in buying."

"You can't sell to your family," Keira protested.

Father laughed. "He's not family yet, daughter!" He grinned and turned to the house, as Keira smiled in amusement.

Keira considered telling Aaron what she'd overheard, but finally decided against it, knowing he would laugh off her concerns about the reeve. Instead, she focused her attention on completing her wedding gown and helping her mother finalize the arrangements for the food.

She was working late one night, plying a needle through the hem of her gown, as mother sat poring over the list she'd been preparing. She might not be in favor of the wedding, but Mother was certainly not going to have the villagers say that she provided poor fare. A dozen geese were being fattened, and Keira's father was expected to gather a party to hunt for wild boar in the woods. The light from the candles flickered around the room, casting moving shadows across the walls. Keira looked up to see Mother staring at her finger intently, and she glanced down to see the ruby sparkling in the light.

"That's a pretty trinket you have there," Mother said. "Aaron Drake has good taste, I see." She leaned closer. "Let me have a proper look, daughter," she said. Keira extended her hand, and Mother caught her fingers between her own, examining the ring. She dropped her hand a moment later. "Hmph," she said as she leaned back. "At least we know he's wealthy, if not worthy." Keira bit off her sharp retort, recognizing that her mother was making a concession, however slight.

Keira continued to manage the market stall as the wedding day grew closer. She saw little of Aaron, but when she did, she could not help stopping what she was doing to stare at him. Soon he would be hers! He always seemed to know where she was, even if his back was to her, and he'd turn and capture her gaze with his own, and quickly hasten to her side to exchange a few words. In church on Sundays, she would feel his gaze on her, and would struggle to listen to the sermon, even forgetting the words of hymns she'd sung since childhood. The priest would frown in her direction, aware of her inattention, and she'd blush, and for a few minutes would pay closer attention to his words, but it soon wandered. If anyone had asked her afterwards which passage of Scripture he'd read, she would have been hard-pressed to give an answer.

The dragon still flew over the village every day, but sometimes, when she was in the fields collecting berries and fruit, he would swoop down low, whipping up the grass at her feet and making the branches sway. Once he'd wrapped his claws around her, carrying her away as she squealed and yelled, until he'd landed in a meadow. He'd changed a moment later, then caught her in his arms, kissing her soundly.

"I couldn't let another day pass without feeling you in my arms and your lips beneath mine," he said huskily. "If the wedding wasn't a few days away, I'd take you away now and never bring you back."

He kissed her again, and when he tried to pull away, she'd held him close until he finally groaned in defeat and wrapped his arms more tightly. He'd flown her part of the way back in his arms, until finally changing form and returning her to the field where she'd been working. Anna had come looking for her, and had raised her eyebrows at the sight of Keira riding on the dragon's back, but said nothing.

Keira had not seen Edmund since the evening at the town hall, but a few days before the wedding, as she walked home from the market, she saw him leaning against the wall of the village inn. His eyes were bloodshot, and his lips curled in contempt when he saw her.

"You think you've outsmarted me," he snarled. He pushed himself away from the wall and stalked towards her. "But mark my words, Aaron Drake has stolen something that does not belong to him, and the time of recompense will come."

Keira's hands suddenly felt clammy, but she lifted her chin. "You might try to hurt Aaron, but believe me when I say you'd be foolish to try. If you value your life, then leave us in peace."

Edmund smiled and lifted his finger to her cheek. She jerked backwards, but his hand curled around her neck, keeping her trapped, and he pulled her closer.

"Never," he snarled, before he pulled her mouth to his and kissed her hard. She fought against him, then stumbled when he released her suddenly. "You're nothing, really," he said with a sneer, "but you're mine, and you will pay."

CHAPTER SEVENTEEN

The morning of the wedding dawned fair and fine. Already the weather was starting to hint at autumn, each morning revealing more trees decked out in reds and golds as the cool morning air hung close to the ground. Keira and Anna woke up early in order to help their mother as she rushed around the kitchen. The geese had been slaughtered the day before and were hanging in the cellar, the wild boar was dressed and ready for the fire, the pastry was made and rolled, and bread was rising on the windowsills. The feast was to be held in the village square, the meat roasted in the large fire pit in the center of the square. When early afternoon arrived, Mother pulled Keira aside and opened her hand to reveal a small cake of delicately scented soap.

"I bought this a few years ago from a traveling tinker," she explained, "and I've been saving it for a special occasion. I think your wedding day is such an occasion." Keira carefully lifted the bar from her mother's hand before looking up and meeting her gaze.

"Thank you, Mother," she said softly. She wrapped her arms around her parent, who stood stiff for a moment, before lifting her own arms and returning the embrace.

"You're most welcome, my daughter," she replied, her voice quavering. "Now go make yourself ready."

When Keira reached her room, she saw that Bess had already dragged the large copper tub into the room and filled it with water heated over the fire, while Mary was laying Keira's wedding garments out over her bed. Steam filled the room, and the air was heavy with the scent of the lavender that had been crushed and tossed into the water. Keira stripped off her clothes and stepped into the tub, sinking into the luxurious warmth.

It was a few hours later when Keira stepped out of her room. Her wedding gown, finished just the previous evening, was made of finely woven dark blue linen. It was cut wide across the shoulders and the bodice fitted her closely. The waist was low and below it the fabric flared in gentle folds. The long pendulum sleeves were cut wide at the wrist, the gold lining contrasting richly against the deep blue. A girdle of gold silk was tied around her hips, the long ends hanging down the front of her gown. Her long, dark hair had been parted and intricately braided with gold ribbons, while a circlet of flowers sat on her brow. As Keira walked into the parlor, Anna thrust a wooden cross into her hands with a small posy of flowers resting on top.

Mother looked her critically up and down, before nodding her approval. "You look well, my child," she said.

Father stepped up and dropped a kiss onto the top of her head. "Come," he said. "Nelly's waiting." Keira stepped outside to see that the family horse had been tethered outside the cottage door with a richly colored blanket spread over its back and crimson ribbons for reins. Father lifted Keira onto the mount's back with a smile.

"You're a good daughter, Keira," he said, "and I pray that Aaron Drake will treat you well."

"He will, Father," she said. "He's a good man."

Father nodded and handed Keira the reins. He led the horse by the bridle, and Mother and Anna followed behind them as they made their way through the village to the village church. The priest was already standing on the steps, while Aaron and another man waited at the bottom. Keira barely paid the second man any attention, but stared at Aaron. He was a dazzling figure in gold and crimson; the clothes covering his splendid frame were rich and luxurious. A shirt of cream silk could be seen beneath a doublet of gold velvet. Crimson dragons were embroidered across the chest, the flames from their mouths reaching up to his neck. His hose were of gold silk, disappearing into his customary knee-high boots of dark brown leather. Over his shoulders was a gleaming cloak of gold, lined with crimson, the gold dragon brooch pinning it together over his chest. At his side hung a sword, with two dragons winding around the sheath, their eyes crimson rubies. The hilt of the sword was covered in precious stones, but Keira had no doubt that Aaron could use it with deadly force if necessary. His head was bare, and his tawny hair was pulled back in a gold ribbon, matching the gold in his hair highlighted by the bright afternoon sun.

Keira's father helped her off the horse and pulled her arm through his as he led her up the path to the church stairs where Aaron waited. Father kissed her gently on the cheek before placing her hand in Aaron's and stepping away. The square in front of the church was full of the villagers who had come to watch the ceremony and enjoy the festivities.

"You look beautiful, my sweet," Aaron whispered. He clasped her hand in his as he led her up the stairs, joining the priest at the door, while Keira's family gathered on the steps below, standing beside the man who had been waiting with Aaron. The sun was shining brightly as they stood on the well-worn porch of the small stone church, where the priest conducted the ceremony.

"Dearly beloved," he intoned, repeating the words used in marriage ceremonies throughout the civilized world. Aaron gazed at Keira as he repeated the sacred vows, his eyes alight when he slid a band of gold onto her finger. The smile that lit his face when she began her vows was exultant, and Keira stumbled over the words until he squeezed her fingers with a grin. As soon as the vows were exchanged, the priest led the couple into the candle-lit church for the nuptial mass, before finally leading them back outside and presenting them to the waiting crowd.

They had just begun to descend the stairs when Anna grabbed Keira and pulled her into a tight embrace.

"I'm so happy for you," she whispered. She pulled back with a little smirk. "And me too, of course." She turned to Aaron. "Well, brother," she said with a cheeky smile, "are you going to embrace your new sister?"

"Of course," Aaron said with a smile, wrapping an arm around her shoulder. "But if you start making trouble, I'm sure I can find a dungeon to lock you into," he added.

"I never make trouble," retorted Anna, but Aaron just lifted his eyebrows dubiously, before turning away. The man who had been waiting with Aaron stepped up and clasped one hand on Aaron's shoulder, while shaking his hand with the other.

"Congratulations, milord," said the man.

"Thank you, Thomas." Aaron turned to Keira. "Keira, this is Thomas, my trusted steward and a good friend. I rely on him in many matters, both business and personal."

Keira looked the man over carefully. Despite being older, in his late forties or early fifties, he stood straight and tall. His hair was thinning, but his eyes were a piercing blue, intelligent and kind.

"Thomas." Keira inclined her head in acknowledgment.

"Milady." Thomas returned the greeting before turning away to join the mingling crowd.

Trestle tables had been set up in the village square, and fowl and boar had been roasting since the morning over a fire that roared in a pit in the center. The wedding table had been placed on a raised dais at one end of the square, while other tables were arrayed around the outer edges, leaving the center open for dancing.

Aaron led Keira to the main table, and they were soon joined by Keira's family. Wine and ale were already flowing freely amongst the revelers, and serving maids carried large trays of meats. News of the wedding had brought a traveling minstrel into the village, and he was soon entertaining the villagers with bawdy songs and heartfelt ballads. As soon as he stopped for a rest, the village musicians took over, their instruments urging people to their feet as they joined hands to dance the traditional wedding carol. Aaron grabbed Keira by the hand and dragged her into the circle, joining the villagers already dancing, and when Anna joined them, he pulled her into the circle on his other side. The one person noticeably missing from the festivities was Edmund, although his absence was met with relief by Keira. His father, the reeve, was in attendance, however; but he spent most of the evening glowering at Aaron and whispering with the few men that hovered around him.

It was already past the midnight hour when Aaron suggested to Keira that it was time to make their escape, a suggestion to which she heartily agreed. Aaron gestured to Thomas, letting him know they would be on their way, while Keira scanned the crowd in search of her family. They were on the other side of the square, where Father stood with other village men, and Mother was deep in conversation with Jane Tanner. Anna was close by, laughing with a group of village girls, their giggles rising above the general hubbub of the gathering. Taking Aaron by the hand, Keira led him over so they could make their farewells, weaving her way between the dancers and musicians still enjoying the revelries despite the late hour. At the sound of their approach, Father looked over at his daughter, and a smile wreathed his face.

"You're a beautiful bride, my daughter," he said. "Your countenance has been radiant all evening."

"Thank you," replied Keira, glancing quickly at the source of her joy with a warm smile. Aaron wrapped his arm around her shoulder, pulling her closer to his side as Keira continued. "We're leaving now, Father." Mother and Anna had joined the little group, and this pronouncement was met with expressions of surprise.

"Surely you don't intend to travel to Storbrook Castle at this hour," Mother exclaimed. "It's already past the witching hour."

"You must stay in our home, at least for the night," Father urged. "You can travel to Storbrook tomorrow, by the light of day."

"No," responded Aaron with quiet finality. "Storbrook is my home, and is now Keira's home as well. I have a horse waiting, and my man Thomas will travel with us. I know the road well, and I can guarantee you that no harm will come to your daughter."

Anna was standing a few feet away, and Keira heard her mutter something under her breath. She thought she caught the word 'fly,' but whatever it was she said, it made Aaron glance her way with a look of stern disapproval before he turned back to Keira.

"Ready?" he asked as Thomas appeared behind the square leading two horses by the reins.

"Yes," she said, then turned back to her parents. "Thank you for everything," she said. She reached for her mother's hand and gave it a quick squeeze before turning to Anna and pulling her into a tight embrace.

"I'll be looking for you in a month's time," whispered Anna. "Don't forget."

"We'll be back soon," promised Keira. "A month will go by quickly."

She turned back to Aaron and placed her hand in his, smiling up at him.

"Let's go home," she said.

CHAPTER EIGHTEEN

Keira leaned against Aaron as they rode along the dark road. The moon behind the trees cast eerie shadows, making Keira shiver, but Aaron's strong arms around her lent her courage. Thomas rode his own horse a few paces behind, giving them a chance for private conversation.

"Is Thomas human?" Keira asked once they were clear of the village.

"Yes," Aaron replied.

"But he knows what you are?"

"Yes, he's one of few who do."

"But what about your servants at Storbrook? Do they know?"

"Thomas is the only one in my confidence."

"But how's that possible?"

"The servants all know that the dragon is free to come and go as he pleases," Aaron said, "but the dragon only enters or leaves Storbrook through the large outer windows. The man they know as their master comes and goes through the more conventional entries."

"But still," Keira said in confusion, "don't they see the chambers the dragon enters?"

"The rear wall of the donjon forms part of the outer castle wall," Aaron explained. "It's not possible for someone to see which window the dragon is flying into unless they are directly outside the wall. Since that side of the mountain is sheer rock face, it's virtually impossible."

"But surely the servants must wonder why the dragon is given free rein of the castle."

"If they do, they keep their conjectures to themselves. Fear of a dragon is quite a motivation to keep quiet. Not," he added quickly as she stiffened in his arms, "that I would ever do anything to harm any of my servants – but they don't know that. Besides, my staff numbers only eighteen, and they seldom have need to venture away from the castle. Thomas takes a cart into the village every fortnight, and whoever wants to go with him is free to do so."

Keira was silent for a moment as she considered this. "So," she said, "Thomas is the only one who knows."

"And the priest."

"The priest?" she repeated in astonishment.

"Yes, the priest," he said, amusement in his tone. "He's a confessor for the prisoners and also reads them their last rites."

"Oh! Of course." In fact, Keira had forgotten about the prisoners, but she was glad Aaron attended to their spiritual needs.

"So, Thomas and the priest," she repeated. "That's not very many people." Keira felt Aaron shrug behind her.

"The fewer people who know, the easier it is to keep my secret." He reined in his horse as he spoke the last words and slipped from the saddle, then turned to lift Keira down.

"This is as far as we go on horseback," he explained. "Thomas will take the horses the rest of the way while we fly back."

"But won't the servants be surprised to find you at Storbrook in the morning? And with a wife, as well?"

"I'm sure Thomas will come up with a suitable

explanation, won't you, Thomas?" Aaron asked with a grin as the man pulled up next to them.

"Of course, milord," Thomas replied.

Aaron unclasped his cloak and swung it over Keira's shoulders, drawing the dragon pin through the folds of fabric at her throat. A moment later he'd stripped off his doublet and shirt and stuffed them into a saddle bag, leaving his chest bare. Nodding once at Thomas, he returned his gaze to Keira and pulled her into his arms.

"Hold tight," he said. He unfurled his wings, and she wrapped her hands around his neck as he lifted them into the air. The air was cool around them, but the heat of Aaron's skin slipped through her clothes and kept her warm. The moon was waning and offered very little light, but Aaron flew without hesitation.

"How do you know where to go?" Keira asked, gazing out into the darkness that surrounded them.

"Humans are so used to relying on their sight, they forget about their other senses," Aaron said with a snort. "Close your eyes, my sweet. Tell me what you hear." Keira did as he instructed, listening to the sounds that filled the air around her.

"I hear your wings beating against the wind," she replied, opening her eyes to smile at him.

He smiled. "What else?" he asked. Keira closed her eyes again.

"A nightjar." She screwed up her eyes, concentrating. "And rushing water." She opened her eyes and looked at him questioningly.

"The waterfall. We're close to Storbrook. Now close your eyes again and tell me what you smell." Keira did as she was instructed and took a deep breath.

"I smell you," she said, keeping her eyes closed. "You smell like smoke."

Aaron chuckled before burying his nose in her hair and taking in a deep breath.

"And you smell of the promise of love," he said.

Keira blushed, but took another deep breath. "I smell ..." She hesitated, trying to place the scent. "Pine."

"Well done."

Keira laughed. "I'm a quick student," she teased. "How does pine help you know where you are?"

"Pine only grows at higher elevations, so I know we're high," he said. "But very little grows at the top, so when the smell of pine fades, I know I'm close. Look down – there's nothing beneath us but rock and a little scrub. Can you see Storbrook?"

Keira tightened her grip around his neck and twisted around. Below them, basking in a soft glow, was Storbrook. Flaming lanterns stood along the tops of the walls at regular intervals, bathing the castle in orange light that flickered in the breeze and cast shadows which danced in time to the notes of music that drifted to them on a breeze. A huge fire blazed in the inner court, and Keira could see people mingling around the flames, while others danced. Someone scraped out a tune on a violin, while another played the lyre.

"Are they waiting for you?" she asked.

"They're celebrating our marriage, but aren't expecting to see us tonight. It will be a few hours before Thomas arrives with the horses, and most of the people you see will have retired by then. If one or two are still around, they won't be in any condition to contemplate why Thomas has arrived with two horses, but no second rider," he added with a laugh.

Aaron dropped towards the outer walls of the castle, then flew into one of the large windows Keira had seen before. The wall was built from stone and stood at least three feet thick, and Aaron landed on the window ledge, which opened up into a very large room. Releasing Keira, he jumped down to the floor then turned back to help her down.

The chamber was dark, but Aaron quickly lit the torches that stood in sconces around the room. A huge fireplace was built into one of the walls, and with a few fiery breaths Aaron had a fire blazing in the grate. As the light spread through the space, Keira looked around. The room was clearly a bedchamber, but was larger than her parents' entire cottage. The ceiling soared twenty feet above her, the light barely penetrating the shadowed depths. A huge canopied bed was on one side of the room, covered in thick quilts and furs.

In the wall opposite the window was a large, heavy door, which Keira guessed led to the rest of the castle. Near this door stood a long table with a porcelain basin and ewer on the surface, and a pile of linens neatly stacked beside it. On either side of the bed, rugs had been placed on the stone floors, their exotic colors and designs suggesting they had been brought from afar. Across the room, near the fireplace, was a sitting area. High-backed chairs covered in cushions stood closest to the fire, rugs were scattered on the floor, and further away stood a wooden table, with a chess board set up with pieces. A smaller table stood against the wall, holding a decanter of wine and two goblets. The floor in the center of the room – an area that stretched thirty feet across – was completely bare of both furniture and rugs.

Aaron watched Keira for a moment before walking over to her. He took her hands in his and massaged them with his thumbs.

"Welcome home, Keira," he said softly. He glanced around the room for a moment before looking back at her with a smile.

"This is the Great Chamber. If you'd prefer to have separate chambers, then I'd be happy to arrange that. But I was hoping..." He hesitated for a moment before continuing. "Keira, will you share this chamber with me? There's a Lady's Bower that connects to this room –"

The words weren't even out of his mouth when Keira responded. "Yes. Yes. Of course, yes!"

Aaron's smile was ecstatic as he pulled her into his arms, his mouth near her ear.

"I have dreamed of this moment, my sweet. To hold you

in my arms and know that you belong here with me." He drew back to look her in the eyes. "All that I have is yours — my home, my possessions, my protection, my life and my heart. I love you, Keira, and have loved you from the first moment I saw you. Your grace, your courage and your beauty captivated me. I may be the dragon, but I am completely at your mercy."

Keira shivered as his mouth captured hers, his kiss passionate. As he drew away, Keira could see the desire blazing in his eyes, and she suddenly felt shy. The way Edmund had yanked her skirts had only filled her with fear and repulsion, and although she knew Aaron's attentions would be an act of love, she wasn't sure what to expect. She pulled back slightly, her eyes downcast as Aaron watched her carefully.

"Come, Keira, let's sit by the fire for a while." Keeping her hand in his, he led her across the room to one of the high-backed chairs and poured her a glass of wine. He handed her the goblet, its liquid glowing ruby red in the firelight, and settled himself at her feet, his hands resting on her knees as he looked at her.

"Your parents provided a lavish feast," he said with a smile. "Anyone would think that they actually approve of our union."

Keira grinned. "Mother would rather die than give the village women reason to say she was miserly. And as for Father, I think he really does like you. Or maybe he just senses that it's in his own best interests not to cross a dragon," she teased.

"And don't ever forget it, wife," Aaron growled playfully. He pulled her from the chair and into his lap.

"Did you see Dame Lamb dancing?" Keira asked as she settled her weight against him. "She hobbled around with her stick, grabbing onto any man near her!" She laughed as she remembered the way the old lady lifted her skirts above her ankles, shocking many of the younger women in the crowd.

"Hmm," responded Aaron. "There seems to be more to Dame Lamb than meets the eye. Dancing, drinking, conversing with faeries. What next?"

The fire grew low in the grate as they continued their reminiscing. Aaron made Keira blush when he recounted some of the bawdy jokes told by the minstrel, while Aaron laughed as Keira repeated some of the wifely wisdom that had been bestowed on her by well-meaning village women.

The firelight caught the band of gold glittering on Keira's finger, and she pulled her hand out of his to take a closer look. Finely etched around the band was a dragon, the flame from its mouth reaching around the circle to catch its tail.

"My father gave it to my mother when they were married," Aaron said, watching Keira as she examined the ring. "Once we have the binding ceremony, dragon blood will forever course through your veins." The binding ceremony was scheduled to take place the following week, allowing Keira and Aaron a few days alone before their guests started to arrive. Keira swallowed hard as she remembered what the ceremony entailed – drinking Aaron's blood.

"I can't wait to taste your blood," Aaron whispered, as if reading her thoughts. "I want to know that my blood flows through your veins, and that we'll forever be a part of each other." He turned her hand and traced his finger over the inside of her wrist. "Nothing will ever separate us," he said.

He turned her in his lap so that she straddled him and brought his lips to hers as his hands slid behind her back and slowly loosened her laces. His fingers were hot against her skin, and when his hand slipped beneath her bodice, she shivered.

"I'll be very gentle, Keira," whispered Aaron. "I intend to give you as much pleasure as you will give me in our joining. This is our most private, intimate connection, and nothing that happens between us should be viewed with shame or embarrassment. I love you, my sweet. Allow me to show you how much."

And when he slowly slid her gown off her shoulders and touched her skin with his lips, she gave herself over to him, following him as he led her into untold delights.

When Keira woke the following morning, she was in the large bed, cocooned in quilts and blankets, her husband curled around her back. Bringing her hand to her mouth, she traced her fingers around her lips, before running them down her neck, over her bare breasts and down her stomach. The warmth crept into her cheeks as she remembered her husband's mouth trailing along the same path, and her stomach clenched as she recalled his caress. He had been so gentle the first time, patiently waiting for her before carrying them both to dizzying heights of passion. They had slept lightly, awakening to an intense awareness of each other, and when he moaned at her caresses, she knew that she could evoke the same powerful responses in him that he evoked in her. She had not known it was possible to feel such pleasure, and she smiled in remembrance as she snuggled closer to Aaron, reveling in his warmth. He rested his hand on her breast, and his thighs were tucked behind hers.

"Good morning, my wife," he murmured sleepily, as his hand slowly trailed down her bare hip and along her thigh. His gentle touch made her shiver, and she turned to face him, her legs tangling with his. He pulled her closer, and his warm breath caressed her face as he pushed himself up on one elbow to kiss her. She wrapped her arms around him and gave herself to the passion that tumbled over her like a sudden storm.

CHAPTER NINETEEN

The sun was high when they finally stirred out of the warm nest of quilts, the mundane needs of food and ablutions forcing their way into their private sanctuary. Aaron waited as Keira wrapped herself in a fur from the bed before leading her into the anteroom. She gaped in astonishment as he opened chest after chest, filled with gowns, petticoats, cloaks and shoes.

"But, how ...?" she began, gazing at the luxurious fabrics and bright hues. Aaron smiled as he stood behind her, his fingers trailing down her spine.

"I told Thomas to hire a seamstress as soon as you agreed to marry me," he said. "She's still here, so if you find that these are not suitable, or you fancy something I've overlooked, be sure to let Thomas know, and he'll remedy the situation."

Keira shook her head. "There are more gowns here than my mother, sister and I own together! I cannot think the seamstress's services will be needed any further."

"I'm sure you'll find something to occupy her time," he said. "But come, we should both clothe ourselves and go in search of sustenance."

Keira gently lifted a gown from one of the chests, marveling at the rich green silk trimmed in gold. Gently placing it aside, she reached in farther, pulling out gowns in pinks, yellows, blues and reds; made in rich silks and velvets; trimmed with beads, pearls, gold thread and fur. By the time the chest was empty, there were over a dozen gowns spread across the floor. Aaron smiled as he watched her, her mouth hanging open in amazement at the rich garments.

"Thank you," Keira whispered as she rose and placed her hands on his chest. She shivered when he brushed his lips over hers.

"The pleasure was all mine," he breathed. His hand wandered up to her neck, pulling her close as the kiss deepened. She wrapped her arms around him, causing the fur wrap to slip out of her grasp, and he pulled away to look at her appreciatively.

"As much as I look forward to seeing you in your new garments, you can present yourself to me like this anytime," he said, his smile becoming a leer as his eyes blazed with gold. Keira pushed him away, the color mounting in her cheeks.

"I think it would be prudent for me to get dressed now," she murmured.

"Your being dressed won't stop me desiring you," he said. "It only adds to the pleasure, like removing the shell to reveal the pearl." He laughed as Keira blushed, then turned away to pull on a pair of hose.

Keira had dressed and was brushing her hair when a knock sounded on the door.

"Come," Aaron called, first glancing at her to ensure her modesty. The door pushed open and Thomas stepped inside.

"Milord," he said. "Milady."

"Thomas!" Aaron said. "You made it back without mishap, I see."

"Yes, milord," Thomas responded with a slight grin. "I arrived back a few hours before dawn. I had to rouse the guard in the gatehouse, and nobody still remaining in the courtyard paid me the slightest attention."

Aaron nodded. "Good." He gestured around the room. "The Lady Keira will be sharing these chambers with me, and the Lady's Bower will also be fully at her disposal."

He glanced at Keira. "You're free to make whatever changes you see fit in this chamber or any other room in the castle. Just let Thomas know your will, and he'll make the necessary arrangements."

Aaron glanced back at the steward, his expressive look indicating that the words were as much for Thomas's benefit. Thomas's eyebrows lifted slightly at Aaron's words, but his expression was carefully blank.

"Of course, milord," he replied. He cleared his throat before continuing. "Cook was wondering whether you and your lady would be joining us for dinner, or whether she should send your victuals to your chambers."

"We'll join you shortly in the hall," Aaron replied. "My Lady Keira will be introduced to the household at that time." Thomas nodded and turned to leave the room, closing the heavy door carefully behind him.

A few minutes later the master of the castle and his fair wife left the privacy of their chambers and headed down the corridor. They soon reached a large sweeping staircase, beyond which, Aaron explained, were further private chambers and apartments. Since the castle had remained empty for so long, these were still closed, but with the imminent arrival of guests, they would be opened and aired. Further guest rooms were on the floor beneath, as well as a private solar and Aaron's cabinet. The Great Hall took up the level below, where the household shared their meals and entertainments were enjoyed, while the lowest level housed the low hall, kitchen, pantry, larder and scullery. And below all of that, explained Aaron, a grin lurking at the corners of his mouth, were the caves. But since the Storbrook dragon had declined these particular living quarters, he said, they housed the castle cellars instead.

By the time he'd finished his description of Keira's new home, they had reached the entrance to the Great Hall.

"Ready, my sweet?" Aaron asked softly. Keira nodded her head, and he tightened his grip around her hand, squeezing her fingers gently. "My servants are good people, Keira," he said. "They'll soon learn to love you." He gave her a warm smile as he led her into the hall.

The room was already full of people, seated on benches at the long tables that stood around the huge room. Their voices blended into a rumble which slowly died away as people became aware of the Master entering with his lady. All eyes turned to them as Aaron led Keira to a table on a raised dais. Thomas stood behind the table, smiling at Keira, and she felt some of her trepidation melt away. Aaron handed Keira onto the dais before hopping up himself, and turning to face the assembly.

"Men and women of Storbrook," he began, "I present my wife, Lady Keira." The room was silent for a moment, and Keira trembled beneath the weight of their stares, but when Aaron swept her into his arms and kissed her soundly, the room broke out into cheers. Aaron pulled away with a grin and turned to look at his staff.

"I know that you'll serve her as well as you do me," he said. He waved his hand towards the door. "Now, let us eat." He nodded to the priest to lead the prayers, then pulled a chair from the table for Keira to sit. The prayers said, serving girls brought in trays of food and placed them on the long tables, then dropped themselves down onto the benches with the other diners as soon as they had set down their loads.

"Are all these people here to serve you?" asked Keira in amazement.

Aaron nodded. "It takes a lot of people to keep a place like Storbrook running smoothly."

"I suppose it does," Keira responded, her tone doubtful. Aaron looked at her thoughtfully for a moment.

"You're a woman of strength and courage, Keira," he said. "It may seem a bit daunting at the moment, but you'll quickly grow into your role as lady of the house. You'll have my support in whatever changes you see fit to make, and Thomas will be around to lend his support as well." Aaron glanced at Thomas, who had seated himself next to Keira, and he nodded in agreement.

"You'll do fine, milady," Thomas reassured her with a smile. "The servants all know their duties, and if there is anything you want done, come and speak to me."

Keira nodded. "Thank you," she said.

She glanced up when a short, stout woman brought a tray over to the dais and dropped a curtsey in Aaron and Keira's direction, her expression dour.

"Welcome, milady," she said, her voice void of expression. "I'm Cook. I expect you'll want to talk to me, so you'll find me in the kitchen."

Keira shot an amused glance at Aaron before looking back at the woman. "Thank you, Cook," she said. "I've already heard about your excellent skills in the kitchen, so I look forward to hearing your opinion on the menus I have in mind, knowing that your suggestions will be improvements to my simple ideas." The cook nodded before turning away, her expression not quite as severe as before. Aaron snorted as Thomas smiled behind his hand.

"You're a natural," said Aaron, a note of pride in his voice. "But I'll be very wary when you start plying me with compliments."

When the meal was done, Keira took herself off to explore the castle while Aaron retreated with Thomas to the cabinet to discuss matters of business. She climbed a small, narrow staircase behind the Great Hall that led to the guest rooms, then lost her way as she wandered from room to room. Slowly, she understood that the castle had been built in the shape of a horseshoe, with two wings on either side of the main building. All the rooms were huge, with windows that overlooked the mountains in all directions. She found her way back to the main staircase quite by accident, and descended down to the lowest level, which was cool and dank, before finally pushing open a door that led to the courtyard. It was paved with stone, and bustled with people who bobbed their heads at her before continuing with their tasks. Behind the workshops she caught glimpses of green, and she headed in that direction to explore the gardens. She'd just stepped onto the garden path when Aaron caught up with her. His arms circled around her waist as his hot breath tickled her ear.

"Did you miss me?" he murmured as he trailed kisses down her jaw and onto her neck.

"Mmm," she responded, all thought of speech snatched from her brain as she melted into his embrace. Aaron laughed softly, and taking her hand, led her to a bench half-hidden in the shade of a tree.

"I was discussing the arrangements for our guests with Thomas," said Aaron, placing his arm around her shoulders as they sat. "They'll start arriving in the next few days."

"How many people are coming?" Keira asked.

"Twenty-five dragons, and about eighteen humans."

"That's a, er, a lot of dragons," Keira said.

"They'll be in human form most of the time. After all, we can't have our guests scaring the servants."

"Not to mention your wife," Keira muttered. Aaron laughed as he pulled her close.

"The only dragon you need to be scared of is this one, my sweet. Who knows when he'll decide to nibble on your flesh?" He brushed his mouth over her neck, and she shivered in pleasure. He pulled away a moment later. "Do you want to hear about our guests?" he asked.

"Yes, I suppose so," Keira said. Aaron laughed as she turned and leaned into his chest.

"I told you before that the dragons coming to the binding ceremony are part of my clan," he said. "I also mentioned my uncle, who is a clan elder. His name's Owain, and he'll lead the binding ceremony. His son, Favian, is my closest friend. He and Cathryn were married about ten years ago, so Cathryn is probably the closest to you in age. They have two young children who'll also be coming."

"Do you see them often?" asked Keira.

"It was Favian who reminded me that I was also partly human. In fact, he tore the strips off me and threw them in my face." Aaron grimaced at the remembrance, before adding wryly, "I suppose that was the only way he was going to get through my thick, beastly mind. But it worked. And so I suppose it is thanks to him that I'm holding you in my arms." He paused for a moment, dropping a kiss onto her sun-warmed hair, before continuing. "It's been my wont to spend part of the year with them. They live with Owain and Margaret, and are my closest family. But you are my family now."

Keira pulled away and turned around to face him.

"I don't want to be the reason you stop seeing your family, Aaron. I'm sure that I'll love them as much as you do, and if you want to spend time with them, then that is what we must do." Aaron smiled at her expression, intense and stern, and lifted his hand to push back her hair.

"I want to be with you," he said. "I love Favian and Cathryn, but it is you who is now my life and my home. There'll be times when we visit them, but it will be because we, you and I, choose to do so, not because I'm lonely for family. You have made my life complete." Aaron ran his hand down her cheek, and bent down to kiss her. She sighed as he pulled away.

"So what other dragons are coming?" she asked.

"Members of my clan. Most of them are related in some way – cousins, aunts, uncles."

"You have dragon aunts?" asked Keira in surprise.

He grinned. "Did you think all dragons were male?"

"Well, no, I suppose not," she said with a blush. "I

suppose I didn't really think about it."

"I have one dragon aunt, my father's sister. Her name's Beatrix, and her husband, James, is also a dragon." Aaron caressed Keira's shoulder as he spoke. "He was rather wild in his younger days, and had already fathered two children with two different human women when he met Beatrix. But he settled down after meeting her, and they've been very happy together. The children, who are dragons, of course, remained with their mothers until they were teenagers, at which time they moved in with Beatrix and James." Aaron rose and pulled Keira to her feet. "As dragons, they should be attending their Master's binding, but I doubt that Max will exert himself enough to come, and since I really don't know Jane, I doubt she'll come either. In fact, I suspect the only reason Beatrix and James are coming is to inspect the woman who has captured my heart."

He glanced at her with a smile. "I've finished with Thomas for the day, my sweet, and I don't believe you've had enough time to fully appreciate our chamber." His hand closed around hers as his eyes began to swirl with flame. "I do think we should ensure the bed is really to your liking!"

Keira smiled. "That sounds like an excellent plan," she said.

CHAPTER TWENTY

Keira stood in the castle courtyard and looked up at the man standing before her. Almost a week had passed since her marriage to Aaron, and this was the first of the guests to arrive for the binding ceremony. She'd expected the other dragons to share Aaron's golden coloring, but this man had flaming red hair, while his eyes were a dark, sapphire blue. He was taller and heavier-set than Aaron, but like him, his skin glowed with light golden color. He raised a fist and placed it over his heart as Aaron strode towards him.

"Favian!" Aaron said. He grasped the man's hand in his own and pulled him close as he thumped his back, then turned his attention to the pretty, petite woman standing at Favian's side. "Cathryn! Welcome to Storbrook." Aaron grabbed Keira's hand and drew her closer. "Keira, this is Favian and Cathryn." Aaron glanced around as Keira greeted them with a smile.

"Where are Bronwyn and Will?" he asked, but the words were barely out of his mouth when Keira saw two small forms hurtling towards them. Taking a quick step backwards, she narrowly avoided being knocked over as the two children flung themselves at Aaron. The combined force knocked him off balance and he tumbled to the ground as shrieks of "Uncle Aaron" rang through the air.

"Urgh, you monsters," Aaron growled in mock ferocity. The children climbed onto his chest and wrapped their legs around his waist as he playfully wrestled with them in the dirt. He looked up and met Keira's eye with a grin.

"Will! Bronwyn!" Cathryn's words cut through the air, laden with horror and embarrassment at the antics of her offspring. "You're behaving like a pair of beasts in front of your new aunt," she scolded. "Get up now. And Aaron!" She swung a ferocious look at the man lying prone in the dust. "You should be equally ashamed, behaving like a lunatic."

Aaron pushed himself to his feet, ruffling the children's hair, the grin never leaving his face as he reached over to Cathryn and pulled her into an embrace.

"It's wonderful to see you again, Cathryn," he said. "It didn't seem quite like you until you started yelling at me."

Cathryn pulled away with a mock scowl which quickly turned into a laugh.

"You really are a monster, Aaron," she said. "I'm not sure what Keira saw in you, but it's a good thing you acted so quickly, before she saw how truly dreadful you are."

"I know," said Aaron, dropping his voice to a conspiratorial whisper. "A monster most terrible. She doesn't know it yet, but I'm going to lock her in one of the turrets as soon as you all leave. That way, I can have my wicked way with her whenever I please." He grinned at Keira as the heat rushed to her cheeks.

"Hmph," was Cathryn's response. "I suspect that you can have your wicked –"

"So, Aaron," Favian dropped his arm over Aaron's shoulder. "Who else can we expect to see over the course of the next few days?"

"Will Uncle Aaron really lock Aunty in a turret, Mama?" asked the little girl. Cathryn glanced around, surprise suffusing her features when she saw her children a few feet away. She blushed, but held her hand out to her daughter. Favian was saying something to Aaron, and they started to wander away, but not before Aaron threw Keira a quick wink.

Keira smiled to herself as she turned to examine the children. Bronwyn was a girl of around five or six with big brown eyes, her gaze solemn and intense. Brown pigtails, splashed with coppery tones, hung down the sides of her face, and bits of grass and twigs were tangled in her hair after her romp on the ground. Her brother, older by a couple of years, stood beside her, his height and size suggesting that he would have the big build of his father.

"No, silly," he responded, answering the question addressed to their mother. "Uncle Aaron is just teasing. He'd never lock someone in the tower unless they'd been really naughty." He stopped and turned an appraising look on Keira. "Have you been naughty, Aunty?"

Cathryn gasped in horror, but Keira burst out laughing.

"Are you Will?" she asked, smiling when he nodded. "Well, I'm very pleased to make your acquaintance, Will. I'll try very hard to not be naughty. I really don't want to be locked in the tower. What about you? Will you be good while you are visiting us?"

"Well," responded the boy doubtfully, "I can try." A small frown furrowed his forehead, before suddenly smoothing out as he grinned. "But Uncle Aaron won't lock me in the tower, even if I am naughty. Isn't that right, Mama?" he asked, turning to his mother.

Cathryn looked at him sternly for a moment, although a smile tugged at her lips. "Well, that depends. The Master can't allow dragons to do whatever they want."

Will nodded solemnly. "I'm a dragon, you know," he said to Keira. "At least, I will be one day."

"Me too, me too," shouted Bronwyn.

Will gave her a look of withering scorn. "You're just a little girl. I'll be a dragon long before you."

"Now, now, children," said Cathryn. "Run off and play while I talk with Aunt Keira."

Needing no further encouragement, the two children took off across the courtyard, chasing a frightened chicken before veering towards the gardens. Cathryn watched them indulgently for a moment, then turned back to Keira with a grin.

"They can be little monsters, but I do love them. Now, believe it or not, this is my first visit to Storbrook Castle, so I'm most eager for a tour. I was so pleased when I heard Aaron had finally found someone, and now that I've met you, I think we're going to be wonderful friends." Pulling Keira's arm through her own, she led Keira across the courtyard and through the door.

Storbrook Castle was a hive of activity over the next few days as more dragons and their mates continued to arrive. Most of the guests arrived late at night, gliding undetected through the dark night sky and arriving through one of the large windows above the sheer rock face.

"We're not going to have someone fly into our chambers in the middle of the night, are we?" Keira had asked Aaron worriedly when the first guests started arriving.

"No, my sweet," Aaron replied with a snort. "They know better than to come uninvited into their Master's personal chambers. Just in case, Thomas has marked the different rooms so each guest knows where to go."

Owain and Margaret, Favian's parents, were the next guests to arrive. Owain was Aaron's uncle, and also one of five clan elders who served as advisors to the Master. As both an elder and surrogate father, Owain would perform the blood-binding ceremony.

As Owain stepped into Aaron's presence, he dropped to his knee and placed his right hand in a fist over his heart.

"Master," he said, his eyes on the ground.

"Welcome, Owain," Aaron replied with a nod. Owain

rose to his feet and gave his nephew an appraising look then clasped him around the shoulders and pulled him forward into an embrace.

"It's good to see you, Aaron."

"And you. Let me introduce my wife, Keira."

Owain turned to Keira. "So this is the girl," he said. "She's quite a beauty, Aaron, and she must be quite an extraordinary women to have won your heart."

"She is, indeed," replied Aaron, reaching out to grasp her hand.

Owain nodded, then startled Keira by pulling her into an enveloping hug. From the corner of her eye she could see Aaron laughing, until he gently pried her out of Owain's arms.

"Careful uncle, she hasn't had dragon blood yet."

"Oh, yes, of course," Owain said.

Margaret stepped forward with a gentle smile and grasped Keira's hands in her own.

"If Owain seems a bit overwhelming, it's because he despaired of Aaron ever finding someone to love! We are delighted to welcome you into the family, my dear."

"Thank you," Keira said.

More guests continued to arrive. Favian's sister, Ayleth, came with her human husband in tow. She was beautiful, and carried herself with regal grace and a cool assurance, and like the other dragons, her skin glowed as though lit from within. She nodded at Keira when Aaron introduced them, but offered no warm words of welcome.

In complete contrast to Ayleth were Aaron's aunt Beatrix and her husband James. Beatrix was a warm, matronly woman, and she immediately encircled Keira in a fleshy embrace, pronouncing how wonderful it was that Aaron was finally settling down. She too had the inner glow that seemed to characterize all dragons, and her ease and familiarity made Keira feel part of the family.

Guests continued to arrive over the next few nights. If

the servants wondered why people arrived so silently under cover of darkness, Keira never heard any whisperings when she sat with them in the Great Hall for meals. She could only suppose that Thomas had concocted a story that presented at least a passable explanation for the strange nightly activity. Each morning, Aaron would enthusiastically introduce Keira to the latest arrivals, and it was clear from the warm welcome Aaron extended to each new guest that he was very fond of his clan members. In fact, only one guest was met without pleasure.

"Jack arrived last night," Aaron said one morning. "Although a request to attend was sent to all dragons, he was one guest I was hoping would decline the invitation."

"Why?" she asked. "Who is he?"

"He's the son of my father's cousin, and is the black sheep of the family. Or perhaps I should say black dragon. He runs wild, with no regard for others, either dragon or human."

"Weren't you like that for a while?"

Aaron glanced at Keira for a moment before turning away and moving to the window. Leaning his shoulder against the wall, he gazed out at the mountains surrounding the castle.

"It's not quite the same," he said. "My behavior was fueled by anger and hurt – not that that makes it right, of course," he added hurriedly. "But Jack is cruel. He cares for no-one but himself. He flouts the rules whenever possible, and snubs his nose at me."

"Isn't there anything you can do?"

"Of course I've tried," he said wearily. "I can banish him, but that won't keep him away. And when he returns, I'll be forced to kill him."

"I see."

Aaron turned back to face her with a strained smile. "Exactly," he said. "He's here for a reason, and the only one I can see for him coming to Storbrook is to force my hand. I don't doubt that he'll do something while he's here to overstep the mark, and I'll have no choice but to banish him."

Keira walked over to where Aaron stood and wrapped her arms around him, leaning against his chest as he folded his arms around her.

"You're a good man, Aaron Drake," she said. "I know that you feel responsible for each dragon, but it sounds to me like Jack has made his own choices, and must accept the consequences of those. You are not answerable for his actions."

"You're right, of course," he responded. "But it doesn't make it any easier."

"You'll do the right thing, Aaron," she responded, lifting herself onto her toes to kiss him. "Now, let's get dressed so that I can meet this dreadful relative."

Whatever Keira had expected when she met Jack in the hall later that morning, Aaron by her side, it wasn't the handsome man who greeted her with a flourishing bow and a kiss on the hand. His coloring was dark – jet black hair pulled into a ribbon at the nape of his neck, and silver eyes that flashed when he smiled at her. His high cheekbones and fine features were almost feminine in their beauty, but his eyes were cold, making his smile seem cruel.

"Cousin Keira," he said softly, leaning towards her so that his breath brushed her face. "It is so wonderful to meet the woman who has tamed this particular dragon. I've heard that Aaron is quite smitten."

"Enough, Jack," Aaron said, his voice sounding harsh after Jack's smooth murmur. Placing his arm around Keira's shoulders, he pulled her close to his side.

"Now, now, Aaron," Jack responded with an airy wave of his hand. "No need to show your claws. I was just being friendly."

"Stay away from my wife while you're here, Jack."

"You cannot expect me to pass up the chance of getting to know my new relative, can you?" He glanced back at Keira. "She looks like a pretty, young thing." Aaron's arm tightened around Keira's shoulder, and Jack grinned. "So it looks like the rumors are true, Aaron. You have fallen in love! It will be interesting to see how far you'll go to protect her."

Aaron frowned. "Come, my sweet," he said to Keira.

Jack's voice trailed after them as they walked from the hall. "Don't worry, Aaron, I have no intention of harming your wife."

"What was that about?" Keira asked as they rounded the corner.

"Nothing. Just don't allow yourself to be alone with Jack. He can be charming when he chooses, but his intentions are never honorable."

"Don't worry about me," she said. "I can look after myself."

"I know you can," he said, "but I'd rather you didn't find yourself in a situation where you had to." He kissed her gently. "I have business to attend to with the elders," he said. He stared at her for a moment, then yanked her into his arms and kissed her deeply. She was panting when he pulled away. "That's so you don't forget that you're mine," he growled in her ear.

"How could I forget that?"

"It seemed prudent to remind you."

"Hmm," she said. "Well then, perhaps you should remind me again – my memory does seem to be a little deficient of late." He grinned and brushed his lips against hers before walking away.

CHAPTER TWENTY-ONE

It was a few hours later when Keira realized that Aaron's concerns about Jack were well founded. She had retired to the Lady's Bower, seeking a little privacy while she reviewed Cook's menus for the coming days. Her desk was placed near the window, and light spilled onto the parchment. Since her arrival at Storbrook, she and Cook had settled into a routine where Cook would tell her what she was planning, letting Keira make whatever changes she saw fit. Despite her grim exterior, Cook had proven herself to be Keira's ally, and had helped to ease her into her new role as mistress of Storbrook.

Keira had just dipped the quill into the small bottle of ink, intent on making some minor changes, when she felt the soft brush of warm fingers on the nape of her neck. Her first thought was that Aaron had returned from his meeting – when a soft voice sent that notion scattering. Jumping up from her seat, Keira spun around to face the intruder into her private quarters.

"Jack, what are you doing here?" she demanded angrily.

"Why, just looking for you, my dear cousin," Jack said. "We are cousins now, and I thought we could spend some time getting to know each other." His smooth voice sent a sliver of fear racing through Keira, and she took a step backwards.

"You're not welcome in my private quarters." Keira's voice came out as a whisper, and she paused, forcing an edge into her tone. "Please leave at once!"

Jack took a step towards her. "Not exactly beautiful," he said, "but there is something quite enchanting about you. I think it must be your eyes. They show a certain intellect quite unusual in humans. I can imagine a man could get quite taken in by such lovely eyes."

He leaned closer, and his hand brushed her breast before snaking around her waist and pulling her hard against him as he lowered his lips to hers. With his other hand, he grasped her behind the neck, preventing her retreat. For a moment Keira stood frozen in shock before her mind sprang into action. His chest was pressed up hard against hers, leaving no space between them that she could leverage to push him away, so she lifted a hand, and curling her fingers into claws, scoured them down his cheek, leaving three long, angry welts marring his smooth skin.

He jumped back with a curse, grabbing her wrists in a steel hold. "Why, you –"

"Jack!" She and Jack spun around as the sound of Jack's name cracked out sharply from the doorway. Pulling her hands free, Keira looked at Cathryn in relief as she entered the room.

"What exactly do you think you're doing, Jack?" Cathryn demanded.

"This has nothing to do with you," hissed Jack through clenched jaws.

"Perhaps not," responded Cathryn, "but I believe Aaron will think it has something to do with him."

Jack stared at Cathryn for a moment, before he shoved past her and out the door.

"Are you all right?" Cathryn asked, quickly crossing the floor to where Keira stood. Pulling the stool closer, she pushed Keira gently onto the seat, and poured her a cup of wine from a jug on the desk. Keira took a few deep gulps before looking up at Cathryn.

"How much did you hear?"

"Enough," Cathryn said. "I saw Jack heading up the stairs. I wondered what he was up to, so I followed him. I heard you tell him to leave."

"I'm very glad you arrived when you did," she said. "I'm not sure what I would've done if he had persisted."

"It sounded as if you were managing just fine," Cathryn said. "But still, it's a good thing you have a witness to what happened. It wouldn't surprise me if Jack tried to insinuate that you were the one seducing him. And the Master does have his enemies – dragons that would use whatever they could to stir up trouble."

"Apart from Jack?"

"His followers. But since I heard what happened, no-one can doubt your loyalty to Aaron."

"Would you have doubted my loyalty?"

Cathryn laughed. "It's clear to anyone who can see that you and Aaron have eyes for no other. I would not have believed Jack."

Keira nodded. "Good."

"Now let's go find that husband of yours and let him know what Jack has been up to."

"I'm not sure that's necessary," Keira said. "After all, nothing really happened."

"Nothing really happened?" she scoffed. "Jack tried to kiss you. Aaron is not only your husband, but also the clan Master. Jack answers to Aaron, and Aaron needs to know what happened, and he needs to hear it from you. It won't do for him to hear rumors whispered between the servants in the low hall. Now come, there's nothing to fear."

With a sigh, Keira led the way to Aaron's cabinet, and waited outside as Cathryn went in to call Aaron. He exited a moment later, his brow furrowed with concern.

"What is it? What's happened?"

"Tell him," Cathryn urged.

Keira drew in a breath and started to relate the events that had happened, and after a moment, Cathryn slipped away. As soon as Keira mentioned Jack, Aaron's eyes began to blaze, and the heat seemed to leap from his skin. For a moment, Keira thought his anger was directed at her – that he blamed her somehow – but when he pulled her into his arms and murmured apologies into her ear, she realized that his anger was completely for Jack.

"Aaron, it's all right," she insisted. "Apart from his kissing me, nothing really happened." Aaron pulled away, and stared down at her in shock.

"A kiss is not nothing," he said. He turned away and slammed his fist against the wall, blowing out a stream of flame as he did so. "If Cathryn hadn't been there, Jack would have made sure a lot more happened. He pressed his advances on you, my wife. Not only were his actions insulting to you, he has shown complete disrespect to me as his Master. This is his final act of defiance. He'll be made to leave Storbrook tonight, and will be banished from the clan."

"No, Aaron, please don't do this because of me," she said. "He's your clansman."

Aaron turned to look at her with incredulity. "Not banish him because of you? Of course I'll banish him because of you! You're my wife, but more than that, you are my very life, and his treatment of you will absolutely not be tolerated. This is just one more in a long line of defiant acts, but mark my words, it will be the last."

Pushing himself past her, Aaron flung open the door of the small room where the other dragons still remained, and slammed the door closed behind him. Keira watched his retreat in astonishment before turning on her heel and marching away.

Keira didn't see Aaron again for the rest of the day, but from the curious looks she received, she guessed that news of Jack's actions had already spread around the castle. She sat with the guests in the Great Hall, and tried to join in the conversation, but her mind was on other matters. Owain and the other elders entered the hall later that afternoon, their loud voices quickly adding to the noise in the huge room, but Aaron did not come.

As soon as supper was done, Keira excused herself from the company, pleading a headache. She felt annoyed and peevish, wishing the ceremony was over so she could have her new home and her husband to herself once again. The bed seemed vast and lonely as Keira pulled the quilts up around her chin, and despite her irritation at Aaron's response, she longed for his warm arms around her, holding her close. She was already fast asleep when Aaron climbed into the bed, but the action roused her enough to turn towards him, snuggling against his chest as she sought out his warmth.

"Jack's gone, my sweet. I'm sorry I took my anger out on you," she thought she heard Aaron whisper through the fog of sleep that still clung to her. She felt his lips brush against her forehead before wandering down to her ear. "I love you, Keira." The words washed over her and she smiled before once more passing into sleep's oblivious embrace.

CHAPTER TWENTY-TWO

Keira woke early as a stiff breeze raced through the window. She pulled the quilts up around her chin and opened her eyes, searching the room for Aaron. Even though a fire was blazing in the hearth, the room was cold – something that Keira didn't usually worry about when Aaron was close by. Aaron wasn't in the room, though, and she curled her feet beneath her, trying to find a pocket of heat, until finally she gave up in frustration. Jumping out of the bed, she wrapped her cloak around her shoulders and hurried over to the fire. The flagstones around the fire were warm, and she spread her toes, enjoying the heat as it spread through her feet. She wondered where Aaron could have gone so early in the morning, forgoing his usual habit of staying with her until she awoke. Curious, she pulled on a gown and slipped on a pair of slippers before cautiously pushing open the huge wooden door that led to the wide passageway.

Glancing up and down the corridor, she quietly stepped out and crept towards the stairs. She could hear the faint but unmistakable sounds of dragons growling as she walked, and she quickly made her way to the low hall, the door of which led to the courtyard. As she approached the doors, the sounds from the courtyard grew louder, and she could tell that there was more than one dragon out there. She paused for a moment, wondering at the wisdom of interrupting the gathering, but when she heard Aaron's voice ringing out amongst the other growls and voices, she pushed open the door and slipped through.

The air outside was cold, and the night sky was paling as the dawn approached. The dragons hadn't noticed her, and she crept along the wall until she stood behind a pillar. As curious as she was, she did not want to alert Aaron to her presence while he was here amongst the other dragons. There were five of them assembled in the courtyard, their claws scratching the ground impatiently. Their colors ranged from orange to red to black, but Keira watched the dragon that glowed gold, his armor rivaling the light of the sun on the brightest day. His wings glimmered in the early morning light, throwing a rainbow of colors against the surrounding walls. While the other dragons sat low against the ground, Aaron stood, his attention focused on something beyond Keira's line of sight.

Peeking around the pillar, Keira saw Thomas emerge from the prisoners' tower, followed by five men. Their hands and feet were bound with rope, and as they followed Thomas into the courtyard, they seemed unsurprised to see the huge beasts that ranged around them; instead, they wore expressions ranging from indifference to resignation. The fifth prisoner, however, a short man with a portly belly and a thick, greasy beard, stopped in his tracks and began to tremble as soon as he saw the beasts towering above them. His eyes darted wildly between the dragons as the sweat trickled down his pudgy face and dripped into his beard. He took a half step back towards the building, then jumped when Thomas addressed him. He stared at Thomas, wide-eyed, before stumbling after the others. As they reached the center of the courtyard, the priest stepped out from the shadows. Again, the first four men appeared unsurprised, and they knelt down on the hard cobblestones as he stooped before them and offered them the sacraments. He made the sign of the cross, then turned to the fifth man, who seemed not to have noticed him. The priest touched his arm, and he spun around, startled. He shook his head at something the priest said, and then again when Thomas joined the conversation. Thomas pointed at the prisoners' tower, and the man glanced at it before turning back to the dragons. His beard shook as he stared at them, and his lips began to move as he murmured something beneath his breath.

Thomas turned away and gestured to the other men to rise to their feet, and they waited silently as he removed their binds then stepped away, leaving them alone in the midst of the dragons. There was a rush of wind, and the dragons rose into the air and perched themselves along the turrets. Aaron landed on the highest, and from where she stood, Keira could see his eyes blazing as he stared at the terrified man.

Aaron cocked his head, and the gesture reminded Keira of an eagle watching his prey. It was in that moment that Keira realized what it was that she was witnessing. She gasped as Aaron lifted his head and let loose a savage roar as flames rolled through the air around him. The sound was so wild that Keira shivered in fear, and she watched in horror as Aaron launched himself from the turret and swooped downwards, his claws stretched out before him. He hit the short man with the full force of his claws, and Keira opened her mouth in a soundless scream as horror froze her in place. The body fell limp in Aaron's claws as he buried his talons into the man's chest, ripping him open, before sinking his jaws into the lifeless form. Fire curled from his mouth, blackening the flesh in the moments before he sunk his sharp teeth into it. Light from his eyes fell onto his victim as he lifted his head briefly before once more burying his jaws in the bloody flesh.

Keira could not move, but stared at Aaron as revulsion rooted her in place. She watched as Aaron buried his snout in the flesh, then pulled his dripping jaws away from the body. He looked up, and his blazing eyes met hers. A tremor passed through the mighty beast, and he pulled back slightly as Keira clasped a shaking hand over her mouth and stumbled backwards. She spun around as Aaron's roar rang through the air, his hot, fiery breath chasing her as she tugged at the heavy wooden door of the castle and threw herself inside. The sound of Aaron's roar only made her move faster as she flew up the stairs, her footsteps pounding against the stone as she raced along the corridor that led to their chamber. She yanked open the door, the bright light of Aaron's transformation from dragon to human flooding the doorway her only warning that he had anticipated her flight and beaten her to the room. He was already striding towards her as she pushed the door closed, his eyes blazing violently as his hands reached out to grab her.

"Don't touch me!" Her words flew out without thought as Keira shrank back against the door. Aaron stopped, his expression turning wary. In his haste he had not clothed himself, and Keira looked away, not wanting to see him in the body that she loved.

"Keira," he said, his voice tight, "you know what I am. A dragon. I've never hidden that fact from you. And you know what dragons eat – what we have to eat in order to survive. I have never hidden that from you, either. I'm sorry if it disgusts you, but you knew from the start what it was you were marrying."

Aaron turned away in frustration, pacing over to the window before turning back to Keira as she stood with her back pressed against the door. She could feel his anger mounting as she stared at the ground.

"Look at me," he said, but when she ignored him, his voice grew cold. "Look at me, Keira!" he repeated, his tone brooking no refusal. Reluctantly Keira lifted her head and met his gaze.

"This is what I am, wife," he growled. Keira watched in

stunned silence as Aaron started to transform before her eyes, his hands stretching into claws, his body growing longer and heavier. She shrunk back, pressing herself against the unyielding surface of the solid wooden door. His skin was stretching, thinning, turning translucent; and Keira gasped when she saw flames rippling beneath it, fire licking through his arms, legs, torso. Gold scales started to form across his body, and a tail grew from his spine as he fell down onto his front claws, his feet already stretching into similar appendages.

She started to turn away, unable to watch, but Aaron's voice stung her like a whip.

"Look at me!"

She turned back again and drew in a deep breath as Aaron's face started to elongate while his nose and mouth grew into jaws as his eyes moved to the sides of his head. His eyes were burning flames, the whites and pupils consumed by the blaze. The light within him was growing, as though seeking a way to get out, but Aaron held it at bay. Horns pushed through the top of his head as his neck started to stretch, reaching up until he towered over her. Along the length of his back slid his wings. Opening his mouth, Aaron breathed out a curling tongue of flame between rows of teeth that were as sharp as needles.

"This is what you married, Keira," he said, his voice hard and pitiless. He gazed at her for another moment before turning abruptly and launching himself out the window, his wings unfurling as a current of wind carried him away from the castle.

CHAPTER TWENTY-THREE

Keira ran to the window as Aaron flew from the castle and disappeared into the distance. Tears streamed down her cheeks, and she sank to the floor, her body shivering uncontrollably. She buried her head in her hands and sobbed, heedless of the cold stone beneath her or the slowly ebbing fire in the grate.

A long time had passed when a knock sounded at the door and Cathryn entered the room. She held a cup which she lifted by way of explanation.

"I thought you could use a libation," she said with a smile. She sat down beside Keira and handed her the cup.

"Favian told me what happened this morning," she said. Keira shuddered at the mention of what she had seen, but she remained silent, her fingers absentmindedly turning the cup in her hand.

"I remember the first time I saw Favian as he truly is – a dragon first and foremost," said Cathryn. "I was absolutely appalled, and horrified that I'd married such a beast. I refused to be anywhere near him for weeks after that. It took a long time for me to realize that the problem wasn't with him, but with me. He was who he was, but I could not accept his dragon nature, even though I loved the man. But by not accepting the dragon, I almost lost both." Cathryn gave a wry smile as she continued. "We were both so totally miserable – I'm sure he regretted taking me to wife many times over. And unfortunately, the lesson needed repeating before I finally grasped that if I loved him as I told myself I did, I needed to accept him completely. I couldn't just pick and choose the parts I liked, and reject the parts I didn't. Love means accepting the good with the bad, and loving the person regardless. It took a long time for him to finally see that I did love him, all of him, and that he could trust me enough to be himself around me." Cathryn stopped, her expression filled with regret as she watched Keira.

"Keira," she said, "don't make the same mistake I did: Aaron loves you, but if you push him away, you will lose both the man and the dragon."

Keira was silent as she gazed into the cup. "It was so horrible," she finally whispered. "Aaron tore a man apart. The blood was dripping everywhere, and he seemed to be enjoying it." Keira's voice dropped as she remembered the horror she had felt.

Cathryn took Keira's hand in hers and rubbed it between her palms, coaxing some warmth into her cold skin.

"The man you know wouldn't even exist if he didn't do these dreadful things, Keira," she said quietly. "When our men become dragons, they allow their beastly natures to rise to the fore, pushing aside any intellectual thought. Do you think he could live with himself as a man if he condemned himself for his actions as a dragon? So yes, Aaron probably did enjoy his meal. But that doesn't change the man. And in time," Cathryn added, a little wryly, "you may actually start to enjoy watching the dragon being ... a dragon!"

Keira looked at her in shock, but despite the color rising in her cheeks, Cathryn met Keira's gaze steadily.

"I'll send someone up with some food, and to stoke up the fire," she said, pushing herself up from the floor.

"I'm sorry," Keira said, her voice harsh from crying and

LINDA K. HOPKINS

raw emotion. "I'm not being a very good hostess. It should be me attending to you!"

"No," Cathryn said, waving her hand airily. "There's plenty of staff here to take care of our needs, so please don't concern yourself. You need to rest before the ceremony tonight. And Keira," she said, waiting for Keira to meet her gaze, "think about what I've said." She smiled before quietly letting herself out of the room.

Keira watched as the door closed behind Cathryn, then pushed herself up from the floor and drew her cloak tighter around her shoulders as she went to stand before the fire. Only coals remained, but the stone floor around the fireplace still retained some heat. Another knock sounded a few minutes later, and the door opened to reveal one of the serving maids with a tray of food, which she placed on the table. She disappeared out the door, only to return seconds later with an armload of wood for the fire.

Wandering over to the table, Keira picked at the food on the tray, considering what Cathryn had said. She knew her friend was right, that she needed to accept Aaron for what he was; but the question was, could she? She'd grown used to the idea of drinking his blood, as much as it still disgusted her, but could she accept what he ate? Could she accept that along with the man, came the dragon?

She thought about the man she had married, and even though it had only been a week, she knew her life would be infinitely less without him. With him, she felt loved. When he wrapped his arms around her, she felt secure. He brought out sensations she hadn't known existed – the racing of her pulse whenever he was near, the tingling of her skin when he touched her.

He hadn't scoffed at her hopes and dreams, and shared his own as they clung to each other after passionate lovemaking. He was a mate who would satisfy her all her days – how could she possibly risk losing that? But then she remembered what she'd seen that morning, and revulsion churned her stomach, and the bile rose in her throat. She'd opened her heart to Aaron, but her mind could not reconcile him with the deadly monster of the dawn.

The sun was already high in the sky when Keira finally found a fresh gown and got dressed. She ran a wet cloth over her face to wipe away the last traces of tears before leaving the room. The corridor was quiet, and although she wondered where everyone was, she was grateful she didn't need to face any judgmental – or worse, sympathetic – glances.

Hurrying along the corridor, she took the stairs down to the ground level and let herself out through a side door instead of risking the hall. Once outside, she glanced around, wondering where she could find Thomas. She searched for a while before finally locating him in the stables, giving directions to a stable hand. He looked up at the sound of her approach, quickly masking the look of surprise that suffused his features.

"Milady," he said with a bow. "How may I be of assistance?"

Keira took a deep breath and looked him in the eye.

"Are there more prisoners in the tower, Thomas?" she asked, her voice giving no hint of the turmoil she felt inside.

"Yes, milady." His expression turned wary as he watched her.

"I would like to see them, Thomas," she said.

"Milady ..." He paused, clearly uncomfortable. "I'm not sure that's a good idea."

"I'd like to talk to them a little, Thomas," she replied, tension making her voice sharp. "Surely there is no harm in that."

Thomas's gaze wandered to the castle. "Why?"

"Because I want to understand why they've chosen to come to the dragon's den," she replied. Thomas turned back to her, and he stared at her for a few moments before slowly nodding.

"Very well, milady, but I insist on being present while you speak to the men."

"I wouldn't expect anything else," she said, gesturing for him to lead the way.

The prisoners' tower was in the far corner of the courtyard with an entrance that faced the outer wall surrounding the castle. Crossing the courtyard behind Thomas, Keira shuddered at what she had seen that morning, but a quick glance showed that all evidence of that morning's grisly activities was gone; even the flagstones had been scrubbed clean of any bloodstains. Thomas led her to the door of the tower, telling her curtly to wait there before disappearing into the gloom of the building. He returned a few minutes later and gestured for her to follow him as he climbed a narrow flight of stairs, stopping outside a large wooden door.

A guard sat on a small stool, and Thomas nodded at him to open the door. The first thing Keira noticed upon entering the room was how warm it was. She had expected cold, drafty quarters with few furnishings, but instead a fire roared in the corner of the room and rugs covered the stone floor. A bed stood against the wall, with a quilt heaped on the straw mattress. A man sat on it, holding a chunk of wood in one hand and a small knife in the other. He reminded Keira of the men from her village – a little unkempt, but with steady eyes and coarse, callused hands. A man who knew hard work.

"This is my Lady Drake," Thomas told the prisoner. The man's eyebrows rose as he looked at her.

"Drake?"

"The dragon's wife," Thomas said.

The man's eyebrows shot up. "But she's human."

Thomas nodded, and the man turned back to Keira. "Milady."

"What's your name?"

"Simon," the man replied.

"You've been condemned to death?"

"Yes."

"Why?" The man looked surprised, and glanced at Thomas before answering.

"I killed a bailiff," he said. "I didn't mean to, but he caught me stealing. The wife was ill, the littl'uns hungry." The man raised his chin slightly as he continued. "It wasn't the first time I'd stolen, but the 'eavy saw me, and afore I knew it, he was dead at me feet. I's caught before I'd a chance to run, and they sentenced me to 'ang."

Keira nodded and cleared her throat before continuing.

"You have chosen to be killed by the dragon instead of the hangman's noose?"

"Yes."

"Why?"

Simon glanced at Thomas before answering. "Well," he started, scratching his head as he considered his words. "Dead's dead, see. It doesn't matter to me how's I die, and Thomas here said that if I let the dragon kill me then the dragon'd take care of the family. Feed and clothe 'em, I mean, maybe even find a place for 'em to live. If I faced the noose my family would be out on the streets – at least this way my death can bring some good."

"You know that the dragon will eat you?" she asked. The man laughed, a hard, dry rasp that lacked humor. "Of course. That's what dragons do. I s'pose dragons need to eat as much as you or me. Thomas here says it won't hurt much. 'Over afore you know it,' he says." Keira felt Thomas's gaze resting on her as Simon spoke, but she ignored him as she considered the prisoner.

"Are you well looked after here?" she finally asked.

The man shrugged. "I sleep on a bed 'stead of a stinking, rotten pallet, and 'ave two meals a day. And I don't 'ave to share the chamber pot. What more could a dead man want?"

"Thank you," she said. She turned to Thomas and nodded, indicating that she was finished. Thomas followed her out of the room and waited for the guard to lock the door.

"Are you sure you want to see any more prisoners, milady?" asked Thomas. "The others are not so pleasant."

"Yes," Keira said firmly. Thomas indicated to the guard to open the next door.

"Stay close to me, milady," he said in an urgent whisper as the door opened. Like the first room, it had a bed pushed against the wall, and a fire burning in the hearth. The room's occupant was standing at the window, leaning against the wall as he gazed through the bars at the courtyard below. At the sound of the door opening he turned towards his visitors and looked Keira up and down in open perusal.

"'Bout time you brought me a woman," he said. "This looks like a pretty filly. I'll give her the ride of her life."

Thomas took a step forward, placing himself between the man and Keira as the man strode forward. He was of average height, with a paunch that strained against his stained tunic. His crown was balding, but long, greasy locks hung down the side of his face, while his leering grin showed a mouth of blackened and broken teeth. He smelled like he was in dire need of rudimentary hygiene, though Keira doubted it was due to an oversight by his jailors.

"Not another step closer," Thomas said. "This is the Lady Drake."

A brief look of astonishment crossed the man's face before being replaced with a sly grin. "Don't know how a dragon can satisfy a pretty thing like you," he said, "but I'd be 'appy to show you what happens 'tween a man and woman."

Beside her, Keira heard Thomas growl, but she held up a hand to forestall his protests even as she swallowed her disgust.

"Why have you been condemned to die?" she asked.

The man's face turned to an angry scowl. "Killed the wife. Stuck a knife through her heart, and watched her bleed out."

"Why?" Keira whispered in horror.

"It was her own bloody fault," he said. "The bitch wouldn't stop nagging. A man needs his freedom, but she was always bitching and complaining. Get a job. Earn some money. Didn't want me hanging with me mates, either." The man's face was twisted in an ugly snarl. "She wasn't even much to look at, 'specially after the brats came along. Should've been grateful to have a man, but she complained she was too tired to service my needs. Had to force her to do her wifely duty."

Keira took in a deep breath, steeling herself as she asked the next question. "Why are you letting the dragon kill you? Is it because of your children?"

"My children?" he said. "Gawd, as if I care what happens to them. Why should the brats have it any better than me? I jes' figured I would live out my last days in comfort – wine, food, a bed. Though I reckon I was deceived 'bout the extent of the comforts. Haven't had a woman to warm my bed since I got here."

The man cast a scowl at Thomas, who shrugged tightly as he turned to Keira. "Milady, are you ready to leave?"

"Yes." Keira suppressed a shudder and turned to go, feeling very ready to leave.

"Milady," the man said with a snigger, "I'll be waiting whenever you're ready for a real man to ride you."

The door slammed on his final words, as Thomas gave her an apologetic look. Keira shuddered before giving him a sympathetic smile. "I know you didn't want to bring me here, Thomas, and you're not responsible for that foul man's words." Thomas eyed her doubtfully as she continued. "Tell me, Thomas, what did happen to that man's children?"

"Milord found a good home for them. They're young enough that they can still be trained."

"Good."

Keira was thoughtful as she walked back to the donjon, Thomas silent by her side. He left her as she slipped quietly through the side door once again and hurried back to her room. She still shuddered at what Aaron had done, but the interviews with the prisoners cast his actions in a new light. As much as Aaron was bound by his dragon nature, his human nature still dictated that he act with as much compassion as possible. The realization made tears spring to her eyes as she remembered the condemnation she had felt towards Aaron that morning. Her reaction had forced him to reveal himself to her in the most blatant way possible, forcing the truth of what he was onto her. Cathryn was right. She needed to accept Aaron for everything he was, and she was suddenly eager to do so.

Keira glanced out the window to see that it was already mid-afternoon. She had not seen any of their guests all day, with the exception of Cathryn, and she felt a pang of guilt before pushing it aside. Her guests seemed quite capable of entertaining themselves, especially since she was barely more than a stranger to them. The ceremony was scheduled to begin at midnight, which meant Keira still had quite a few hours before she needed to be ready. She could only hope that Aaron would come back before then.

CHAPTER TWENTY-FOUR

Keira's eyes fluttered open as the sound of Aaron returning penetrated her dreamless sleep. She'd loosened her laces and lain down on the bed after her visit with the prisoners, and quickly drifted off. Aaron eyed her warily as she sat up on the bed. His wings were closed on his back and the late afternoon sun glinted off the scales that covered his huge body. She slipped from the bed and walked over to him, then paused, wondering how to proceed. Mere words seemed too trite in light of all that had happened.

A smile tugged at the corners of her lips as another idea occurred to her. Reaching up, she slipped the sleeves of her gown down her arms, until it dropped to her waist and then onto the floor. Aaron watched her cautiously as she loosened the ties of her chemise and pushed it down her body until it joined the gown, leaving Keira naked in front of the dragon. His gaze roamed over her, his eyes brightening as he took in her form, while sparks flew from his nostrils. Keira took a step towards him, swaying her hips evocatively, and reaching a hand up to his chest, stroked the thick, leathery skin.

"What are you doing, Keira?" Aaron asked in a strained voice.

171

"I love you, Aaron Drake, no matter what you are," she whispered.

His bony eyebrows rose as he pulled back in surprise, before he bent his neck in a downward curve and brought his eyes level with hers.

"Do you mean it?" he asked.

Keira smiled and ran her hands down the length of his jaws before pulling him closer and kissing him along the side of his mouth. A soft growl rumbled through his chest as her fingers scraped along the hard, scaly skin. She stretched her hands up to the crest of his head, then pulled herself up on her toes as she grasped the horns curling from his crown. They curved back over his skull, the surfaces hard and smooth and ending in sharp points. Wrapping her hands around them, she leaned her head back, feeling his breath wash over her. It stroked her skin in warm, sensuous waves, making her shudder. She closed her eyes a moment before a flash of light filled the air, and suddenly she was falling into Aaron's human arms, his mouth dragging over her skin as he carried her to the bed, his wings still unfurled behind him.

"I love you," he murmured. His lips slid down her jaw before meeting hers, and his tongue sent jolts of pleasure spiraling through her as he pulled her closer. His arms wrapped tightly around her as his wings covered them both like a silky canopy.

It was much later when Keira lay curled in his arms on the bed, their legs intertwined as her head rested on his chest. Aaron traced a pattern on her back as he held her close.

"Keira," he started, then hesitated a moment. She lifted her head to look up at him, her gaze meeting his as his eyes continued to blaze brightly. "I never wanted you to see me like that," he said savagely. "I'm so sorry."

Keira looked at him for a moment before pulling herself up and startling him with a fierce kiss.

"Don't ever apologize for what you are," she said as she pulled away. "It is me who should be apologizing to you. I realized today that I cannot love only half of you. You are both dragon and man, and without the one, there is no other. I love you, Aaron Drake, every part of you – even the parts that terrify me. I don't ever want to lose you, Aaron."

The words were barely out of her mouth when Aaron pulled her back down, his mouth savage against hers. "You'll never lose me," he growled into her ear before pulling her mouth back to his, their mounting passion leading them to dizzying heights.

It was already dark by the time they floated back to earth, and Keira pushed herself reluctantly away from her husband. He grabbed her hand and pulled her back for one last kiss before finally letting her go.

"I need to get ready for the ceremony," she said with a smile. "I don't want to shame you in front of everyone."

"Impossible," he growled, his eyes sparkling.

Keira bounced off the bed while Aaron lay back against the pillows, his arms behind his head. He watched appreciatively as she brushed her long hair and twisted it into a braid, before pulling on a scarlet gown with gold embroidery trimming the hem and sleeves. Keira spun around in a circle, holding her arms above her head.

"Will I do?" she enquired coyly.

"You know very well that you look beautiful," Aaron said. He stalked towards Keira and wrapped his arms around her from behind. His mouth dropped to her neck, and his warm breath tickled her as he caught her earlobe between his teeth and nipped her gently. She shivered as he reluctantly pulled away and turned her around to face him. Taking her hand, he turned it over, his gaze tracing the path his fingers made over the inside of her wrist.

"Are you ready for tonight, my sweet?" he asked, lifting his eyes to meet hers.

"Yes," she breathed. "I want to be yours completely."

He smiled as he kissed her hard on her lips then pushed her away again with a groan.

"We should go downstairs before I throw you back on the bed," he said. "Do you want to fly down with me or meet me in the hall?"

"I'll come with you," she replied.

"For the last time, turn around," he said. "The next time I transform, you will be watching me in all my splendor," he added with a smirk.

Keira waited as the light flashed through the room, then turned back as his tail swept around her waist and lifted her onto his back. He launched himself out the window, and took a turn around the castle before flying through the large window into the Great Hall where the guests were already assembled and waiting. Thomas was the only servant in the room, his knowledge of Aaron's secret allowing him entry into the ceremony. Aaron had explained to Keira exactly what to expect, so she was not surprised that Aaron was the only one in the hall in dragon form.

"Just till after the ceremony," he promised.

Aaron glided over to the dais, and settled gracefully on the raised platform as Keira slid down his back and landed on her feet with a thump. Aaron looked out over the gathered crowd, as the members of his clan each dropped to one knee and thumped a fist over their heart, acknowledging Aaron as their Master. Lifting his head, Aaron let out a roar that rolled out with a steady stream of flame, and the clan members roared in response. Flames rose through the air and swirled around the blackened rafters before dissipating. Over the lowered heads, Keira caught Cathryn's smile and she smiled in return.

The clan rose to their feet and Owain stepped out from the crowd and pushed his way to the front where he stepped onto the raised dais. He was dressed in a long, white robe, embroidered with flames that twisted their way up the garment, with a cloak of gold clasped around his neck. In his hand he held a large gold goblet. The outside of the cup was studded with gems that sparkled in the light of the rush torches that had been lit around the hall. Keira suppressed a shudder when she realized what would soon be in that cup. She watched as Owain lifted it above his head and waited for the murmuring in the room to die down. Despite his years – Aaron had already told Keira that Owain was nearly three hundred years of age – his presence was commanding, and in a few moments, all attention was focused on the elder.

"As dragons and mates," he said, his deep voice resounding around the room, "we have assembled to witness the formal binding of Aaron Drake to his chosen wife and lifelong mate, the Lady Keira." He turned to face Aaron, inclining his head to indicate that he should proceed.

Aaron's gaze burned into Keira's as he stepped towards her. She lifted her hand, palm up, and stretched it out to him. He took it in his claw and placed a sharp talon against her wrist. She nodded slightly, and he pressed his talon into her flesh and scored the soft skin. She flinched as blood welled from the wound, but he tightened his grip on her hand and held her steady. Owain had already positioned the goblet to catch her blood as it spilled from the wound, and Keira watched as it dripped into the chalice. It was a quarter full when the last drop trickled from her skin. Owain turned to the crowd and lifted the cup above his head.

"The blood of this woman, freely given," he cried. He gave the goblet to Aaron, who took it between his claws. His eyes were still on Keira as he blew on the crimson liquid, then lifted his head and poured it down his throat. It seemed to Keira that she could feel her blood slipping into him, mingling with his; and when he looked back at her with brightly burning eyes, she could feel the strength of his emotions. His love and desire wrapped around her, and she shivered. He glanced at her stained wrist, and lifting her hand, ran his tongue over her skin, cleaning the wound. His eyes held hers, and she felt a clenching in her lower belly that had nothing to do with revulsion.

"Keira Drake, I choose you to be my lifelong mate," he

said. "As your blood runs through my veins, we are bound together until we are parted by death."

He released her arm as Owain stepped forward once more, and Keira turned to see that Owain held a short silver dagger, which he held towards her. She stared at it a moment, then took it from his hand. It was heavy, with a slightly curved blade, and the handle had been inlaid with jewels. She glanced up at Aaron, and he nodded.

"You can do this," he whispered. He reached out a claw and wrapped it around her hand as it clasped the handle. Pulling her closer, he placed the blade against his skin, just above his heart. She stared at it for a moment, then looked up at Aaron. He smiled, and she placed her other hand against his chest and pressed the blade down, but his tough hide did not give way.

"Use some force," he whispered.

She drew a deep breath and pulled the blade back, then swinging her arm forward with as much force as she could muster, plunged the blade into his chest, burying the blade up to the hilt. He grunted, but when she pulled back, his claw was immediately over her hand, holding the blade in his flesh. He dragged the blade down, causing his skin to burst open as it left a trail of blood running down his chest. Owain thrust the goblet at Keira and she hurriedly pressed the cup against Aaron's skin, trapping the blood in the golden chalice as it continued to spill out. The blood was already slowing, and Aaron pushed the blade to the side, opening the wound further. Only when the cup was full did he release his grip over her hand, and she pulled the blade from his skin.

She handed the goblet to Owain, who raised it above his head. "The blood of this dragon, freely given," he cried.

He offered the cup back to Keira. Her hands were trembling as she wrapped them around the bowl of the cup. She turned back to Aaron, and met his gaze as she lifted the cup and brought it to her lips. With a deep breath, she tipped back her head and drained the contents. It didn't taste like the blood she'd tasted on her own wrist so many weeks before; but instead the flavor was like that of a heady liquor, sweet and potent at the same time. The heat curled around her as it hit her stomach, and she could feel the liquid spreading through her veins, reaching to her hands and her feet. She willed every drop from the cup into her mouth before she finally dropped her hands and stared at Aaron.

"Aaron Drake, I choose you to be my lifelong mate," she said. "As your blood runs through my veins, we are bound together until we are parted by death."

The words were barely out of her mouth when the room blazed with light. It took only a moment for Aaron to change his form, but Keira noticed with surprise that she could see the light expanding from within him, exploding from his every pore, before falling back in on itself, pulling Aaron's shape from that of a dragon into that of a man. In a flash Owain swung his cloak off his shoulders and onto Aaron's, covering his bare form. If Aaron noticed this gesture, he completely ignored it as he stepped towards Keira and took her in his arms. He dropped his lips to hers, his kiss savage and jubilant.

"You've given my life new meaning, my sweet," he whispered in her ear. "My cup runneth over."

"I love you, Aaron," Keira whispered. She wrapped her hands around his neck and pulled him down to her lips once more, ignoring the titters that ran through the crowd. Aaron's expression was exultant when he finally turned towards the guests, his arm around Keira's waist.

"Clan Drake, my mate!" he exclaimed as the crowd broke into shouts and applause.

Aaron pulled Keira off the dais and wove his way through the crowd, responding to the slaps and yells of his family and friends with good humor. The doors opened and servants brought trays laden with roasted game, fowl, sweet meats, wine, and ale, which they offered around as they moved through the hall. Aaron tightened his grip on Keira and led her to the far side of the room.

"I'm going to our chambers to clothe myself," he whispered. "Will you come with me?"

The smile on Keira's face gave him his answer, and he pulled her hurriedly through the door and dragged her up the steps as she laughingly followed. He had made it to the top of the grand staircase when he whirled around and pinned her against the wall, his mouth claiming hers as she responded with just as much eagerness. He pulled away with a groan before swinging her into his arms and hurrying down the corridor to their room. He kicked the door closed with his foot as his hands tangled in her hair and he kissed her again. She pushed Owain's cloak aside and ran her hands over Aaron's bare flesh, her breath coming in short gasps as she felt his heat searing into her. Impatient, he pulled her skirts up before carrying her over to the bed. The climax came hard and quick, and they collapsed in a tangle of sheets and skirts minutes later. Turning to face her, Aaron ran his hands lightly over her face.

"Do you feel it?" he asked. "The bond that ties us together? We're a part of each other now. Nothing can ever separate us."

"Yes," she whispered, "I feel you. And when you changed, I could see everything. You looked as though you were exploding with light."

"My blood protects you from the light, making you stronger, and your senses clearer. And look at your arm – the wound I gave you is already healing."

Keira glanced down at her arm to see that the gash had already closed, a slash of pink skin the only evidence of Aaron's scoring. Her mouth dropped open in shock as Aaron smiled in amusement.

"This morning I was able to see you transform, but there was no light," she said.

"I'm so sorry about this morning, my sweet. I was angry at your revulsion, and felt quite entitled to act as a beast." His expression was rueful as he continued. "I wanted to force every dark, ugly aspect of myself onto you. Only a Master can control the transformation like that, commanding each element of the change, keeping the light trapped. I wanted to horrify you."

"I was horrified," she said. "But as soon as you were gone, I was more worried that I'd lost your love."

"Never," he said. "You'll never lose that!"

She smiled. "You should have told me how good your blood tasted," she said. "I think I'll want to drink you every day."

Aaron rolled over her, trapping her beneath his weight. "You have my permission to drain me dry, my sweet," he said, his voice heavy with innuendo, before once more claiming her lips as his hands explored her body with a thoroughness that left her gasping.

Twenty minutes later saw them both downstairs once more, mingling with their guests. If her hair looked a little disheveled, or his cloak was a little askew, no one commented. Keira saw Cathryn at the other end of the room, and leaving Aaron's side, she headed over to her friend.

"Thank you," she said with a smile. "You were so right about everything."

Cathryn pulled her into a tight embrace. "Aaron is fortunate to have found you," she said. "I can see that you'll both bring each other much happiness."

Keira turned to look at Aaron across the room, laughing with Favian and some other dragons as they slapped him across the back. She couldn't stop smiling as she turned back to Cathryn.

"I think I'm the fortunate one," she said. "To have a man to love and respect, and who loves and respects me, is the desire of every woman, but only a few get to see that wish fulfilled. I not only have my dearest wish, but I get to enjoy that happiness for longer than even a child of destiny. So believe me when I say, I am truly blessed." Linking her arm through Cathryn's, she glanced around the room. "Let's find something to eat," she said. "I'm famished."

CHAPTER TWENTY-FIVE

Aaron's arms were wrapped around Keira as they lay in bed the next morning.

"Aaron," Keira said, "should I be scared of you?"

Aaron pulled back in surprise, his eyebrows raised.

"Scared of me? Why would you be scared of me?"

"Well ..." Keira said. She hesitated for a moment, wondering what imp had possessed her to bring this up.

"Yes?" prompted Aaron when she didn't continue.

"Cathryn said you give yourself over to your animal instincts when you feed," Keira said slowly. "Should I be worried if I come upon you when you're feeding?"

"Ah!" Turning away from her, Aaron rolled onto his back, his eyes gazing up at the ceiling as he folded his hands behind his head.

"I heard you went to visit some of the prisoners yesterday," Aaron said.

"Yes. Are you angry?"

"No, I'm not angry," he said. "I'm glad you wanted to find out more, though I'd prefer you not make a habit of it. Most prisoners are truly wicked men."

"I understand."

"Keira, if there is one thing I could change about myself, it would be my need to eat human flesh in order to survive. I hate the fact that my survival is dependent on people dying. If I could change this aspect of my nature, I'd do it in a heartbeat." Aaron turned to look at her. "But I am a dragon, and I refuse to hate myself. There have been those who drove themselves mad, denying who and what they are, destroying themselves in the process. Jack's father was one of those, but I will not do that."

"Jack's father?" she said in astonishment.

"Jack's father died just a few years after mine," he said. "But unlike my father, who was killed at the hands of others, Jack's father died because he refused to accept who, or what, he was. He went mad before he died, unwilling to feed and eventually too weak to even get out of bed. But God said that his creations are good, and I choose to believe that this includes dragons, and that I too am fearfully and wonderfully made." He gave her a brief smile before continuing.

"Cathryn is right when she says that we give ourselves over to our animal instincts," he said. "I have to give myself over to the beast. Killing my prey while thinking as a human would drive me crazy. And I cannot consider my actions in the light of human emotion, either." Aaron gently stroked her cheek before continuing. "But Keira, I never lose myself. I am always fully aware of who I am, where I am, and who it is that I love. When I kill my prey, I know what it is I am doing, and I try to make it as quick and painless as possible. So could I ever hurt you, even when I'm like that? The answer is no, never. It would be like destroying a part of myself if I were to hurt you."

"What if I was the last person left on earth?" Keira asked, the teasing note in her voice deflecting the strain of the question.

Aaron grimaced. "Absolutely not. I'd rather die than hurt you."

"And would you die? I mean, what would happen if you

didn't eat ... well, you know."

"Humans?" he said. "Yes, I would eventually die, but I'd probably go crazy first, like Jack's father. Most of us have trained ourselves to go for longer and longer periods without it, but we still need to feed that part of ourselves eventually. Without it I'd weaken to the point of sickness, and then death."

"So how long can you go without it?"

"It depends," he said. "Usually a few months, but more frequently if I'm expending more energy. Yesterday was the first time I'd fed on human flesh since before I met you."

Keira considered this for a moment.

"Aaron?" she said, then hesitated.

"Hmm?"

"Do you enjoy it?"

"Enjoy it? What do you mean?"

"I mean ... never mind."

Aaron stared at her for a moment as a blush crept into her cheeks.

"Are you asking me if I enjoy my meals?" he asked incredulously, laughing when Keira remained silent. "Oh, Keira," he groaned. He rolled onto his side to face her. "When the body needs nourishment, even the most unappetizing meal is as welcome as a cup of cold water in the middle of a burning desert. My body begins to crave what it needs, and is satisfied when it receives it. There, does that answer your question?"

She nodded, but refused to meet his gaze. He watched her for a moment, then placed his hand beneath her chin and forced her head up until their eyes met. "Keira, my sweet, I may not always like your questions, but you must never be shy with me," he said. "I love you, and I'll always answer your questions as honestly and openly as I possibly can. You have taken a beast into your arms, into your bed and into your heart, and you're entitled to know who it is you have married."

Keira smiled shyly as Aaron bent down to kiss her.

"I love you too," she whispered back.

They lay there for a few more minutes before Aaron suddenly pushed her away and, springing out of the bed, strode over to the window.

"The mountains are so beautiful in the early morning light," he said. "I haven't taken you anywhere since our guests started arriving, so come, let's take a quick flight."

"But aren't the other dragons expecting you to join them?" she asked in surprise. Aaron shrugged.

"They've had plenty of my attention all week. They can manage without me for a few hours. Now come along, lazy bones." He grabbed her hands and yanked her up, spilling the quilts onto the floor. "Get yourself dressed, and hurry. I'm getting impatient."

Keira laughed. "Patience is clearly a virtue you need to learn. Perhaps I'll send for a bath before I get dressed."

But when Aaron sprang at her, growling, Keira held up her hands in surrender. "I'm going, I'm going. Wouldn't want to rile the beast – I could end up being a meal." She skipped away from his reaching hand as he growled, and laughed as she went into the antechamber to don a gown.

Anyone scaling the sheer rock face minutes later might have looked up to see a fearful dragon soaring out of the castle window, his golden armor gleaming in the light of the sun which was rising over the mountains. If they had squinted against the light, they may have seen a figure riding the dragon's back without any fear of the beast, thick brown hair streaming out behind her as she leaned forward and gently stroked the thick neck of the monster. They might have noticed the dragon turning his head back to look at the lady, astonished at the gentleness in the dragon's gaze, before the creature straightened himself out and headed towards the ever-brightening horizon. But there were no such climbers, and the moment passed without anyone spying on the beast and his wife.

CHAPTER TWENTY-SIX

Favian and Cathryn were the last of the guests to leave Storbrook Castle, one week later. They were traveling by carriage, a fact that surprised Keira since all the other dragons had flown to Storbrook, carrying their mates on their backs. She had asked Aaron about it the night before Favian and Cathryn's departure.

"It's because of the children," Aaron explained. "They don't have wings yet. Only when they reach puberty will their dragon traits emerge. Favian could carry them all, but the children grow weary traveling long distances and can slip from his back, so he prefers more traditional means of travel for them. He'll probably fly a lot of the way, but will stay close to the carriage to ensure his family's safety."

"I pity any highwayman that holds up that carriage," Keira said with a laugh.

Because of the rough mountain terrain, Favian had arranged for the carriage and coachman to meet them in the village. Thomas had already taken down their luggage in a cart, and Favian would fly his family down the mountain. They said their farewells in the courtyard at Storbrook Castle.

"Promise me that you'll visit as soon as you can," Cathryn

pleaded, holding Keira's hands in her own. Early morning light bathed the courtyard in a soft, pink glow, and a kitchen maid hurried across the stones from the direction of the stables. She paid no attention to the huge red dragon.

"Of course we will," Keira assured her new friend. She bent down to gather Bronwyn in a hug before solemnly shaking hands with Will.

"Are there any towers at your home that I should be concerned about?" Keira asked him.

"Oh, no! We don't live in a castle like Storbrook," he assured her, "so you'll be quite safe there."

Keira swallowed a laugh and nodded gravely. "Then we'll come and visit you soon, if that's acceptable to you."

Will nodded his head as Bronwyn gave him a shove. "Of course Aunty can come and visit us any time she wants," she said. "I'll even let her stay with me in my room."

Keira stood up with a laugh as Cathryn hustled the children onto the back of the waiting dragon. He bent down to look at Keira.

"Take care of yourself, cousin," he said, "and keep an eye on that husband of yours – he can be quite a dragon if you're not careful." With a sparkling snort, he pulled away and lifted himself into the air.

Aaron put his arm around Keira and pulled her closer, whispering into her hair. "We have our privacy back, my sweet, so what would you like to do?"

Twisting in his arms, Keira looked up at him with a smile. "I think we should go into the village."

"The village?" he asked in surprise. "Haven't you spent enough time with other people over the last two weeks?"

"Yes, but they were your people," she said. "Now I want to see my people."

"And who is it that you really want to see?" he teased. "Anna and your parents or is it Edmund that you're pining for?"

"Definitely Edmund!" She laughed at Aaron's grimace

before turning serious. "I want to check that Anna is all right and that Edmund hasn't turned his attentions to her."

"If you want to see your family, then that's what we'll do."

It was a few hours later when Keira walked up the path to her old home, Aaron by her side. Anna was outside, helping Mary hang wet washing on a line strung between the trees.

"Mistress Keira, 'ee've come home!" Mary cried. "Your parents will be pleased to see 'ee. I'll jes' go find 'em." As she turned away, Anna draped a shirt over the line and hurried over to give Keira a warm embrace.

"Why, Anna," teased Aaron with a grin, "one would think you actually missed your sister."

Anna rolled her eyes before taking Keira by the hand. "I was worried you wouldn't return," she said. "You haven't forgotten your promise, have you?"

"No, Anna, we haven't forgotten. We came because ..." She stopped and stared at her sister. "Anna," she whispered. "What happened to you?" A dark bruise spread over Anna's cheek, and the clear marks of a tight finger grip stained her arm.

"It's nothing," replied Anna, turning away, but Aaron caught her gently by the arm.

"Who did this to you, Anna?" he asked, a frown creasing his forehead. "Was it Edmund?"

"He was waiting for me, just inside the alley near the church," she said. "I managed to get away, but not before inflicting some damage of my own." She lifted her head and looked at Keira with a ghost of a smile. "He has some new scars to match the ones given to him by a certain dragon."

Keira smiled wryly. "Good for you. But why didn't you want to tell me right away?"

Anna lifted her chin and threw Aaron a quick glance before replying. "I didn't want you to think I was looking for sympathy so that I could come to Storbrook sooner."

"But of course you must come with us. Isn't that so,

Aaron?" demanded Keira, turning to look at her husband.

"Of course," he said. "You can come back with us now if you like, and I'll send Thomas to collect your things. But first we need to speak to your mother."

No sooner had the words left his mouth than the person in question emerged from the house, wiping her hands on an apron that covered her kirtle.

"Keira!" Mother said. "Milord Drake! You're back. We were wondering if we'd ever see you again."

"Madam Carver. How lovely to see you," Aaron said. "But come, we're family now, so you must call me Aaron. And how should I address you? Jenny? Mother?"

Keira hid a grin as her mother sputtered before her, then felt a flash of shame at the amusement she derived at her mother's expense. Taking Mother by the arm, she led her towards the house, throwing a look of reprimand over her shoulder at Aaron. Far from looking remorseful, he grinned back and winked, before turning to Anna and offering his arm.

It took Anna and Keira some time to convince Mother that it was in Anna's best interests to be allowed to return with Aaron and Keira. Father had arrived from his workshop shortly after Mary served refreshments, but it wasn't until Aaron started adding his weight to the argument that Father joined the conversation.

"Jenny," he said gently, "we both know this would be better for our daughter. Let her go with your blessing."

"You want me to lose both my daughters within the space of a few weeks?" she said. "What kind of a husband are you?"

Father slipped from his seat and gently took her hands in his own as he knelt before her.

"Jenny, we have endured many losses over the years, but we're not losing our daughters. We always knew the time would come when they'd leave us, and there were never any guarantees that they'd stay in our little village." He glanced at Anna, before returning his gaze to Jenny. "We cannot place our desire to keep Anna here above her need for safety – and from all we are hearing, Edmund is not the young man we thought him to be."

Mother stared at her husband for a long moment, their shared gaze weighted with their years of marriage. Finally she broke their silent communication, her shoulders slumping.

"Very well, Anna," she said. "If you feel that it would be better for you to be with your sister and her husband than here with us, then go."

Anna smiled, not responding to the bitter barb buried in the words, and turned to Aaron. "When do we leave?"

Despite Anna's impatience, Keira and Aaron tarried for another hour before finally taking their leave. Anna had grabbed a small satchel in which she stowed a few personal items, and she slung it over her shoulder as they headed out the door and into the sunshine.

"Where are your horses?" Father asked, looking around in perturbation.

"Keira wanted to walk through the village," Aaron said, casting a quick glance at his wife, "so we left them tethered near the church."

"She did?" replied Father. "Well then, I'll walk with you. I have some business with the reeve."

Keira cast a frantic look at Aaron, but he smiled nonchalantly. "Of course," he replied.

Keira's heart pounded as she wondered how they would either get rid of her father or explain to him when there were no horses waiting for them. Anna was walking next to Father, and judging by her serene gait, Keira guessed it hadn't occurred to Anna that they were not traveling by horse. Keira sighed, and Aaron squeezed her hand as it lay on his arm, but when the tension remained he bent down with a sigh of his own. "Stop fretting, my sweet. There's no need for concern."

Turning to look at him, Keira raised her eyebrows questioningly and Aaron bent down once more, his warm breath tickling her ear and sending shivers down her spine.

"Didn't you say you wanted to stop at the milliner's?" he said.

Keira looked at Aaron and smiled. She hadn't planned on stopping at any of the village shops, but Father didn't know that, and Keira knew that he would rather be bound by the feet and pulled through a field by a racing horse than spend any time waiting for his daughters at the milliner. She was about to tell Aaron this when her father turned back to them, slowing down until he walked abreast of Aaron.

"I trust you to look after my daughters with your life, Milord Drake," he said, his gaze heavy on Aaron's face.

"I've already bound myself to Keira, offering her the protection of my life, my household and my extended family," Aaron replied, "and I'll extend that same protection to Anna as long as she remains in my household."

Keira's father stared at Aaron, weighing up the words, before nodding slowly.

"You will also protect them from the passion of the dragon?" Father said.

Aaron's expression indicated no surprise at the question, but Keira felt his hand tightening over hers.

"I swear by my life that the dragon will never harm your daughters," Aaron promised.

"You can give such a pledge?" asked Father, although his voice sounded unsurprised. Aaron stared at the man before him for a long minute, his expression thoughtful, as Father returned the gaze unblinkingly.

"Yes, I can," Aaron finally responded, his eyes never leaving Father's face. Father considered the words for a moment, then nodded.

"Very well," Father said. "I'll hold you responsible if ever the dragon so much as singes a hair on either daughter's head."

Aaron nodded. "I wouldn't expect anything less," he said.

As Keira expected, Father bade Aaron and his daughters

farewell outside the milliner's.

"You still want to shop?" Anna moaned. "I thought we'd go straight to Storbrook!"

"And so we will," Keira said. "Just as soon as Father has gone."

"Why?"

Keira smiled. "Because we aren't traveling by horse."

Anna frowned for a moment, then slowly turned to look at Aaron with eyebrows raised.

"You're going to fly us there?" she said, her voice rising as she stared at Aaron.

"Shh," Keira hissed, glancing around. She took Anna by the arm. "Come, Father's gone. Aaron can't change near the village."

"I hope you're not afraid of heights, Anna," Aaron said with a grin. "But don't get used to traveling like this – Keira's the only one I'd usually carry."

Anna gasped when the light of Aaron's transformation filled the air, even though it was at her back; and when she turned to face Aaron, she stumbled back in fear before catching her sister's amused glance. She trembled the entire way – although Keira wasn't sure whether Anna was more scared of the beast itself, or of falling off the beast's back. But once they arrived, Anna relaxed, her ease in Aaron's presence returning when he reverted to his human form.

Keira led Anna up the stairs and down the east wing, where she opened a door to a large guest room. Windows opened with views of the mountains in three directions, and Anna turned around in amazement before looking at her sister.

"I'm staying here?" she said.

"Yes," Keira replied with a smile. "As long as you behave and Aaron doesn't throw you in the dungeon!"

Anna smiled. "I always behave," she said.

That night, as they lay in bed, Keira asked Aaron about her father.

"Do you think he knows what you are?" she said.

"I think he was guessing at first, but my response gave him the confirmation he was seeking."

"Aren't you concerned that he'll tell others?"

"No," Aaron said slowly as he gazed at the ceiling. "I don't think I have anything to fear from him. He's just concerned about you, and as your father, his concern is perfectly reasonable." Rolling onto his side, Aaron pulled his wife closer, sliding his hands through her hair and letting it spill over her shoulder as his fingers trailed down her back. "It's a good thing his concern only extends to the dragon," he whispered, "as he could never protect you from the passion of the man." If Keira had planned to respond, her thoughts were scattered as his lips covered hers, while his hands roamed over her body, chasing away all reasonable thought.

CHAPTER TWENTY-SEVEN

Keira sat at the table in her Lady's Bower, tip of the quill hovering over a sheet of blank parchment as she looked over the list Cook had given her that morning. She glanced up when a knock sounded on the door and Thomas stepped into the room.

"Your parents are in the Great Hall, milady," Thomas announced. "They wish to speak to milord."

"My parents?" she said in surprise. "Very well, please take them to the solar and inform Aaron that we have company."

"Yes, milady," Thomas said with a small bow.

Keira wondered what reason her parents could have for coming to Storbrook as she checked her appearance in the mirror before heading downstairs. They were both seated when she stepped into the room, but Father rose and hurried over to her.

"Daughter," he said, "I trust you're well. Is Aaron here?"

"I'm here," Aaron said, stepping into the solar. "What brings you so far from the village?"

"We have news," Father said. "The reeve is stirring up trouble for you."

"That doesn't surprise me," Aaron said. "But why should

I be concerned?" He went to the small table and poured a glass of wine which he passed to Father, then poured another for himself.

"He's roused the whole village against you," Father said, "and is bringing a delegation to Storbrook, armed with swords and clubs."

Aaron snorted. "What will that achieve?"

"He believes if he comes to Storbrook, he'll find the dragon and kill it."

"Ah!" Aaron said. "The reeve thinks he can kill a dragon!"

"He believes history is on his side."

"Then he'll soon learn the error of his ways."

Father placed his glass on a table. "Please, Aaron," he said. "The last time a Hobbes came against a dragon, many innocent people lost their lives. We should do what we can to avoid further bloodshed. Let us meet the villagers and talk them out of this action."

"You think the villagers are innocent?" Aaron drained his wine and threw the glass into the fireplace where it smashed against the stone wall. Mother gasped as she stared at Aaron in shock, but Aaron paid her no attention. "They arm themselves against a creature that has never harmed them! They come to my home bearing weapons! How are they innocent?"

"You cannot blame them for being ignorant, Aaron. The reeve has been whispering in their ears since you arrived, telling them tales about the last dragon, stoking their fears. And when you took Keira from Edmund, you shamed him before his neighbors."

"Aaron couldn't take me from Edmund," Keira said, "I was never his."

"I know that," Father said. "But you still rejected his son."

Aaron turned away and paced the room. "The last dragon died for something he never did," he said. He paused to stare out the window as the others watched in silence. "But I understand that the loss of lives could have been avoided," he said. He turned back to Father. "Very well, I'll go with you to speak to them." He glanced at Mother. "Why did you bring Jenny?"

"I thought if we failed in our mission, she'd be safer here."

"Yes, of course."

Mother rose to her feet. "I'm sure I'd have been fine if I'd stayed at home," she said. "I've known these people all my life – they'd never harm me! It's only the dragon that I fear."

"You know nothing about the dragon," Aaron said. He glared at Mother, then swung his gaze to Keira when she touched his arm.

"I love you," she whispered.

He frowned at her for a moment, but then the expression eased, and he gave a wry smile.

"You must remain here with your mother," he said. "Your Father and I will go talk some sense into these villagers."

"Let me come too," she said.

"Absolutely not. Your presence will be a hindrance." He lowered his voice and leaned towards her. "You are my life, and if anything happened to you, it would surely kill me. I will do everything in my power to convince them that they should turn back, but if things should turn nasty, I don't want you to be caught in the middle. I won't give them a dragon, though, so you needn't fear."

Ignoring a scandalized gasp from Mother, he slid his hand around her neck and pulled her mouth to his as he kissed her deeply. It was Keira who pulled away first, and he rested his forehead against hers, lingering in silence for a moment before suddenly drawing away and nodding at Father.

"Let's be off," he said. He strode to the door, Father close on his heels, and exited the room.

Keira watched as they left, then sunk into a chair and

buried her head in her hands, as her mother watched her in silence.

"You really love that man, don't you?" Mother said after a while.

"Yes," Keira replied softly. Mother nodded as the sound of footsteps pounding on the stone passage floor reached them. Anna ran into the room, pausing when she saw her mother.

"Thomas told me you were here, Mother," she said. "Where's Father?"

"He and Aaron have gone to talk the villagers out of trying to kill the dragon," Keira said.

"Kill the dragon? Is he crazy? Does he know –?"

"No," Keira said tightly.

Anna glanced between Keira and Mother. "Well, what are you going to do?" she asked Keira.

"Do? Wait until they come back."

"How spineless! You should go after him," Anna said. "That's what I would do!"

"Anna, I can't just run off after him."

"Well, I don't see why not," Anna retorted.

"It's not safe!" Keira said.

Mother rose to her feet. "Well, I'm not staying here."

"You can't leave," Keira gasped. "Father said –"

"Keira, I have no intention of remaining in this stone fortress, hiding from my own people. If I leave now, I can be home again before night falls."

"You cannot travel alone," Keira said.

"Then come with me," she said. Keira glared at Anna as she choked back a laugh.

"I'll come with you, Mother," Anna said.

"No!" Keira exclaimed. "You are not going anywhere." She turned back to Mother. "If you insist on doing this, I'll come with you."

"I insist," Mother said, smoothing down her skirts.

"Very well. I'll ask Cook to pack some food and we'll go."

She turned to Anna. "If you leave Storbrook, you'll no longer be welcome here. Do you understand?"

Anna nodded. "I'll stay. I promise."

Keira nodded. "Good."

A half hour later, Keira and her mother passed under the portcullis and onto the steep path leading down the mountain. It was slow going down, and more than once Keira and her mother had to dismount and lead their horses along the path. They made up time, however, when they entered the forest, following a well-worn track thick with needles from the surrounding pines. Only a few rays of light made it to the forest floor through the densely packed trees, and the path followed a winding trail around thick trunks.

They had traversed about half the distance down the mountain when they pulled their mounts to a stop near a stream. Tired and hungry, they agreed to pause for a few minutes to refresh themselves before continuing on their way. Kneeling down next to the burbling brook, Keira splashed the cool water over her face before sitting back on her haunches next to her mother, soaking up the fresh pine-scented air. Up in the trees, birds twittered and fluttered between the branches, while squirrels clambered up tree trunks and jumped between limbs, chattering noisily.

A sudden screeching of birds was Keira's only warning of danger before a heavy hand fell on her shoulder, shoving her into the dirt. Her stomach sank as she twisted around and looked up into Alan's leering face.

"Look who I've found," he drawled. "Again."

A quick glance around showed Mother similarly sprawled on the ground, her eyes wide with dread. Keira pushed away her own fear – the wife of a dragon should not be scared.

"No monster here to rescue you this time, girl," Alan said with a grin.

"What are you doing in these woods, Alan?" she asked sharply. "These are private lands."

"Drake lands, eh? Soon there won't be any Drakes around to care whether I trespass on the land or not," he said.

Keira stared at him in horror. "You plan to kill Aaron."

"Your husband will enjoy the same fate as the dragon. Now get up," he said. He gestured to Mother. "You too." Taking Keira by the arm, he shoved her forward onto the path, making her walk ahead of him. Mother stumbled beside her, and when they didn't move fast enough, Alan jabbed them from behind with a stick.

They had been walking for a while when Keira heard the sound of voices drifting through the trees.

"You come against with me with sticks and swords and demand that I hand over the dragon. Why would I do that?" Aaron was saying.

"The dragon will destroy our village," someone shouted.

"Nonsense," said Aaron. "The dragon will only attack if you provoke it. And trying to kill me is definitely a provocation!"

"Let's all calm down," Keira heard Father say. "Matthew, for the sake of the people in the village, back away from this fight."

"Back away! I'm protecting our village! Since when did you care more for a dragon than your own people?"

"It's because I care for our people that I'm begging you not to do this!"

"Your loyalty to your daughter is misguiding you, Richard. Now, Master Drake, I think you need an incentive. How would your new wife enjoy being a widow?"

"You could try to kill me, but you'll –"

His voice stopped abruptly as Alan prodded Keira in the back one more time and she stumbled into a clearing, her mother close on her heels. On one side stood a group of men that Keira recognized from the village, crude weapons clutched in their hands. The reeve stood at the front of the group with a sword hanging loosely in his hand. Standing behind him were faces that Keira recognized – Jem Young, Daniel Draper, and even quiet Harry Turner amongst them. They were facing Aaron, who stood a few feet away. Keira's father stood beside Aaron, his hands out in a gesture of appeasement, but they dropped to his side as he stared in horror at the two women.

"Keira," Aaron said. The single word was loaded with a mixture of reproach and resignation as Aaron strode towards his wife.

"I'm sorry," she mumbled to the ground. "It's just ... I couldn't ..."

Her head hung low as Aaron placed his hands on her shoulders.

"I know," he whispered into her ear. "I love you, too." She looked up in surprise, and he met her gaze with a wry smile. "But don't think I'm not still annoyed with you."

She opened her mouth to respond, then closed it again when she realized there was nothing to say. Aaron leaned forward and gave her a quick, hard kiss on the lips before turning back to the reeve.

"My wife and I will be leaving now," he said. "We can finish this another time."

"I don't think so," said the reeve. He looked at Alan with a sly smile. "I see you brought me an incentive. Well done."

The reeve gestured towards Mother, and Aaron shot forward in a sudden movement, but it was too late. Before Keira realized what was happening, Alan had grabbed her mother by the hair, pulling her head back and exposing her throat. The blade of a dagger pressed against her neck and a thin red line welled up. The reeve laughed, a cruel sound that made Keira shiver.

"No!" exclaimed Father, turning to face the reeve. "You cannot do this."

"Ah, Richard," said the reeve, "but I am doing it. Convince your son-in-law to hand over the dragon, and I'll allow Jenny to go free." He turned to Aaron, his expression ugly. "Choose, milord. The dragon or this woman?"

A stunned silence filled the air as the villagers looked at each other in shock, their eyes wide as they shifted uncomfortably.

"Um, Reeve Hobbes." Jem Young stepped forward, glancing at the others for support before continuing. "We didn't come here to hurt anyone. We just came for the dragon."

"And this is how we get the dragon," snapped the reeve. He turned to the man who had spoken. "Remind me, Jem, how much money do you owe me?" Jem looked down at his feet, shuffling in discomfort, before moving back into the group.

Ignoring this exchange, Aaron slowly turned to look at Keira's father, his expression unfathomable as he met the pleading stare of his father-in-law. After a long moment, he turned to the reeve.

"Very well," he said. "I'll bring you the dragon, but you'll pay for your foolishness. Now let my wife and her family go."

The reeve laughed again before responding. "Do you take me for a fool? You may have your wife back when the dragon is dead."

Keira stepped towards Aaron. "No," she whispered, her eyes fixed on him. "You mustn't do it."

"I must," Aaron said, his voice too low to be heard by anyone but Keira. "I'll try …" he paused. "I won't hurt the villagers, if I can help it. But the reeve won't be satisfied until he faces the dragon. It is to his own detriment."

He turned back to the reeve. "You're a foolish man to demand the presence of a dragon." He glanced around the group of men, meeting the stare of each one before continuing. "If my wife or any member of her family is harmed in any way – a scratch, scraped and bloody knees or even a missing hair – the dragon will hunt down each of your family members and devour them slowly, drawing out an agonizing death."

His gaze settled on Daniel Draper. "You, Daniel, you have a daughter, don't you? I'm sure she would be a tasty morsel. And you, Smithy," he continued, looking at the next man, "you have a young son apprenticing with you. I'm told dragons favor young blood. And Reeve Hobbes," he said, turning to face the reeve, "you have four sons. Keep their faces before you as I leave, and make sure your actions while I'm gone are motivated by a desire to see your sons alive tomorrow."

Keira felt her blood rush from her face as she heard Aaron's threats. The men shrunk back, pale-faced and mumbling between themselves, but Aaron ignored them, and turning his attention to Keira once more, dropped his voice.

"All will be well, my sweet," he said to her. "For your sake, I'll keep a leash on my annoyance. I promise that you'll be safe. Yes, your parents too," he added, answering the unspoken question in her eyes. He squeezed her fingers before turning away and disappearing through the trees.

CHAPTER TWENTY-EIGHT

Keira glanced at the sky as she wondered how much longer it would be before Aaron returned. She judged that a full hour had gone by since he had disappeared between the trees, but she suspected that he wasn't far away and was just biding his time.

The men had started mumbling as soon as he left, until finally the reeve, clearly irritated at such open insubordination, had rounded on them and branded them all as cowards. They'd fallen silent after that, but shifted nervously as they waited, darting looks between each other. Alan had dropped the dagger he held against Mother's throat, and she'd fallen to the ground in a heap. When Father dropped beside her and pulled into his arms, she'd clung to him, weeping into his chest.

A few more minutes passed before Keira heard the heavy beats of a dragon's wings. She looked up and watched as a large shape appeared in the sky, blocking the light of the sun for a moment as it circled above them. A thick tail streamed behind a huge body, while the sun glinted on iron-hard scales. A steady stream of flames spewed from the creature's mouth, spreading heat around them, and as it drew closer, a long, loud roar tore through the air, reverberating across the mountains and sending a shiver down Keira's spine. The barbs on its neck and along its tail reached up like a wall of spears, standing in sharp profile against the blue of the sky, and its claws were stretched to their fullest extent, the strength and brutality of them on full display.

For a moment Keira couldn't reconcile the wild, savage creature circling above her with the man that she loved, and she drew back slightly as a wave of fear lapped at the edges of her mind; but at that moment he looked directly at her, as though he sensed her confusion, and in his bright burning gaze she saw him. He circled around once more, then dropped to the ground with a thud that shook the earth, forgoing his usual grace.

The men gripped their makeshift weapons with whitened knuckles as they scrambled away from him, the fear evident in their expressions as they watched the huge beast. Even the reeve pulled back, a momentary look of dread crossing his face as his hand clutched his sword.

The dragon swept his long tail over the ground in a wide arc that stretched across most of the clearing, lifting leaves and dust into the air, while the men pushed and shoved each other in an effort to get away from the deadly appendage, tripping when they were not hasty enough.

As the dragon settled on the ground, Father walked towards the enormous creature, his expression calm as he met the beast's gaze. His actions were in such stark contrast to the other men that they stopped to stare at him in astonishment, but Father ignored them all as he met the gaze of the dragon towering above him. Man and beast, they stared at each other for a moment before Father moved back to stand next to Smithy, who clutched a pitchfork in his hand as though it was all that stood between him and death. The dragon swept his gaze around the circle, lingering for a moment on Keira, then lifted his head and let out another long, low roar.

Turning towards the reeve, Keira gestured to the dragon. "You wanted the dragon. Now let us go."

The reeve had recovered from his momentary fright at the sight of the beast, and he looked at Keira with eyes narrowed in calculation. "Not so hasty, girl. We need to rid our village and these mountains of this monster. You can leave when the dragon is dead." A low growl filled the air at his words, and the reeve's hand tightened on his sword.

"Your actions will only bring about your own demise," Keira said, amazed at the man's stubbornness. She was about to say more, but from amongst the men came a voice of support.

"This has gone on long enough," Daniel Draper said. "Let the girl and her mother go before we find ourselves paying too dear a price." He gestured towards the dragon. "We stand no chance against such a mighty beast, and the fact that we're not already dead makes me inclined to think that we should let it go in peace."

"What are you saying?" the reeve snarled. "We are talking about a dragon – a mindless monster." He pointed his sword at Daniel. "Are you willing to sacrifice your family in an effort to save this girl?" he shouted. "Because that is what will happen if we allow this monster its life. It will attack and burn our village as surely as the last one did. When the creature is dead, the girl can go free."

"No," Keira shouted, but her voice was overridden by the reeve's.

"Kill it!" the reeve screamed, spinning towards Aaron and charging him with his sword outstretched.

Later, Keira would remember the events as they played through her mind in slow motion, each expression and action discrete; but at the time, they ran together in a confused explosion. Taking advantage of the momentary distraction caused by Daniel's words, the reeve raced towards Aaron. The motion caught Keira's dragon-sharpened eye and her cry reverberated through the surrounding forest. The reeve faltered, and instead of piercing the dragon, his sword sliced through Keira's upper arm as she leapt towards Aaron. Aaron's massive claws smashed into the reeve and sent him flying through the air, and he landed on the ground with a crash. Keira's father, too, had seen the reeve's actions and he surged forward, startling the man beside him. Pitchfork lowered, Smithy swung around, catching Father in the stomach and impaling him on the tines.

Keira's gaze was on Aaron as she leapt forward, but she saw her father fall from the corner of her eye, and she spun around to see him grasping the pitchfork with his hands as blood seeped between his fingers. Around her, the other men stood frozen in place, glancing between the dragon and Father, until fear and dread forced them into action, and en masse they turned and ran. The reeve, lying on the ground, groaned as he pushed himself to his knees, then scrambled back with a scream as a stream of flame caught his legs, blistering and blackening the skin. His body thrashed in the dust, causing the flames to slowly subside as he lost consciousness and fell still.

Mother ran to Father and fell in the dirt beside him, while on his other side, Smithy dropped to the ground and slowly eased the pitchfork from his stomach, his face a mask of horror.

"I'm so sorry," he moaned. "I'm so sorry. I'm so sorry." The words flowed from his mouth in an endless litany that grew more and more frantic as Father's blood seeped out from the wounds. "Please, you can't die. I'm so sorry."

"Help him," Keira shouted at Aaron. Blood was pouring from the gash in her own arm, the pale white bone exposed where the tissue pulled apart, but she barely noticed the pain. "He's going to die," she yelled. "Help him!"

"The dagger," Aaron said, "Get Alan's dagger. You'll have to do this – do you think you can?" His voice was low enough that the others couldn't hear.

Keira nodded as she picked up the knife, holding her

wounded arm close to her chest. She stepped over to where her father lay. Small bubbles of blood escaped from his mouth, and she could see that he did not have long to live.

"Mother," Keira said, grabbing her by the shoulders, "the dragon can help Father, but we need to hurry."

"No," Mother hissed, as Aaron moved to Father's side, his clawed feet next to Father's broken form. "Keep that monster away from him. He cannot have Richard."

"Mother," Keira said, struggling to keep her voice calm. "You have to trust me." She looked at Aaron in despair.

Smithy still crouched beside Father, but at Keira's words he stopped mumbling and glanced between Keira and the dragon, then walked around to where Mother knelt on the ground and gently took her by the shoulders, drawing her away. She tried to fight free, but his grip was unyielding. He nodded at Keira, and she smiled gratefully.

Rising to her feet, Keira stood opposite Aaron and placed the dagger against his chest. She stared into his eyes, drawing her strength from him. She drew in a deep breath, pulled back the dagger and plunged it into his chest. Behind her, Smithy gasped, but Aaron remained still as blood began to drip from the wound. Keira's hand shook as her own blood loss crested in a wave of dizziness, and Aaron placed his claw over her hand and forced the blade to the side, opening the wound enough for the blood to flow freely. The crimson stream splashed onto Father as he lay prone on the ground, the blood seeping into his wounds and running down his chest.

Looking down, Keira watched in amazement as the wounds started to knit together, the skin pulling taut before her eyes and closing the gaping holes left by the tines. She looked up at Aaron and smiled in relief as she tugged the blade from his hide. Another wave of dizziness hit, and she leaned against his chest as he clasped his claws around her and lifted her away from the others, turning so that his bulk hid her from their sight. The dagger still hung loosely in

Keira's grip, and Aaron wrapped his claw around her hand and guided the blade back to his chest, forcing the quickly healing wound open again. The blood welled up once more, and he pulled her closer so that it dripped over her arm and into her wound. Her flesh tingled as his blood mixed with hers, and she felt a slight tugging as the muscle knitted itself back together. She looked up at Aaron and caught her breath as he bent his neck down in a graceful arch and brought his mouth close to her ear.

"Drink my blood," he whispered, his hot breath lifting the hair about her neck. "It will build your strength," he said.

"What about my father? Must he drink your blood too?"

Aaron laughed, a low sultry sound that made her shiver. "Definitely not," he said. "Now come, drink."

Keira nodded slowly and drew in a deep breath, releasing it in a long stream as she brought her hands to his chest. She cupped them beneath the wound, which was still flowing freely, and watched as the blood pooled in her hands. She brought them to her lips and drank. As before, she felt the warm liquid hit her stomach and spread languorously through her limbs. The dizziness lifted as the blood flowed through her veins, and she cupped her hands beneath the wound again, drawing more of the elixir into her mouth.

Aaron's head was still bent down to hers, and she pulled back a little to meet his gaze. His eyes were blazing with flames that leaped and sparked, and she smiled as she bent forward, slowly pulling the blade out of his flesh. Blood continued to trickle from the wound as it began to heal, and she leaned forward to lick the drops from his skin. She felt him shudder as a rush of hot air swirled around her, and she leaned back to look at him once more. He met her gaze with an intensity that made her catch her breath, before lifting her arm and slowly licking the blood that had flowed from her wound. His forked dragon tongue curled around her arm, running down its length, and she shuddered as she stared into his burning gaze. A soft growl sounded low in his throat, and his grip on her arm tightened.

"Never fear the dragon, my sweet," he whispered, "for it is you who have power over the beast."

CHAPTER TWENTY-NINE

Keira's father lay on the ground in the clearing, his wife crouched beside him. Smithy stood a few feet away, his eyes not leaving the prone figure as the color slowly returned to his skin and his rasping breath steadied. The dragon stood behind Keira as she knelt beside Father and took his hand, smiling when he turned his head towards her.

"Where's the dragon?" he asked, his eyes seeking out its great form. "Your mother says he spilled his blood over me, healing my wounds."

Keira nodded. "Dragon blood heals, and he saved your life. He'll carry us back to Storbrook, where you can rest and recover."

Mother turned to face Keira, dismay shrouding her features. "Carry us?" she asked in a whisper, casting a furtive glance at Aaron. "That creature may have helped your father, but surely you don't expect me to go near it. It's a wild animal. It could turn on us at any time."

"Mother," Keira replied patiently, "he's not going to hurt us. He's already helped Father – surely that shows that he means us no harm. And I'll be there, too. You won't be alone."

"I'm not sure –" Mother said as Father clasped her hand.

"Jenny," he said, "Keira's right. There's no need to fear the dragon. With all that it's already done for us, we owe it some trust. Let it take us back to Storbrook."

Mother dropped her head, nodding her acquiescence. Squaring her shoulders, she stood up and turned to face Smithy.

"Thank you for staying with us," she said.

"Yes," Keira said, rising to stand beside her mother. "And please let people know that there is no need to fear the dragon."

Smithy shot a furtive glance at Aaron before nodding. "I'm sorry for all the trouble we caused, Mistress Keira. And for your injury," he said, turning to Father. He glanced once more at Aaron, then turned and walked away, disappearing between the trees.

"What do we do with him?" Keira asked, pointing at the reeve lying on the ground. He was slowly regaining consciousness, groaning in pain as his breath rattled through his chest.

"Leave him," Father said, pushing himself onto his elbows to look at the man. "The others will come back for him eventually. In the meantime, he's suffering his just desserts."

"But he could die," Mother protested.

Father just shrugged. "Perhaps the dragon wants a meal."

Mother gasped in horror, but Keira saw an amused glint pass between Father and the dragon. Planting her hands on her hips, she shot each of them a glare before turning to her mother.

"He's not going to eat the reeve," she said. "Now come, help me get Father on his feet."

It took a while for Keira to get her parents onto Aaron's broad back, where they settled behind his neck, Mother shaking with nervousness and Father gasping from exertion. Keira climbed up last of all and positioned herself between

Aaron's spread wings. A few moments later they were in the air as Aaron glided on wind currents which carried them upwards towards the summit of the mountain. Although he flew slower than usual, it didn't take long for him to reach Storbrook, where he dropped into the courtyard as people scrambled to get out of the way as he landed. Thomas ran out to meet them as Keira slipped off the dragon.

"My father's been badly injured," she said to Thomas. "Please arrange for a bedchamber to be prepared, and ensure that my father has all he needs to aid his recovery."

"Yes, milady," Thomas responded. He placed a hand on Father's back and gave him his support as he led him away, while Mother hovered at his other side. Keira watched them go, then turned to face Aaron. Before she had a chance to say anything, he grabbed her in his claws and swung her into the air. He cleared the outer wall and flew out of sight of any observers before transforming in midair and pulling her against his chest. She gasped in surprise, but when his lips met hers, she wound her hands around his neck and hooked her feet around his, pulling him closer. He moaned, a low guttural sound, and slipped his hands beneath her thighs, molding her body to his. His wings beat gently as they hovered in the air, and Keira slid her hands down his back and caressed the place where they broke through his skin. She could feel the powerful muscles just below the surface, flexing beneath her fingers as they moved the enormous appendages through the air.

"You were such a wild creature today," Keira said when he pulled away.

"Hmm," he murmured, dropping kisses onto her shoulder. "Were you scared?"

"A little," admitted Keira. "You looked so ... lethal. For a moment you didn't look like you at all."

Aaron pulled away at her words and gazed down into her eyes.

"I'm always me, my sweet." He drew her back into his

211

arms and rested his chin against the top of her head. "It's difficult to explain, since you'll never experience it. Sometimes I have to allow the monster inside me to take control, but I am allowing it. The creature within never trumps who I am. I may allow it to take the reins, but I – the moral, rational, thinking man that I am – am still in ultimate control. There may have been times in my angry past when I allowed the beast to be dominant, but even then I was still in control – I gave the beast the power to do whatever it wanted."

Aaron sighed in frustration as Keira struggled to understand. "I'm making it sound like there are two creatures warring within me, but that's not right. I am man and beast at the same time, and together they make me who I am." He paused and pulled back to look at her. "Is any of this making sense?"

Keira considered for a moment before slowly replying. "Yes, in a way. I think what you're trying to tell me is that you're still you, even when you look very ferocious, and you could never hurt me."

"That's it." His face broke into a grin. "I, the man and beast merged into one, love you."

"And I love you too, my wonderful, scary monster."

Laughing, Aaron lowered his lips onto hers, kissing her deeply. She could feel his desire pressing against her, and she responded hungrily, fanning the flames of passion as he hurriedly propelled them through the window of their bedchamber.

The sun was already slipping towards the western horizon when Keira rose from the bed and reached for a gown. Aaron watched as he lay over the quilts, and Keira allowed her eyes to wander over his long body in appreciation, before slipping the garment over her head.

"Aaron?" she said as she smoothed down the gown.

"Hmm?"

"Why did it take you so long to get back to the clearing?"

"I need to prepare myself."

"Prepare yourself, how?"

"You've already told me that I appeared more ... wild ... than before," he said. "When I'm with you, I'm more in touch with my humanity, so I needed to let the dragon out. Also, the longer I stay in human form, the weaker I become. I needed to build my strength." He rolled onto his side to face her as Keira sat down at the edge of the bed.

"How do you do that?" she asked.

His eyes met hers. "I needed the taste of fresh blood," he said bluntly.

Keira swallowed as she returned the gaze, and her voice dropped to a whisper. "Human blood?"

"No." He stroked her leg as he spoke. "I tracked and killed a deer in the woods. But I was never far away. Perhaps too far for you to hear me, but never so far that I couldn't hear you."

"You stayed near the men even though you were hunting?"

"No," he said. "I stayed near you even though I was hunting. I would never leave you unprotected. You are my life."

"Oh. I'm glad," she whispered. She bent down and kissed him, then pulled away and swatted him with her hand. "Come on, lazy bones. We cannot linger here all day."

He grabbed her hand and pulled her back against his chest. "Why not?"

"Because my parents are here," she said. "I need to ensure my father is comfortable."

"You should look to your husband's comfort first," he whispered in her ear.

She laughed and pulled herself away. "If I tend to your comfort any more, you'll turn into a very fat, lazy dragon."

"Fat? With all the exercise you give me, that's impossible," he said with a leering grin.

"You're impossible." she said. "Now come on, get up."

Aaron smiled, but did not release her hand. "Actually, there is one more thing we need to discuss, my sweet."

"Oh?" She looked at him in surprise. "What's that?"

"The fact that you followed me when I told you explicitly to wait here." His voice was gentle, but beneath it Keira could hear an undercurrent of steel.

"Oh," she gulped. "Well, you see ..." Her voice trailed off as Aaron lifted an eyebrow questioningly. She took a deep breath and tried again. "I didn't follow you," she said. "Mother insisted on returning home, and I couldn't let her travel alone."

"It didn't occur to you to ask Thomas to accompany her? Or even better, prevent her leaving?"

She straightened the sleeve of her gown. "I thought if I went with her, I could help," she whispered. "I couldn't bear the thought that you might be injured, or worse."

"Keira," he said. "I'm a dragon." His voice was filled with incredulity. "The chances that I would be hurt or killed by the reeve and his men were infinitesimal. The chances of you being hurt or killed, however, were incredibly high, as was proven today." He gestured to her arm, which nonetheless was now completely healed.

"Yes, I know." She rose from the bed and started pacing. "And I'm sorry that I made things more difficult for you, but I was concerned. I don't think I could live without you."

Aaron sighed and got off the bed, grasping her by the shoulders and looking down into her eyes. "I do understand," he said. "The only thing I'm afraid of losing is you. But I cannot understand why you would risk your frail, human life in order to protect a dragon – a creature that is practically unvanquishable."

Keira smiled as she placed her hands on either side of his face, looking deep into his golden eyes.

"It's called love, Aaron," she said. "And I love you. I cannot promise that I won't do something foolish again in my feeble attempts to keep you safe, but I will heed you next time you ask me to stay behind." She stood on her tiptoes and kissed him on his lips before adding, with a sly grin, "Even though the waiting will probably drive me crazy, and you'll return home to a woman demented."

"At least you'll be alive," he rejoined with a laugh. "And perhaps you'll be more amenable."

She raised her hand to swat him and he caught it, then caught the other one as it too flew through the air. Holding her imprisoned in his grasp, he kissed her deeply. Her knees went weak and she placed her hands against his chest, leaning her weight into him; but when he released her, she shoved him away with a laugh and darted behind a chair.

"Come now, milord," she chided, "Isn't someone past the century mark too old to play games? Get yourself suitably attired for someone of such advanced age, and accompany me to my parents' chambers."

She soon learned her error in thinking she could best a dragon in physical prowess: she was on the ground, rolling with laughter, before he finally released her and dusted off her gown. He was still grinning when a few minutes later they left their chamber in search of her parents.

CHAPTER THIRTY

Keira's parents had been given a guest bedchamber on the same floor as Anna, and it was here that Keira and Aaron found them a short while later. Father lay on the bed, propped against a pile of pillows, with a thick quilt covering his legs. Mother sat in a chair beside him; she held a damp cloth in one hand and a cup of wine in the other. Father looked up with a wide smile as the pair walked in.

"It's good of you to join us, Keira," Mother said. "And Aaron! I was wondering what happened to you. We didn't see you again after you left to find the dragon. You didn't run away, did you?"

Keira looked at Aaron, startled. She'd forgotten that Mother didn't know Aaron's true identity, and from his expression, she guessed the thought had slipped his mind, too.

"Well, er," he stammered. It was the first time Keira had ever seen him at a loss for words. "By the time I returned to the clearing, everyone was gone, so I made my way back to Storbrook."

"Why didn't you return with the dragon?" Mother said. "It carried us on its back. Surely it could have carried you, too."

"Oh, no," Aaron replied. "A Drake cannot be carried by a dragon."

"Oh?" Mother said. "Why not?"

"Tradition," he said. Mother frowned as Father watched in amusement.

"I'm sure there's an explanation beyond our comprehension, Jenny," he said gently. Mother looked at Aaron with narrowed eyes and pursed lips.

"I'm sure you're right," she reluctantly agreed.

"Aaron," Father said, turning to look at him. "Son. Thank you for all you've done. You were forced into a difficult position, but your actions were honorable. I'm proud to have you in my family, and hope you'll consider me part of yours."

Keira looked at her father in astonishment before turning to Aaron. He stared at Father for a moment, then strode forward and clasped the injured man's hand in his own. "I am honored to be called your son, and my blood ensures you'll forever be bound to me and my family." A look of understanding passed between the two men before Aaron stepped back and glanced around the room.

"Where's Anna?" he said. "I thought she'd be with you."

With a flash of guilt, Keira realized that she had forgotten her sister.

"We haven't seen her," Mother said. "We thought maybe she was with you." Aaron threw Keira an amused glance, and she looked down as a flush rose in her cheeks.

"I think they were otherwise occupied, my love," Father said with a laugh.

"I'll go look for her," Keira said, suddenly anxious to leave the room. She heard amused laughter trailing her as she turned and fled, while Mother's confused voice demanded to know the source of the humor.

Anna was not in her chambers, nor in any of the common rooms. Vexatious girl, thought Keira. There were many smaller rooms where she could be hiding within the castle, or she could even have gone to the chapel; but as the light was beginning to fade, Keira decided to search the gardens first. She made her way through the low hall and headed into the kitchen garden. It was a small enclosed area, with a low bench against the wall. Anna wasn't there, and Keira turned towards the pleasure gardens. She had just started searching through the trees, calling Anna's name, when she heard footsteps behind her. Turning around, she saw Aaron approach through the lowering light.

"No sign of her?" he asked.

"No," Keira said. "I've looked in all the obvious places, but nothing. I thought I'd search the gardens before the light is completely gone, and if I don't find her, head back inside to search some of the smaller rooms." A rustling sound made her turn to search the shadows, but she saw nothing.

"Come out," Aaron called. "I can see you hiding in the brush."

Keira watched in surprise as a young girl crept out of the bushes towards them. She glanced at Aaron warily before turning her attention to Keira.

"Excuse me, mum," she said, her voice quavering. "I didn't mean to spy on you, it's just that I was in the gardens and you came this way, see? And I couldn't help but hear you talking about Mistress Anna."

"You know where she is?" asked Keira.

"Yes, mum," she said. "I mean no, mum. I mean, I saw her leave the castle earlier today."

"Saw her leave?" Aaron said, his voice harsh after the girl's timorous utterances. She shrank back a little as she glanced at him, then turned back to Keira.

"She wasn't leaving with anything, mum. She just looked like she was taking a walk. She left the castle gates and headed down the path."

"What time was this?" Aaron asked impatiently, and Keira shot him a look of annoyance.

"Um, I'm not sure."

"It's all right," Keira said. "You did the right thing telling us. What were you doing when you saw her?"

"Coming back from the stables. I'd taken a message that you wanted the horses saddled, mum."

Keira felt the color drain from her face as she looked at Aaron. "That was hours ago. Where could she have gone?"

Aaron nodded at the girl and flicked his fingers to indicate her dismissal. She turned and ran, disappearing into the shadows.

"Keira, there is something you should know," he said. "When we returned with your parents, I smelled something. I thought the scent had been carried by your parents, and didn't pay it much mind. But in light of your sister's disappearance, I believe it's significant."

"What, Aaron? What did you smell?"

"Did you notice someone missing at the clearing?" he asked. "Someone who would've jumped at the chance to see me at a disadvantage?"

"Edmund," she breathed, shocked that she hadn't noticed his absence before.

"Yes."

"We must go find her," she said.

"Not we, I," he said, folding his arms against his chest.

"No Aaron. She's my sister, and I need to see her safe."

"Keira, we've already gone over this. I'll find her and bring her back, but it's not safe for you to be with me."

"Why not? It is only one man. A boy. He's no threat to me with you nearby, and certainly no threat to you."

Aaron shook his head, his expression closed, and Keira grabbed his arm.

"Please, Aaron," she said. "This situation is not like before. Don't make me stay here, wondering whether you or my sister are safe."

"You know I'll keep her safe."

"Please, Aaron." She looked up at him beseechingly, and he let out a sigh.

"Very well," he said. "Against my better judgment I'll let you come. But promise me you'll stay away from Edmund."

"Thank you." She threw her arms around his neck.

"Don't make me regret this," he growled in her ear. "Now, let's go, before we waste any more time."

Aaron and Keira paused only to tell Keira's parents that Anna hadn't returned from a walk and they were going to search for her, omitting any mention of Edmund. In their bedchamber Aaron removed his shirt before strapping a sword around his waist. Keira watched in surprise as he fastened the buckle.

"You're going like that? Why?"

"You do know that I'll kill Edmund, don't you?" he asked, grabbing a dagger and shoving it under the belt.

"Yes," Keira said.

"Edmund will know the man that is sending him to his grave, and I'll look him in the eyes as his lifeblood drains away." Keira shivered at his words, and he turned to look at her. "He's brought this on himself, Keira. He's tried to harm not just you, but now your sister as well. Given the chance, he'd take your life without giving it a thought. He does not deserve the life he's been given, and now it will stand as forfeit for his deeds."

Aaron finished arming himself and jumped onto the window ledge, reaching out a hand to pull Keira up as well. He wrapped his arms around her and threw himself from the ledge, and his wings unfurled behind to catch them in their descent. It was already too dark for Keira to see more than a few feet ahead of her, but she knew that Aaron could see movements in the forest even from this height. Below them was the path leading from the castle, and Aaron followed it until it disappeared under the trees.

"She passed this way," Aaron said into Keira's ear. "I can smell her." He swooped downwards, and Keira tightened her grip around his neck as he skimmed the tops of the trees.

"There," he said, pointing with his chin. "I can hear noises." Keira strained her ears, but the wind whipped away any sounds. A few more moments went by until she heard a cry, and Aaron picked up his speed and headed towards the sound. Through a break in the trees Keira could see Edmund dragging Anna by the arm as she tripped and stumbled behind him. He jerked her back to her feet angrily.

"This is your sister's doing," Keira heard him shout, the dragon blood in her veins sharpening her hearing. "She was supposed to be my wife. She thinks she can leave me and marry someone else, but she'll soon learn that I'm not a man to be trifled with. She'll pay for her insolence. And when she finds your lifeless body, she will know that she should never have crossed Edmund Hobbes!"

He yanked Anna's arm again, and she fell to the ground with a cry. Her knees were already bloodied, and long scratches ran down the length of her cheeks, with tears, blood and dirt mingling in brown streaks.

Aaron closed his wings against his back as they drew closer, and dropped silently towards the forest floor, releasing Keira when they were just a few feet above the ground. He plowed into Edmund, dragging him away from the traumatized girl as she lay helplessly on the ground. Edmund rolled over, shock written across his face as he stared up at Aaron.

"You," he spat. His face was twisted in anger, but as Aaron rose to his feet, the expression was replaced with horror. Aaron stretched his wings to the fullest extent allowed by the trees, while his inhuman eyes blazed with flames.

"Who are you?" Edmund gasped, pushing himself away.

A stream of flame curled from Aaron's mouth and brushed against Edmund's skin. "I'm your worst nightmare," he said, his voice low.

Kneeling beside Anna, Keira gathered her sister in her arms. She pulled Anna against her shoulder as sobs wracked her frame. The girl seemed oblivious to the scene playing out before her, and Keira shifted herself so that Anna could not see what was happening.

"You're the dragon!" Edmund exclaimed, fear making his voice rise in pitch.

"Exactly," Aaron said. Edmund trembled, and Keira felt a flicker of pity for him, but it was quickly gone. Aaron took a step backwards.

"Stand up," he said. "I could kill you in an instant, but I have a very strong sense of fair play. Since you were unaware of my true identity, I'll fight you not as a dragon, but as a man." He pulled the sword and dagger from his belt, and holding them both by the blade, extended the handles to Edmund. "Choose your weapon."

Edmund chose the sword, leaving the shorter dagger for Aaron. Despite the longer reach of his weapon, Edmund did not look very confident as he faced his opponent.

"I'll kill you quickly, to save my wife's sensibilities," Aaron said, flicking a glance over at Keira. Edmund looked at her in surprise, and Keira wondered whether he'd even realized she was there. Edmund looked back at Aaron and then, without waiting for a signal, rushed towards him with the sword outstretched. Aaron spun away from the weapon and turned to face Edmund, who charged again. The sword went wide, and Aaron brought the dagger up into Edmund's chest as he rushed past. He collapsed onto the ground with a groan as Aaron stepped over to him and yanked out the dagger. Blood gushed from the wound and Edmund groaned.

"Look at me," Aaron growled. Edmund lifted his eyes to meet Aaron's, and they widened in fear when he saw Aaron's face start to elongate as the skin pulled taut and split as it formed into scales; his eyes moved around to the sides of his head; and his hair vanished as horns grew from his skull. The last thing Edmund saw before he breathed his last was fire curling from between a row of sharp teeth while a forked tongue flicked out of the mouth.

Aaron stared at Edmund as his features returned to their human form, then turned towards Keira. He held her gaze for a moment before glancing at the girl in her arms.

"How is she?" he asked. Keira shook her head.

"She's been badly hurt. She'll soon recover from her superficial wounds, but it will take far longer for the deeper ones to heal."

Aaron ripped the bottom of Edmund's tunic, then slashed his own wrist with the dagger. Blood quickly welled up from the wound, and Aaron held the cloth against it, saturating the rag before handing it to Keira.

"Wipe her wounds with this," he said. "It'll help them to heal." He turned away as Keira gently wiped the bloodied cloth over Anna's face and arms, then lifted her skirts and wiped her knees.

Anna's eyes fluttered open as Keira worked, and she gazed at her sister as she finished.

"You came," she said in a whisper. "Thank God you came – he was going to kill me. He said it was all your fault – that he was going to teach you a lesson. I tried to get away, but I couldn't." Anna's voice broke as she choked on a sob.

"Sshh," Keira soothed. "It's finished. Edmund is dead."

"Really?" Anna whispered.

"Yes, really. Look." Taking Anna by the shoulders, Keira turned her around to where Aaron stood over the lifeless remains. Anna pushed herself to her feet, grabbing Keira as she stumbled, then walked over to where Edmund lay. Her lips curled as she stared at the body, and she spat on it before she turned away.

"I'm glad he's dead," she said. She walked over to a tree and slumped down against the trunk as she buried her head in her hands.

"Come," Aaron said, "let's get out of here."

"What about the body?" Keira asked.

"I'll take it to the village tomorrow," he said. "At least

people will know what happened."

"No," Keira exclaimed. "You can't do that. People will blame the dragon."

"He was stabbed with a dagger. No one can say he was killed by a dragon."

"Do you think that will stop people blaming you?" she said.

"What are you suggesting, Keira," he asked quietly.

"We need to destroy the evidence. Get rid of the body."

"Get rid of the body?" he repeated. "How?"

Anna lifted her head from her hands and gave him a sly grin. "She means," she said, "you should eat him." Aaron's eyebrows flew up. "I don't mind," she added.

"No," Aaron said, glaring at his wife.

"Why not?" Keira asked. "You are a dragon, after all, and here is warm flesh waiting to be eaten."

He turned away from her, flinging a reply over his shoulder. "Absolutely not!"

"Oh come on," Anna said, leaning against the tree as she rose to her feet. "No need to be bashful. I'll just go wait behind those trees while you do what you have to do."

Keira's mouth dropped open in astonishment as Aaron turned around slowly to stare after his sister-in-law. He looked back at Keira, his gaze meeting hers.

She stepped towards him and wrapped her arms around his waist. "You are a dragon."

"Are you sure?" he whispered.

"Yes," she said softly.

Aaron pulled away from her embrace. "You must wait behind the trees with Anna."

Keira nodded and turned away. As she reached the trees she looked back to see Aaron, his back to her, pulling his pants down his legs. A flash of light blazed through the air, and instead of the man stood the dragon. He lifted his head and sniffed the air, then slowly twisted his long neck around and met her gaze. She dropped her eyes and hurried over to where Anna sat on the ground, her back pressed against a tree.

Keira sank down below her sister and took her by the hand. "I'm so sorry, Anna," she said. She blinked away the tears that filled her eyes.

Anna shook her head. "This is not your fault, Keira. Edmund was evil, and was determined to hurt us. I'm just glad he's dead."

"Me too," Keira said, leaning back against the tree. "Me too."

They sat together in silence as soft growls reached their ears from behind the trees. Anna's body relaxed slowly as her eyes closed. Keira waited a few minutes before leaning forward to listen to her breathing. Its slow, steady rhythm assured Keira that Anna was asleep; and slowly, with as little noise as possible, she rose and tiptoed towards Aaron. When she had drawn close, she quietly bent around a tree trunk to see what he was doing. His claws were buried in the body before him as his teeth ripped off pieces of blackened flesh. She drew in a deep breath and closed her eyes, steeling herself against the sights before her, then opened them again. Low growls rumbled through Aaron's chest as he pulled apart more flesh while Keira watched. Through the trees she could see the rising moon, and its light threw down faint shadows around the dragon.

Aaron lifted his head, and his eyes met hers. He pulled back, watching her warily, as Keira returned the gaze. Slowly, keeping her eyes on him, she inched around the tree until she was standing directly in front of him, the tree pressed against her back. Aaron continued to watch her for a few more moments, then lowered his head and tore off another piece of meat, looking back at her to meet her gaze once more. The growls from his chest grew louder, and his gaze did not leave hers except when he lowered his head to pull off more flesh.

As Keira watched, the connection in her mind between the man and dragon began to dissolve. She no longer thought of him as a man, but as a wild beast, ferocious and beautiful. She paid no attention to what he was eating and marveled at the magnificence of the creature before her – fierce and primal, silhouetted against the moon. The dragon continued to watch her as he ate, and she watched in return, with a feeling of awe. A sound behind her pulled her attention away, and fearful that Anna had awakened, she quietly tiptoed away, looking back one more time to meet his gaze before stepping behind the trees.

Anna was mumbling in her sleep, turning her head frantically as she tried to get away from the monsters in her dreams. Keira sat down beside her and wrapped her arms around her sister. Anna fought for a moment, then relaxed against her as her body grew heavy. Keira must have fallen asleep as well, because when she opened her eyes, Aaron was squatting against a tree across from her, his arm hanging loosely over his knee. He'd been watching her as she slept. She met his gaze, catching her breath when she saw his smoldering eyes burst into flames. Anna remained sleeping next to her, and Aaron and Keira stared at each other in silence as the moon made its way across the sky.

CHAPTER THIRTY-ONE

The early morning light was filtering through the trees when Anna rolled out of Keira's arms. Her eyes flew open as her body tensed in startled apprehension, then relaxed when she saw Keira and Aaron watching her cautiously.

"Enjoy your meal, brother?" she asked.

"You're clearly feeling better, Anna," he replied.

He pushed himself up from his crouched position and stretched his legs, then reached down a hand to help Keira to her feet. She fell against his chest, and his arms immediately went around her, his mouth descending in a kiss.

"Urgh," said Anna. "Can you not find some place in private to do that?"

"I'm saying good morning to my wife. You can always look away if that disturbs you," he replied, unperturbed, applying himself to his task once more as the object of his desire responded with equal ardor. Anna huffily turned her back to them, tapping her foot as she waited for them to be done. Keira was grinning when she pulled away.

"The horses you and your mother rode yesterday are close by," Aaron said. "I'll go fetch them and we can ride them back to Storbrook."

"They weren't attacked by wild animals?" Keira said.

"The only creature they need be afraid of is a dragon," he replied with a grin. "Other predators tend to stay away when they smell dragons close by. And since the only dragon in the area had already eaten, they were perfectly safe." Anna made a face and Aaron laughed. "I'll be back in a few minutes," he called over his shoulder as he walked away.

By the time the three stragglers returned to the castle, the sun had risen above the horizon. Keira helped Anna to her bedchamber, then called for a maid to fill a tub with hot water. The memories that had been held at bay finally crashed over her, and Keira rocked her sister in her arms as she wept. She finally fell into a deep slumber, her body and mind exhausted, and Keira sighed in relief, glad that Anna could find some measure of escape from the terrible memories of the previous night. She felt herself trembling as she considered what might have happened if she and Aaron had not arrived when they did. She looked down at her sister's sleeping form and gently touched her cheek. Anna looked so young, lying on the white sheets, her hair spread around her face; but Keira knew that beneath the surface Anna had a resilient spirit – a spirit of courage and strength that would help her move on from the terrible events of the night just passed.

Keira watched her sister for a few more minutes before creeping from the room in search of Aaron. She finally found him in the solar, where he had been joined by Keira's father.

"I need to know, Aaron," Father said. "Was Edmund involved in Anna's disappearance?"

"Yes," was Aaron's curt reply. Father nodded, as though that was the answer he had expected.

"Did he force himself on her?"

"No. But he threatened to kill her."

Father's jaw clenched in anger, but he returned Aaron's gaze steadily. "Is he dead?"

"Yes." At Aaron's response, some of the tension left

Father's shoulders, and he nodded again.

"Good." He held Aaron's gaze. "I'd like to keep this from Jenny. It will just distress her to know the extent of Edmund's duplicity."

"She'll learn of it soon enough," Aaron warned.

"Perhaps," Father said. "But I'd like to protect her as long as I can."

"Very well," Aaron said. "That's your decision. She'll not hear of tonight's events from me."

"Thank you."

Aaron watched as Father left the room, then turned to Keira. "I promised to protect his daughters, and I failed him."

"No!" Her response was emphatic. "Aaron, you might have strength and power on your side, but not even you can predict every possible situation. You cannot control the actions of others. Anna chose to wander beyond the safety of Storbrook, and Edmund chose to attack her."

Aaron shook his head. "I should've realized that Edmund was up to something when he wasn't with the other men. And then again when we returned and I caught his scent."

"Well in that case, Father and I are just as responsible – we should have noticed that Edmund was missing."

Aaron smiled bleakly. "You aren't going to convince me that I don't bear responsibility for this, but thank you for trying to lessen my guilt." He took her hands and pulled her into his arms. "I thought I was so strong, Keira. Invincible. I am, after all, a dragon. But I'm beginning to realize that I am, in fact, weak and vulnerable. All those years spent indulging my anger were years of weakness. It is only with you that I can be strong." He traced the lines of her face with his finger. "I love you so much, Keira. You have filled my life with so much meaning and purpose. I cannot imagine spending another day without you by my side."

He gently drew his fingers across her mouth before replacing them with his lips. His arms encircled her and he pulled her close. Despite his words, his embrace was strong and secure, and Keira melted into him. Whatever he might say, Keira knew that it was she who had been blessed, by being loved by a beast. She could never tame the dragon, but she held his heart, and that was enough.

EPILOGUE

Anna leaned against the window and stared into the garden below. She could see Aaron and Keira strolling along the path that wound between the shrubbery. Aaron's arm held his wife securely by his side, while Keira's laughter, trilling lightly, floated up to where Anna stood. Anna turned away from the sight in irritation.

It had been two weeks since Edmund attacked her – two weeks of conflicting emotions raging within. The outside wounds may have healed, but inside, Anna felt empty and hollow. Apart from meals, she spent most of that time in the privacy of her chambers, alone with her thoughts. Each day, Mother had come to sit with her for a short while, but she had been of little comfort. Mother never asked Anna what had happened that day, and Anna suspected that she knew very little of the events that had touched her daughter so deeply. While Anna was angry that Mother was spared the hurt and pain of Edmund's actions while she herself had to suffer, she was relieved that she did not have to deal with Mother's guilt.

Father had come by only twice to see her. The first time was the day after the attack, when he had held his youngest daughter and rocked her in his arms as tears rolled down his cheeks. He'd expressed his regret at what had happened, and Anna had cried too, clinging to the man who had always seemed so strong and in control. The second time had been that morning, when Father came by to say goodbye. He and Mother were returning to their home in the village, though it seemed to Anna that Father was rather reluctant to go. Keira had told her that Father spent hours with Aaron each day, grilling him with questions about his life as a dragon. And despite the fact that Aaron was older than Father by almost sixty years, Aaron welcomed the new father-and-son relationship.

Anna sat down on her bed as another wave of self-pity washed over her. Keira would come soon to see Anna, as she did every day. She was the only one who talked to Anna about what had happened, and at first, Anna had been grateful to have someone to confide in. Keira was the one person who really understood, since she too had suffered at the hands of Edmund. But as time went on, Anna began to feel annoyed and irritated with her sister. After all, if it hadn't been for Keira, Edmund would never have turned his sights on her. She knew that such thoughts were unfair to Keira and that her sister was not responsible for what had happened, but she just couldn't help snapping at Keira whenever she was near. The thoughts refused to be dismissed and the words just flew out. Anna always felt bad when she saw the look of hurt that always flashed across Keira's face. But Keira had had a happy ending. Just seeing her with Aaron made Anna's gall rise. Where was her happy ending? Where was her golden dragon? Her knight in shining armor?

Anna curled her legs beneath her and buried her face in a pillow. The truth was she wasn't even sure she wanted a knight in shining armor anymore. She had always dreamed of that perfect, happy marriage. A nice home, children, a loving husband. But that night had shattered her dreams. Men could be so cruel and mean. And there was nothing a woman could do about it when her husband beat her. There were plenty of women in the village who had husbands like Edmund, although there were good husbands, too, of course. Anna just had to look at her own father to see that. But how did you know what really lay beneath the shining armor of the knight you were marrying? It just didn't seem to be worth the risk.

Climbing off the bed, Anna went over to the window once more as she considered her options. She definitely did not want to return to the village, even though the threat of Edmund had been removed. Somehow she felt like she had moved beyond the confines of small village life. She could take the veil, but Anna knew she wasn't cut out for life as a nun. She lacked the patience and sweet temper that would have made Keira a good candidate. Of course, she could remain with Aaron and Keira – in fact, Keira had already told her that she was welcome to stay with them – but Anna could not help wishing, most perversely, that Aaron and Keira were not quite so happy. She sighed, annoyed with her thoughts again.

She would remain at Storbrook, of course. And when the children came along, she would be the loving, indulgent aunt who'd help them learn their letters and numbers. The poor, dependent relative that people looked at sympathetically as she passed by. She would gracefully decline into old age, helping her sister until she died. Anna smiled. The picture had a certain appeal – an indispensable spinster that the family depended upon. She nodded to herself, satisfied with the image that played out in her mind – unaware, at the tender age of sixteen, that life has a way of unraveling the best-laid plans.

GLOSSARY OF TERMS

The setting for this story is the Medieval period or the High Middle Ages, which covers roughly the time period from AD 1000 to 1300. In the course of the story I have used terms that not everyone is familiar with. Below is an explanation of these terms.

Bower – a private study or sitting room for the lady of the house.

Cabinet – a study or library.

Carol – a dance (not a song) where everyone holds hands and dances in a circle.

Doublet – a tight-fitting jacket that buttons up the front.

Great Hall – a multi-purpose room for receiving guests, conducting business, eating meals, and when necessary, sleeping.

Kirtle – a gown worn over a chemise and laced across the front, side or back.

Reeve – an overseer of a town, reporting to the local lord. (In this story, Aaron Drake is referred to as 'milord', a title used for someone of superior social standing. However, he is not the lord of the district, and the reeve does not report to him.) The word 'sheriff' comes from the word reeve. The reeve carries a white stick as a symbol of his authority.

Solar – a private sitting room used by family and close friends. The word solar does not refer to the sun, but rather to the fact that the room has sole or private use.

Tunic – a garment pulled over the head that reaches around mid-thigh. It is worn over a shirt and cinched at the waist with a belt.

A note about meals. During the Early and High Middle Ages, the entire household typically ate meals together. There were only two meals a day, although the working classes would usually eat something small, such as a piece of bread, when they first arose and before they started working. The first meal, called dinner, was served at around 11 a.m. and was the larger meal, with numerous courses. A second meal was served in the late afternoon.

If you are interested in learning more about the Medieval period, head over to the author's website, www.lindakhopkins.com.

CONTINUE READING FOR A PREVIEW OF THE NEXT
BOOK IN *THE DRAGON ARCHIVES*,
LOVED BY A DRAGON

CHAPTER ONE

It was early winter, but already the weather was cold. Snow lay on the ground, and the rivers and lakes were covered in a thick layer of ice. Keira stood at the edge of the frozen river watching the five wolves on the opposite bank. She and Aaron, her husband of three months, had just been in the village, visiting her parents, but they had stopped in the forest before continuing their journey home to Storbrook. The wolves were huge; big gray beasts, with yellow eyes that stared at her alert and unblinking in the dull light of dusk. They watched her with an intense hunger, but made no move to cross the icy wasteland. At the front of the pack stood the alpha male, his posture tall and erect, while a smaller female stood at his side. They were gaunt, the deprivations of winter obvious in their dull coats. The male stood still, growling low, but his eyes were focused not on Keira, but on the creature that stood behind her. The breeze shifted slightly, blowing away from Keira and towards the wolves, and the ears of the male rose upright as he bared his teeth, his growl becoming louder. The female moved nervously at his side, but her eyes were on Keira, and after a moment she took a tentative step forward. The male's growls grew louder, but the she-wolf ignored him, moving cautiously across the ice.

Keira could feel the hot breath of the wild beast standing behind her, its hulking presence an impenetrable barrier to her escape. It was infinitely more dangerous than the wolves, but Keira felt no fear. Instead, her attention was completely focused on the small pack across the river, and she watched them curiously. The alpha male was watching the beast nervously, but the female, clearly not familiar with the threat, continued to pick her way across the ice. Keira was well aware of her precarious position – if the wolves managed to reach her, she could be ripped to shreds. But she knew that the beast behind her would attack the wolves before they got that close. The she-wolf was growing bolder, her tentative steps becoming more confident as she stood near the middle of the river, where a thin channel of water cut its way through the ice. A low growl rumbled through the air behind Keira, and the female paused, her eyes seeking out the threat as she sniffed the air. She glanced back at her mate, still standing on the riverbank, but before she had a chance to retreat, a burst of flame shot over Keira's head. The blaze caught the wolf's coat, and with a yelp she turned and ran, bounding between the other wolves and disappearing amongst the trees as the rest of the pack turned and followed.

"You set that wolf alight," Keira said, her eyes still on the retreating forms.

"Don't spare it too much pity," the dragon said. "It would have killed you if given a chance. Besides, it will soon seek relief in the cool snow, which will put out the flames."

Keira turned to look at the dragon. "Like other wild beasts, it was just looking to assuage its hunger."

"That is true," the dragon replied, "and if it had set its sights on any other creature in this forest, I would not have interfered. But it was hungering after you, my sweet, and that is quite unacceptable."

Keira smiled as she stretched out a hand to stroke the smooth scales on the dragon's neck. "I love you," she said.

The dragon smiled, revealing a mouth of sharp, pointed teeth. His scales glimmered and shone a pale gold in the dull light, while huge wings lay folded across his broad back. A tail, armed with fierce spikes, curled around his body, the tip stretching beyond where Keira stood and curling around her protectively. He bent his long neck, lowering his massive head with its sharp horns which stood stark against the light, and brought his eyes down to her level. They were blazing as brightly as the fire that had streamed from his mouth, and his breath was hot and musky. "And I love you, my beautiful wife."

CHAPTER TWO

Keira looked down at the list in front of her, tapping the shaft of her quill against the pot of ink. A streak of sunlight fell from the window across her shoulder, highlighting the rich chestnut browns of her hair. Adjusting the quill in her hand, she added something more to the list, before setting the instrument back in its stand and nodding to herself. It was the season of Advent, and with the Christmas Feast Day fast approaching, Keira wanted to make sure nothing had been overlooked. The menus for the Christmas season had already been planned with Cook, while Thomas had been tasked with finding a troupe that would entertain the residents and guests at Storbrook Castle. It would not be a large gathering – Keira's family would be the only guests for the season – but it was the first time she would be celebrating the feast with Aaron, and she wanted everything to be perfect.

Keira smiled to herself as she leaned back in the chair, jumping in surprise a moment later when a pair of warm hands descended lightly on her shoulders. She looked up with a smile into Aaron's tawny eyes as he stepped around the chair, his warm lips descending on hers for a quick kiss. When he pulled away a moment later, the color of his eyes had been swallowed up in a blaze of flames, reminding Keira that the man she had married was not like other men, for just beneath the surface of his human guise burned a creature of such strength and power that just the mention of the beast made people hide themselves in fear. The thought excited Keira, and she reached up her hand to pull the beast back to her, opening her mouth to him as he responded hungrily. His hands were tangled in her hair when he pulled himself away with an audible intake of breath. He pushed himself upright and leaned his weight against Keira's desk.

"You seemed very intent in what you were doing," he said.

"Just putting some finishing touches on my plans for Christmas," she said. "Thomas has found a troupe willing to risk their lives and provide entertainment at Storbrook." In fact, most people refused to venture anywhere near Storbrook Castle, where a dragon was rumored to have its lair. What they didn't know was that the dragon could disguise himself in human form, and often walked amongst them.

"Thomas is certainly resourceful," Aaron replied, "and seems to have no qualms about spending gold from the dragon's hoard. I wonder how much this entertainment is going to cost me." In Aaron's tone there was a grudging respect for his steward, one of the few people who knew the true identity of the dragon. Keira stood up and slipped her arms around Aaron's waist.

"Is the dragon really so miserly that he begrudges a few coins spent on the entertainment of his guests?" she asked. The dragon laughed, and pulled his wife hard against his firm body.

"The only thing the dragon truly treasures is you," he said, his eyes glowing as he kissed her. He pulled away a moment later, resting his forehead against hers.

"It looks like we will have another guest for Christmas," he said, drawing away to look into her eyes.

"We will? Cathryn and Favian?"

"No. Max."

"Max? Who is Max?"

"Do you remember Beatrix and James?" he said, and Keira nodded. Beatrix was Aaron's aunt, and she and her husband James had been at Keira and Aaron's blood-binding ceremony a few months before. "Do you remember me telling you that James had fathered two children before he met Beatrix?" Again Keira nodded. "Max is James's son. From what I've heard, he is earning quite a reputation in the city as a rake and a cad. It must run in his genes," Aaron added cynically. "Beatrix has asked me to send for him in the hopes I can talk some sense into him."

Keira pulled herself out of Aaron's arms and took a step back. "Can you?"

Aaron shrugged. "I can only try. As Master, it falls to me to bring him into line." Keira nodded slowly.

"All right. So tell me about him. How old is he?"

"He's thirty-five, charming and handsome. Women adore him, his friends admire him, and his enemies, which includes most of the husbands in the city, are jealous of him. He treads a fine line between recklessness and caution, and it is amazing he hasn't spilled the secret of what he is over the whole city. Or maybe he has, but his friends have been too drunk to give it any attention," Aaron added dryly.

"So you think that being away from the city will help?"

"I'm not sure, but Beatrix thinks I will be able to influence him where others have failed."

"Why?"

Aaron turned away and stared out the window at the mountains surrounding Storbrook. "Because my own past has been rather checkered," he finally replied.

"Yes, but Aaron, you rejected humanity. You stayed away from people. You didn't drink and carouse with them."

"You are right, but only partly," Aaron said, turning around to look at her. "For many years I did shun all humanity. But for a while, after Favian tracked me down and forced me into the human world, I went to the opposite extreme. Part of it was because I could – humans are attracted to dragons without knowing why. And part of it was to prove that I was right all along – that people are selfish and irresponsible, and that love makes you weak. I used people, and they allowed themselves to be used. I took advantage of all that the women had to offer, both giving and taking a momentary pleasure that their married lives did not afford." Aaron smiled grimly. "They loved me for it!"

Keira stared at Aaron wide-eyed as she drew in a deep breath before he went on. "I drank with their husbands, matching drink for drink, and they thought I was a great sport even though I trounced them at cards. And the women could not stay away from me – I could ask for anything and they were happy to give it. So you see, I know what Max is doing – I know how powerful and important it makes you feel, and I know how meaningless it all is." Keira took a step backwards, holding up her hand when Aaron started to move towards her.

"I knew you had been with other women, Aaron, but married woman?" she said. "How many?"

"Keira," Aaron said, "they did not mean anything to me. And I certainly didn't mean anything to them either."

"Really? Did you just sleep with them once, or did you have ongoing affairs?"

"Keira, please."

"Tell me, Aaron."

"Sometimes once or twice, other times more. But Keira, that's in the past. They meant nothing to me."

"But you still slept with them. How do I know that I am not as meaningless to you as they were?"

"The fact that I married you should tell you that!" Aaron said sharply. He took a deep breath, running his fingers through his hair as he did so. "I love you, Keira," he said, his tone softening. He reached for her hands, grabbing them when she tried to move away, and took a step towards her.

"I cannot take back things I have done, as much as I may wish to," he said. "But believe me when I say that you hold my heart, and there is no-one else I have ever loved as I love you."

Keira stared up at him, still unsure for a moment, but when Aaron wrapped his arms around her, she allowed him to pull her close, resting her head against his chest. It stung a little, knowing there had been so many others before her, but she could not doubt the love he had for her. They stood in silence for a few moments until she finally pulled away.

"So you want to invite Max for Christmas?"

Aaron nodded. "But only if you are comfortable with him being here."

"What about Anna?"

Anna. The name hung between them as the memories of what had happened came rushing back. Anna had been abducted the previous autumn by Edmund, who had planned to kill her as revenge against Keira and Aaron. They had found the teenage girl before Edmund could carry out his threat, but ever since the attack she had become even more difficult and self-absorbed than she had been before.

Keira pulled her thoughts back to the present as Aaron responded.

"Anna is far too young and naive to interest a man like Max, and Max is too worldly wise to allow a rude and distrustful girl like Anna to get under his skin. I would never do anything to place Anna in harm's way. I have failed her and your father once, but I will not do so again. However, I suspect she will ignore Max, and he will do the same."

"You are not responsible for what happened to Anna, Aaron. If it hadn't been for you, we would never have found Anna in time."

"If it hadn't been for me," Aaron responded wryly, "Edmund would never have turned his sights on her. It was my presence that flamed his jealousy for you, and when he turned his anger to Anna, it was only because you were beyond his reach."

Keira shook her head, knowing the futility of continuing the argument. "Go ahead and invite Max for Christmas," she said. "It will be nice to have more company over the festive season, and if he is as charming as you say, he will be a welcome diversion through the dreary months of winter."

CHAPTER THREE

Anna pulled her cloak tighter around her shoulders as she slipped out the side door and picked her way through the snow towards the distant corner of the gardens. The air was frigid, and Anna curled her hands into fists within her mittens in an effort to maintain the warmth in her fingers. Before her the gardens were covered in a shimmering blanket of silver-white, while behind her the pristine covering had been marred by the trail of her fur-lined feet pushing through the snow, a record of her passing. The trees had long since lost their leaves, and hoar frost clung to the bare branches, the delicate feathering sparkling in the weak rays of winter sun and presenting a stark contrast against the deep blue of the sky. Silence hung in the air, with just the faintest voice occasionally drifting on a wayward breeze from the direction of the towering heap of stone that formed the walls of Storbrook Castle. To Anna, the walls of Storbrook seemed at times to be more like a prison than a sanctuary, and it was at these times that she felt the need to escape the thick walls, dark passages, and smoky halls. Treading through the snow, Anna filled her lungs with the cold air, then released it slowly, watching as it hung in a small cloud for a moment before dissipating. Peace flooded her mind with each breath, blowing away the dark, depressing thoughts which so often plagued her.

There was a wooden bench in the far corner of the garden, and it was to this that Anna made her way. The seat of the bench was buried under three inches of snow, smooth and unspoiled until Anna swiped her hand through the thick powder and pushed it onto the ground below. She sat down cautiously – the seat of the bench was cold – before slowly relaxing against the backrest. At her approach, a robin had flown into the branches of a nearby tree, but after a few moments it fluttered back to the ground, foraging around the base of the tree as Anna watched. The winter sun was shining feebly on the glittering landscape, and Anna lifted her face so she could feel the warming rays on her cheeks. She closed her eyes and allowed the serenity of the moment to filter through her mind.

A shout in the distant courtyard startled her, nudging open the door that held back the memories of her abduction the previous autumn. They no longer had the power to terrify her, as they had at first, but they still managed to bring a mild sense of panic. She had been nothing more than a tool in Edmund's hands – an opportunity for him to exact his revenge against Keira for her rejection, and when Anna had stumbled across his path that fateful day, he had seen in her the means by which he could obtain his retribution. Anna no longer recalled the individual events of that terrible afternoon, at least not in her waking hours. The way he had dragged her, pulling her stumbling through the woods, was now just a blur, but she could not forget the terror that had gripped her that day. And although she could not recall the exact moment when Aaron had arrived, pulling Edmund from her, she remembered the flood of relief when she realized she was free from him, and that her persecutor was dead.

It had been Aaron that had saved her life that day, but in

the deep recesses of her mind Anna could not help blaming him and Keira for all that had happened. After all, it was Keira's rejection of Edmund that had made him focus on Anna. And surely Aaron should have realized her predicament sooner. If he had, she would not have suffered as much. And not just Aaron and Keira. Perhaps if Father had spoken more forcefully against Edmund, once he realized Edmund's true character, events would have played out differently.

But it was Mother's actions that hurt the most. Long before he set his sights on Anna, Edmund had attacked Keira, but Mother had clung to the belief that the son of her dead friend was a man worth defending, even when it meant denying her own daughter. Perhaps if Mother had stood by Keira, Edmund would not have persisted in his belief that she belonged to him. And Mother still did not know how evil Edmund truly was. Father had chosen to protect her by keeping her in ignorance of the terrible events that had affected Anna so deeply, and so she knew nothing about Edmund's plan to kill her daughter. Father knew Mother would be devastated that the son of her closest friend could have done such terrible things. Edmund's mother had died years earlier, but as she lay on her death bed, Mary had begged Mother to watch over her boys. Anna guessed that if Mother admitted Edmund's true character, she would feel that she had failed her friend. Her thoughts returned to the attack, and she shivered slightly. Anna could still remember the feeling of helplessness she had felt when Edmund had taken her; the surety that she was going to die, and there was nothing she could do about it. She never wanted to feel that helpless again. Never wanted to find herself at the mercy of a man again.

Anna clenched her teeth, grinding them together in annoyance at where her thoughts were leading her. All this reflective thinking was making her miserable once more, and Anna was sick and tired of feeling miserable. She wanted to leave all of this behind her, but where could she go? She knew she could never go back to life in her little village. She had outgrown it, somehow. The girls she had grown up with seemed silly and immature now, thinking only about boys, marriage, and children.

If she was honest with herself, Anna had to admit that in unguarded moments she wondered what it would be like to be in love. To have a man love you the way Aaron loved Keira. But then she would remember how the actions of a man had made her suffer so much, and she would push the thoughts away. There was no point chasing after a rainbow that only promised an illusion of happiness. She would never be able to trust a man enough to spend the rest of her life with him. She would rather remain a spinster forever. When she had told Keira, her sister was horrified.

"But Anna," she had remonstrated, "you cannot measure the behavior of all men against that of Edmund. His actions were not the norm, and he received his just desserts for his behavior."

"Are you so sure?" Anna had retorted. "What about Widower Brown? Some say he murdered his last wife, although I'm not sure how he managed that since he is barely ever sober. And Gwyn's father beats her mother."

"Yes, but look at Father," Keira pointed out. "He has never raised an angry hand to Mother, and Aaron would never hurt me."

"Two, Keira!" Anna had shot back. "You can only name two worthy men! And Aaron doesn't count! So one man. That is hardly a glowing recommendation!"

"There are plenty of others, Anna," Keira had argued, but Anna remained unconvinced.

"Maybe there are, Keira, but I would prefer not to risk my future happiness on that chance."

Anna shivered again as a slight breeze ruffled her hair. Although it was still early afternoon, the sun was already dropping towards the western horizon, giving way in defeat to the long winter night that followed closely on its heels. Her toes were starting to feel numb through the thick fur-lined boots that wrapped around her feet, and she wiggled them against their confines to get the blood moving once again. Pushing herself up from the bench, she retraced her footsteps, the light glowing in the windows of the castle a beacon that promised a warm fire to chase away the chill.

I am thrilled to offer my readers free short stories from The Dragon Archives. Head over to my website, www.lindakhopkins.com and click on the tab, Short Stories, to learn more..

ACKNOWLEDGMENTS

It is friends and family that make the journey through life worthwhile as they love and support us. Cathy, Lynn, and Belinda, your support and encouragement are so appreciated. Claye, Kristin and Bethany, thank you for allowing me to pursue my dreams.

ABOUT THE AUTHOR

Linda K. Hopkins is originally from South Africa, but now lives in Calgary, Canada with her husband and two daughters. Head over to her website, www.lindakhopkins.com, to learn more about the author.

BOOKS BY LINDA K. HOPKINS

Books in *The Dragon Archives* Series
Bound by a Dragon
Pursued by a Dragon
Loved by a Dragon
Dance with a Dragon
Forever a Dragon

Other Books
Moondance